# SEC[illegible]S ON

# WAR STREET

N.R. DOWNS

ISBN: 978-1-9193270-0-6

Backstory Books

www.backstorybooks.com

Join the community!
Follow *backstorybooks* on social

Also follow *War.street.author* on
Tik - Tok/Instagram & War Street Story on
Facebook

## DEDICATION

To all who lived on the Home Front during the Second World War - in honour of their resilience, their bravery, and the memory of those who were lost.

# CONTENTS

## ACKNOWLEDGMENTS

My sincere thanks to the countless factual resources, blogs, and works of historians that have helped shape this story, and to the phenomenal team at the Imperial War Museum. Their dedication to preserving history has allowed me to research this piece of historical fiction in detail and with accuracy. Their work is vital in ensuring that the real voices of the past continue to be heard.

# *1939*

# 1 Nippy

It's just a normal Friday. My feet ache something terrible, a dull, persistent throb, but I don't stop. You're not allowed, see. That's why they call us Nippies; we're always nipping between tables, quick as you like. You must look brisk, efficient. No hanging about.

'Don't drop the tray, and don't you ever drop your smile,' Mrs Miller, the manageress, barks at us constantly.

I've been at this Lyons tearoom for three years now. Relentless work, but I do enjoy it most days. You meet all sorts here, and I've made some wonderful friends. At twenty - two years of age, I suppose I'm a bit of a veteran. Sometimes people ask if I fancy moving to one of the bigger Corner Houses in town, those massive, bustling places with thousands of customers, but I'm quite happy here in Putney. The customers are mostly decent, if always demanding. We get all sorts too: professionals, doctors, businessmen, then labourers and shopkeepers. A lot of the girls have met their boyfriends here. I'm pretty sure half the chaps come for us, not the tea.

The downside to the job is Mrs Miller. She's a cruel woman, and I'm certain she's got it in for me. She stands at the end of the room, watching us like a hawk. If your collar's crooked or your apron not white enough, you'll hear about it sharpish. Lean on the counter? You'd think you'd committed murder. So, no matter what, even if my legs are screaming, I stand up straight, smile fixed, and keep moving. You've got to.

And it's not just about keeping busy; you've got to look smashing too. We wear black dresses, starched white aprons and cuffs, and our hair must always be neat, our lips touched with a bit of lipstick. That's the Lyons way. A Nippy should always look fresh, even when she isn't.

And Mrs Miller certainly has high standards when it comes to our appearance. I think some of it is jealousy; she's no oil painting herself, I have to say it. No amount of lipstick can disguise her masculine looks. We girls joke about it, quiet-like. Mister Miller, we call her. It's ever so cruel, but you should see her - Churchill in a wig, if you ask me.

The best part is working with Sheila Warner. We've been best friends since we were little, only a couple of years between us. She's the younger one, twenty years old and full of life. She grew up next door to me at Number 1 Turner Street, though her house was far more crowded than mine. She lived with her mum, dad, and five siblings in a little two-up, two-down. She spent a lot of time at my house, just for a bit of room. Sheila still lives there now, though most of her siblings have moved out, except her older sister Pat - nearly thirty and not married yet. Pat's too busy getting involved in politics and volunteering. Looks exhausting if you ask me, possibly more exhausting than working here.

What's striking about me and Sheila is we're total opposites. I'm a brunette, really dark, black as the night some days, whereas Sheila's blonde. Turns heads, that one. More than me, I reckon, not that I don't get the odd gaze myself. Also, unlike me, she's got these sharp, striking cheekbones, like she's been carved from stone. My face… well, it's not chubby or round exactly, but I don't look skeletal like Sheila, that's for sure. You'd never believe it, the way she packs it away though. Any leftover cake? Gone in a second if Sheila's about.

We're a good group of girls, all grafters, except for Lorraine, or Lazy Lorraine, as we call her. Honestly, how she's not been given the elbow by Mrs Miller, I'll never know. She can't even pour a cuppa without looking wiped out. And then there's Chatterbox Catherine who, as you can probably tell, loves the sound of her own voice. Always chatting. Well, everyone likes a natter, don't they? Round here they do, anyway. A lot of the talk now is about whether there's going to be a war. The answer depends on who you ask. Some seem convinced it's all bluster, that Hitler wouldn't be mad enough. But then… this is Hitler we're talking about. He doesn't exactly come across as the most reasonable of men, does he?

I try not to let thoughts of war get to me. I know what a battlefield can do to a man. My old man fought on the Somme and came back completely different, like he survived but didn't. The joy, the happiness, the passion wiped right out of him. I was born during that war, so I only know the post-war father I've had to live with my entire life. But my family tell me often how he used to be, and sometimes, just sometimes, I think I catch glimmers of it, like he's temporarily forgotten to be scarred.

The signs of war are all around us now, London getting itself ready for whatever's coming. I think of my brother Henry. I think of my husband George. It's hard not to panic, really. Blimming Germans. Always a nuisance.

Tonight, Sheila's off to the Locarno ballroom over in Streatham and she's been pestering and pleading for me to go. She loves a dance, Sheila. Anything where she can lose herself for a moment. She often says she dances in her head at work. Dancing? Singing I understand, but dancing in your head is beyond me.

But I can't go tonight, nor any night really. My George wouldn't have it. He'd be furious if I went to a place like that with the girls. Besides, my feet ache as it is. How they muster the strength to dance the night away, I don't know.

I suppose you could say Sheila is single, although she does speak fondly of some gentleman studying medicine at St George's Hospital. Samuel, his name is. I think she's playing hard to get. Wise strategy if you ask me, because once they've got you, it all changes. Married life is quite a different life.

My priority after work is to get home and get George's tea on the go. He'll be late tonight. It's Friday, so he'll stumble into The Old Swan with my brother Henry. Christ knows when he'll get home, but nevertheless, tea must be ready. Cold but there. Ready.

When I finally clock out of Lyons, it's always a mad dash. It's not a long hop into Battersea, and the walk from the bus stop to home isn't far, but after hours on my feet, with blisters practically sprouting blisters, every step feels like a monumental effort.

I live on Turner Street, the only place I've ever called home. It's a long row of houses, always bustling, always alive. The occasional plume of smog from Battersea Power Station hangs heavy in the air. It can't be good for you, but there's a strange comfort in it, a warmth that speaks of home. In the distance you can hear the rhythmic clatter of Clapham Junction, a constant companion, a never-ending hum of life and machinery.

All sorts live here, and I pretty much know everybody, to varying degrees. From my best friend Sheila to the mystery man at Number 45, who we've only ever seen leave the house once or twice. Folks I went to school with still live on this street. Heck, folks my dad went to school with still live here. Even my old school teacher lives on Turner Street.

Most of the street is made up of these typical Victorian two-up, two-downs, crammed together as if they were built from a single mould. Each with a generous garden, all things considered. On the corner, a little parade of shops provides us with everything, saving you a trek: the greengrocer's, the chip shop, a baker's and, of course, my dad's butcher's.

It's like a place that exists on its own. You can loiter about Turner Street and the few roads that feed into it and you'll have everything you need. You won't need to go any further, and for some people, that's exactly what they do.

On the other end of the street, you'll find the newer houses, built about fifteen years back. A mix of terraces and even some semi-detached places, all boasting their own indoor bathrooms. We call that the 'Posh End', and the rest of us are from the 'Down End'. Funny thing is, I live at the posh end now, Number 96, with Mrs Dreyfus. Or Esther, as she insists, we call her.

Esther always looks radiant. Her brown hair is carefully arranged in a tight chignon at the nape of her neck, not a single strand daring to escape its perfect form. She has these sharp dark eyes, deep brown, like two wells, and in them you can see the weight of what she has endured and the strength she still possesses. Eyes that have seen a lot but also hold a wisdom and a kindness.

Esther and her husband, Maurice, moved onto the street when the posh end was first built. They are both Jewish and had come over from France. Esther has a voice like an angel, and she taught singing to others. Maurice played the violin beautifully; he would play, and Esther would sing. He also worked at the pictures, playing in the orchestra for the silent films. But then the talkies came in, and Maurice struggled to find decent work. You could see the hurt in his eyes, but they kept going and managed to hold onto the house. That was the main thing. Number 96 meant everything to them.

Then, about five years ago, a horrendous accident struck. Maurice fell into the Thames and drowned. Esther was utterly distraught, as you can imagine, like her heart had been ripped clean out. She even said she'd never sing a note again.

A couple of years back, Esther asked if George and I would like to rent two rooms in her house and share the rest. It wasn't dear, and it helped us out no end - plus, it meant we could finally live somewhere with an inside lavatory. I was reluctant at first, leaving Dad, but I soon realised it was perfect for now. Same street, not far, but it gave me a real sense of independence. And it was the posh end. Ideal, really, until we can afford a place all to ourselves.

Despite sharing the place, it feels like home. It's quiet, it's welcoming.

However, a few months back, I had the shock of my life when I came home and found a young girl sitting in the living room. She was about ten years old, with short rusty brown hair and the palest little face. She looked absolutely petrified.

'Oh, blimey, I didn't mean to scare you,' I said to her gently.

But before I could say another word, Esther rushed in, quickly speaking to the girl in another language. Not French, but German.

'This is Nadine,' Esther then told me, already slipping an arm around the girl's shoulders. 'She's come from Germany. She's my brother David's child. My niece. I've only met her once before and now… now I will care for her.'

Nadine just looked at me, utterly lost.

It turns out Nadine came here through the government's Kindertransport programme, where Jewish children were sent to safety, away from the horrors of the Nazis. Esther's brother had moved to Germany as a young man, made a family there, and now he'd sent his only daughter to his sister, desperate to keep her safe.

So, here's Nadine, living in her aunt's house, a woman she hardly knows. Unable to speak more than a word or two of English, but luckily with good French. Poor little thing must miss her parents something awful.

'It is only until things get better,' Esther explained. 'My brother is hoping to go back to France… then Nadine can join them there, to be with them.'

I gave Nadine a welcoming smile, as warm as I could manage.

Esther didn't waste a moment in trying to make the place feel like home for her: toys, books in a jumble of French and German, alongside a few simple English language books. I could see her slipping into the motherly role so easily.

I think Esther wishes she'd had a child of her own - and tragically, she nearly did. Twice, in fact. Both lost at birth. Now she has the chance to be the loving aunt, even if her relationship with her brother has always been rather distant.

I'm trying my best too, to make Nadine feel welcome and safe. George, of course, is less happy about it.

'They're the enemy,' he said, rudely.

'She's ten years old, George.'

'She could be a spy.'

'She's *ten years* old, George,' I repeated. 'You know what they're doing to Jews over there. Poor love, she might never see her family again.' I said the last part quietly, making sure she couldn't hear me from downstairs.

It does change the dynamics of the house, having a young refugee under the roof, but this is the world we're in now. You just have to get on with it.

And get on with it I must. George's tea won't make itself. So when I get home I'm usually straight into the kitchen. This evening it's sausages and mash. We're never short of sausages in this house, something we've got in common with the Germans, I suppose. In fact, we're never short of meat at all, not with George working at my dad's butcher's.

Growing up, I soon got used to Dad bringing home the off-cuts and organs nobody else wanted. It wasn't uncommon to see a pig's head sitting at the back of the garden for whatever reason. It was like growing up on a farm of the dead. Grim, really, but you soon get used to it. With George and Dad keeping us well stocked in meat, and me bringing home stale cakes from Lyons, I reckon if there is a war, we'll do all right for a while.

Still, as expected, George doesn't come home. Not on time, anyway. So, I wait. And even though it's late July the sun soon gives in and the light fades away. He really is very late.

It makes me wonder, in this little reprieve, no cooking, no washing, maybe I should've gone out with Sheila after all. Sure, my feet are red raw, but if I'm strong enough to work all day, I can surely manage a dance or two. Or at least try. But no, it'd be more trouble than it's worth, dealing with George after. So here I am, staying at home, waiting. Wondering.

I always worry, even though I know he's at the pub. I just worry. I daren't eat; I'll wait. My feet could do with a nice soak, that'd be lovely, but then I picture myself soaking them when he comes in and I'll look like a right slouch, like Lazy Lorraine at work.

But in the end I think, *sod it.* It's late, I'm missing out, and George is clearly having a brilliant time. So I wind up the gramophone, put on one of my favourites - *My Woman* by Al Bowlly. Oh, it's a marvellous song. You can't help but move when it starts. It just sticks in your head; you can't shake it off.

So here I am, dancing on my own, my feet begging me to stop but my heart keeping me going. I imagine myself with Sheila and the other girls, like I'm really there. I close my eyes, twirl about, arms loose, heart full, ears brimming, a smile escaping - pure joy. Dancing in my head. This is what it must be like. Although I am also staggering across the room in a disorganised mess.

When I open my eyes, my brother Henry is standing in the doorway, steadying George, who's barely upright. Barely awake.

I strike the needle off - it screeches to a halt.

'Didn't know you were having a party,' Henry jokes as George flops onto the sofa with a thud, groaning. 'Put it back on, we'll have a dance,' Henry adds, with that cheeky grin of his.

'You're all right,' I shoot back, turning my attention to George, who's moaning and shifting uncomfortably. 'He ain't all right though, is he?'

'One too many,' Henry says, still smiling, though he himself is swaying ever so slightly.

'What am I gonna do with you two?' I sigh.

'I helped him home. I'm his carer,' Henry says defensively.

'Well, ain't you a blimmin' saint,' I snap, watching him head for the door. 'At least you can hold your drink, Henry,' I call, waving him off.

When I turn back, George is suddenly standing. His face has dropped, his eyes somewhere else. He looks hurt in some unspeakable way.

'I can hold my drink, Vera,' he says sternly, pointing at me.

I say nothing. Just stand still. But George isn't finished.

'You love showing me up in front of your brother, don't ya?'

'What you on about?' I reply, trying to avoid an argument but genuinely curious all the same.

'You… you,' he stammers, steadying himself on the table. 'You make me look stupid, Vera. Like I can't control myself. Like I'm a boy.'

He stumbles to the cupboard and pours himself a whisky, still going on. 'You embarrass me. Belittle me in front of your family. All the sodding time.' He takes a sip, shakes his head. 'You make me feel… I dunno… worthless. Inadequate.'

I've had enough now. I shouldn't say it, but I do - tired and angry.

'You're being daft, George,' I say, my voice raised just enough.

That's when he cracks.

His whisky glass flies across the room and smashes against the wall beside me. Tiny shards spray, little spikes catching my arm and neck. Harmless but sharp. I try not to flinch. I don't think he meant it for me.

'Daft?!' he shouts. 'I ain't bloody daft, Vera!'

He pushes me hard in the chest, and I hit the wall behind me. I stay as still as possible. Try to give him nothing. Or maybe I can't feel anything at all.

He staggers past and out the door, still cursing as he goes, until the silence finally returns.

I shouldn't have said anything. I know what he's like. It's not the first time.

It's just a *normal* Friday.

# *Before*

## 2 The men

My old man, Albert - or Bertie, as most people call him - is known by pretty much everybody round this way.

Dad met my mother, Mary, by her saving his skin - something she ended up doing quite a lot, as it goes.

Dad was working at a bakery back then, a delivery boy but hardly a boy; more a young man with no real sense of purpose or direction. Not ideal for a delivery driver, really.

It was 1913. Dad had just turned twenty-one, and the fair was on at Battersea Park. Always a popular attraction, all lights and music and noise spilling out across the south and beyond.

He went to the fair with his three best friends: John, Timpson (another John, but known by his surname to avoid confusion), and Eric. Those four were always up to no good, worse when together. Dad said they were hoping to win a few pennies back on the coconut shy and maybe impress a girl or two while they were at it. Trouble was, he got accused by one of the stallholders of pinching a penny bun off the counter - ridiculous, considering he spent half his life surrounded by bread - but Dad, being Dad, didn't take kindly to the accusation and gave him a mouthful back. There was a bit of pushing and shoving, and next thing he knew, he was being frogmarched to the edge of the park by a constable. Dad, stubborn as ever, refused to keep quiet. John, Timpson, and Eric quickly fled the scene, leaving Dad to face the music like a lone soldier.

That's when she came along - my mother - basket on her arm, coming home from the jam factory. She stopped, looked Dad up and down, and said, calm as you like:

'You've got yourself in a two and eight, haven't you, Harry? Your sick mother will be fuming, and your father… turning in his grave, no doubt.' Then she looked directly at the police officer. 'Lost on the Titanic. Not even a grave to turn in. He'll never get over it.'

She said it with a sombre tone.

Apparently, Dad just stared at her, mesmerised by her beauty, her adorable curly dark hair and long lashes, confused by what was going on but nodding in agreement nevertheless.

Mum then took the police officer aside and, after a bit of muttering and a sharp warning from the officer, Dad was let go. She handed Dad his cap back, told him to keep out of trouble, and went on her way.

But the next Friday, Dad was waiting outside the jam factory for her, grinning like a fool, with a fresh bun in his hand.

'Paid for this time,' he said, and then: 'I know why you got the job here at the jam factory.'

'Why's that, then?' Mum asked.

''Cos you must be the sweetest girl I've ever seen,' he said, with a ridiculous smile.

And that was that.

Mum later told me she'd never seen a lad look so handsome and yet rough at the same time, and she was drawn to him like a magnet - that's why she helped him get away with it. She knew he'd come looking after. I envied that confidence of hers. From that day onwards, Mum always called Dad Harry, which confused a lot of people, but that was their thing.

A few months later they were married and moved into Turner Street, Number 3, and then, right on cue, my older brother Henry was born nine months later - just as the world fell apart and went to war.

Dad, John, Timpson, and Eric were quick to put themselves forward. I think it gave them real purpose. They ended up being banded together; they called them the Pals Battalions - groups of friends, brothers, neighbours who all signed up together, thinking it would be grand, all of them marching off side by side. They ended up in the East Surrey Regiment and soon found themselves on the Somme - hell on earth.

And that cheeky, naughty, funny Albert (or Harry) disappeared on the battlefield. He would never be the same. But he was indeed the lucky one; John, Timpson, and Eric never came home. Dad was the lone soldier once again.

In late 1916, Dad was granted leave after receiving what they called a blighty wound - a survivable but painful injury that meant he had to go home. He had taken a shrapnel wound that tore into his leg and scarred one side of his face. He felt terrible about it, leaving the boys behind, but eventually all the men were praying for a blighty wound themselves, so they too could go home.

When Dad got home, I was conceived - born in the summer of 1917, with the war still raging. Despite his injury, Dad was called back once he had healed well enough. Limping into battle, but eventually he came home for good. The war was over, and for him, it was like starting his life again. Only now he had a wife and two young children to feed.

Ever determined, Dad started up his own butcher's, setting up a tiny little shop round the corner. It was often said that after the war he was so used to blood, guts, and death that opening a butcher's felt like a natural choice, like he was at home.

And in many ways, that shop was his home. We rarely saw him growing up - always grafting, always providing, but incredibly distant. Mad, considering it was so close to home. He became very well known; with his limp, scarred face and clutching a meat cleaver, he wasn't someone you'd forget easily.

My brother Henry idolises my father; he was quick to join him at the butcher's. He'd been working there on and off since he was thirteen, but as soon as he could pack in school, he had a meat cleaver in his hand, and he's never been happier.

The little shop's gotten bigger over the years. I can't say I'm not proud of them both, seeing *Wright & Sons* painted on the sign above - our family name. We've done all right, considering.

If he's not working at the shop, Henry's other love is football. And he's pretty good at it. He's always hoping he'll get scouted by one of the big clubs - Chelsea or Fulham, maybe - though it hasn't happened yet. Not that he's giving up. Every Sunday he's out there playing at Battersea Park, come rain or shine. Now and again, I'll go and watch, usually with Joy - that's the girl he's courting. Lovely girl, quite posh. Her beautiful red hair makes her stand out from anyone. I can see why Henry was drawn to her, with her adorable freckles on her face. She's from Wimbledon and went to university. I doubt her parents imagined her ending up with a butcher, but love does funny things to you. She was always at the playing fields cheering on the boys, but it was my brother who got her attention. They've been together for quite some time now.

It's also how I met my George, through Henry's football and their friendship. George William Hopkins. Tall, dark, handsome. A missing bottom tooth that bizarrely makes him more attractive. A wicked smile, piercing blue eyes that will make you blush. He's scrubbed up well considering he's from the roughest part of Battersea. His father, Frank, was killed in the war when George was just a year old, so he never really knew him. That left his mother, Maureen, to bring up George and his three siblings. She couldn't cope, took to the drink, and in the end it was his grandmother, Vera, yes, same name as me, who brought them up.

It was a hard life for George. They were terribly poor. I mean, we didn't have much, but we always had food on the table, a roof over us. It wasn't like that for him. George used to tell me he would pick out the weeds from the pavement and eat the root because he was so hungry.

My dad took to George straight away when Henry put him forward for a delivery job. I think it's because George had lost his father in the war and Dad knew what that loss felt like with his friends. Also, George was undoubtedly looking for a father figure. So Dad gave him the job, running deliveries and such. Funny, really, the shop's called *Wright & Sons*, plural, and I think Dad sees George as another son now. In fact, I'm certain of it.

I'd only seen George a couple of times at the park playing football, but he never really stood out to me at first - horrible thing to say, I know. It wasn't until I saw him in the shop, up close, that I really, really noticed him.

I remember it so well. It was four years ago. I was popping into the shop to see Dad and Henry. That scent hits you the second you walk in - a mix of sawdust, salt, and raw meat that just lingers in the air. Henry was at the counter, his white apron already splashed with the day's work, and Dad was somewhere in the back; I could hear him banging about with the cleaver.

'Watcha, Vera,' Henry said, weighing out mince.

And then the door to the back swung open with a smack of wood, and there he was. George. Back from a delivery, cheeks flushed, hair a little windswept, a paper bag in one hand and his cap shoved in his pocket.

He saw me straight away, and that smile of his, just the faintest curve at the corner of his mouth - missing tooth showing. Well, it was like a switch in me just turned on.

Henry properly introduced us. George shook my hand, gentle, considered. From that moment, he made it his quest to make me his. Luckily he had Henry, who I don't think minded. He trusted George, even if he had a temper and liked a drink - I mean, which man doesn't?

A few weeks later, just after my eighteenth birthday, Henry and I went to see *The 39 Steps* at The Grand. Henry must have given George a heads-up, because when we were coming out, there George was - all smart and sophisticated - waiting on the pavement.

He offered to walk me home, which was slightly odd seeing as Henry was heading home too, but Henry let us walk ahead, the two of us wandering arm in arm through Battersea, with him trailing behind like a royal bodyguard. I spent half the walk talking about the film, trying to make head or tail of it. George just listened, smiling, laughing at all the right bits. He seemed so charming, polite, kind.

And that was the beginning. What a whirlwind those first few months were. Dad was over the moon - now George really would be part of the family. Usually, it's the man asking the father to wed his daughter, but I'm sure in this instance it was the other way round.

George didn't hang about, either. We'd only been together six months when he got down on one knee and popped the question. Christmas Day, it was, very special.

That evening, though, George had one too many, and Henry didn't like it much. They kept arguing over football - can you believe it? How worked up and passionate they get over a load of men kicking an inflated ball about a pitch. Anyway, it ended in a punch-up just after Christmas lunch, spilling out onto the pavement outside. Dad was raging, I've never seen him so angry, so embarrassed. It became the talk of Turner Street, that's for sure. Both of them ended up with black eyes and bloody noses, though Henry came off worse - not that I'd dare say it.

They soon made up. By New Year, they were best friends again.

New Year's Eve is one of the rare times I'll go to the pub, the local one, anyway. Such a boisterous, lively, wonderful evening of drunken hugs and silly jokes. I think that might have been one of the happiest nights of my life.

George leaned in and whispered in my ear that he wanted me to have a baby in '36. I laughed it off - we needed to get married first, and besides, it takes nine months to cook one. We'd only have the start of the year to make it happen. But George just smiled at me, that smile of his - part flirty, part deadly serious. A man with a plan. I think that's why we rushed to get married - a small service, few people, not much fuss. I wasn't wanting much more, but it all happened so quickly. It feels like only yesterday I was leaving school, and now here I am, a ring on my finger, Mrs Hopkins.

Around the same time, I got the job as a Nippy at Lyons. I was made up, beats cleaning at Dad's place, rotten and smelly it was. I much prefer tea and cake to blood and guts.

It's amazing how quickly life just seems to slot into place. It sort of comes together before you've even noticed. No baby yet, mind. That's something that's playing on both our minds - but what will be, will be. We've rushed everything else so much, maybe the Lord's taking His time when it comes to that. Some things you just can't rush.

## 3 The women

My mother Mary was one of the most outgoing, confident, outspoken people you could ever meet. She always had an opinion, always gossiping; she'd be the first to hear the news and the first to tell you exactly what she thought of it. I adored her. She was everything you'd want from a parent: nurturing, caring, loving, wise - but you couldn't put much past her. She was sharp as a tack, always alert.

She'd worked her way up to supervisor at the jam factory before she packed it in to focus on bringing us up. We could just about afford to get by. It was hard, but we had each other. And Mum had plenty of friends too - people who helped us. She was very sociable.

When Dad came back from the war, though, their relationship had changed. Still loving, still respectable, but not as fun anymore. It was like she was constantly reaching for the old joy they used to have, but could never quite get her hands on it. Like slippery soap in the bath. So, in many ways, they lived separate lives.

Then, when I was ten, Mum got ill. It all started with just a little cough. That's what she kept saying: *just a little cough, don't fuss.* But it wasn't little for long. Within weeks she couldn't get through a sentence without stopping to catch her breath. And her skin… it went this strange greyish colour, like she was slowly being drained away.

The doctor came, Dr Clarke. He didn't say much at first - just prescribed some tonic and told her to rest. But by the time he came back the following month, she was already too weak to stand. Dr Clarke told Dad it was tuberculosis. Whispered it, as though saying it too loud might finish her off right there and then.

She went to bed that day and never got back out again. It was so quick. She looked like she'd aged fifty years in five weeks. Her hair thinned, her hands shook, and her lovely full cheeks - just like mine - completely sank in. Even her voice sounded like it belonged to someone else.

They moved me in with Doris across the road at Number 2, so Mum could have my bedroom to herself. I hated every minute of it. Doris and her vinegar tongue, always finding little ways to remind me I was a guest, not family. But they said it was for the best - to keep me out of the way, to keep the air clear for Mum, to avoid catching anything.

I'd watch Doris peering through the net curtain, waiting for news, like she was excited by the fact my mum was on her last legs. She didn't like my mum much, and Mum despised her.

Doris's husband, Harold, was completely blind and barely spoke. He just made noises - another victim of the war - which meant Doris could get up to all sorts and he'd be none the wiser. Honestly, she's an evil woman, I'm convinced of it. I used to watch her rearrange the furniture just to upset Harold, who'd bump into it. Worst thing you could do to a blind man. Sinister, really bloody sinister.

Living there was unbearable, so I'd often sneak back across the street when I could. Just to sit by the door and listen. Listen to my mum wheezing, sometimes crying out, sometimes just silence. I remember once Dad came out and shut the door very softly behind him. He didn't even see me sitting on the stairs. He just stood there for a long time, staring at nothing, before he went back in.

When Mum finally passed, I didn't even get to say goodbye properly. She was only thirty-four. But she looked about eighty when they carried her out.

For my dad, it was like being at war once more - not the physical strain, but the mental one. The loss, the sadness. Like losing his best friends all over again. Everything he seemed to love ended up dying. He never spoke about losing Mum, like he never spoke about the war really. Tight-lipped, dry-eyed. Occasionally he'd just wander off and leave me and Henry. I'm convinced he went to have a cry, but he'd never say so. I don't think we even hugged when Mum went.

Now I think Dad just… exists. Because what else is there to do?

Since Mum passed, Doris has been ever-present, often round for cups of tea. She's the only woman Dad really talks to. I wish he'd talk to me instead. Meanwhile poor Harold clings on at home, still trying to master the new living-room layout.

Not having a mum around was a loss I couldn't put into words. Her absence is felt every minute of the day. My role went from little girl to the lady of the family overnight. The responsibilities were overwhelming, but you just had to get on. That's what we do. That's what Mum would have told us: just get on with it.

I miss that she hasn't seen me grow into a woman - seen that I've got hair just like hers, seen that I've kept that upbeat, positive spirit she always had, and that Dad's misery hasn't rubbed off on me. I wish she'd met George. She would have liked him - not his temper or his drunkenness, mind - she'd have soon put him in his place, that's for sure.

Violet Ball at Number 5 sort of took on the mother role in many ways. She's always been there to help and support me, even when it came to… private lady matters. She's nine years older than me and has such a sensible head on her shoulders.

Stanley Ball, her other half, is a lovely man, kind as they come. He works on the river as a bargemaster, navigating the water with heavy cargoes of coal. Both Violet and Stanley are an example of an idyllic married couple, a fine pair, always good to each other. I envy them, really.

They've got two children now, Rita who's seven and James who's five, lovely little kids. I'm often over there playing with them, teasing them, bringing them leftover treats from Lyons. They call me Aunt Vera. Now and again I mind them, just to give Violet and Stanley a break so they can go to the pictures or out to dinner in town. I play with the kids, thinking about what it'll be like when I have my own. Good practice, I keep telling myself.

I read them a bedtime story, but little Rita prefers it if I make one up like her mum does - so I do. I tell tales of lost worlds and mythical adventures, mermaids and fairies. They love it. I love it. I'm glad I'm still only down the road from them.

A year ago, Violet was recruited as an Air Raid Precautions warden. She practises running air raid drills and all that, just in case the war comes. I keep asking her if she's got some insider knowledge - you know, whether she knows things we don't, things the wireless keeps quiet about in case of panic. She just smiles and says the government's simply readying themselves, and better that than being surprised by the Germans. She does her warden role alongside her part-time job as a receptionist for a solicitor's. I've no idea how she finds the time. A miracle woman, really.

Stanley's gone for now, volunteered for the Merchant Navy. They said his skills on the river would come in handy, and a few weeks back they called him up. Off he went, now carrying coal and supplies across foreign seas. Feels like war's already here, even though they've not said the word yet.

I think Violet's role as an air raid warden keeps her distracted from the fact Stanley is gone. She has a plate outside her front door which proudly states *Warden* and she's become well occupied with a mountain of information and procedures. Sheila and I even attended a gas mask safety session inside the school hall, where Violet showed how to properly put one on. Ghastly things they are, frightening too, but they've now become a constant companion, tied to us all.

Opposite Violet and Stanley at Number 6 is my old schoolteacher, Mrs Henderson. We still call her Mrs Henderson now, never by her actual name, Dot - it just wouldn't feel polite.

Mrs Henderson taught me at St Mary's, just around the corner. She still teaches there now, in fact - same no - nonsense bun, the smell of chalk dust clinging to her skirt. She has this sharp way of looking at you, like she's still marking you out of ten.

When Mum died, she always made sure I was managing. Now and again she'd even pop in and give me some extra lessons. She was desperate for me to succeed. She wasn't a shoulder to cry on or anything - very firm, very matter-of-fact - but she showed her care through her knowledge and persistence.

Her husband, Frank Henderson, works down at Clapham Junction on the railways - a quiet, steady man with hands like spanners and a cap that never seems to leave his head.

They've got twin lads I grew up with, Arthur and Kenneth, they're the same age as me, though we were never close. Boisterous, cheeky chaps; they used to run rings round Mrs Henderson, which always surprised me, considering how strict she was at school yet how little control she had over her own boys.

I say I wasn't close, but truth is I had my first kiss with Arthur… and my second with Kenneth. I didn't know at the time, of course, they're so alike, they thought it hilarious to swap places and see if I'd notice. What a rotten trick. Safe to say, I told them exactly where to go after that. That was seven years ago now, and I've not had a proper conversation with either since.

These days, Ken works at the power station, different job to his dad, but still comes home stinking of coal. Arthur drifts from job to job, mostly warehouse work, an aimless lad without ambition. There are plenty of those round here.

# *1939*

# 4 Blackout

'*The Black - Out Begins at 10 p.m. - All lights out!*' That's what the flyer says. They've dropped a load of them. Over the course of the summer, the preparations for war have been relentless. Soon London will fall into darkness, if only for a practice. It is summer now, so it doesn't get properly dark until later, but come winter we'll all be hunting for our way home in the pitch black. Must be what it's like for poor Harold every day.

But you see, it is all just precaution, a way of readying ourselves. We've had our gas masks for the best part of a year. Awful things they are - the stench of stale rubber and dust is enough to make me gag even when you don't have to wear it. The one time I did, everything turned into a foggy, claustrophobic nightmare. I always forget to take it out with me; you quickly realise when you get a judgmental glance from someone.

Of course, a lot of this blackout is down to us ordinary folk to sort, to darken the streets. We've got to extinguish or black out every lamp, every glimmer, after 11.30 p.m. at the very latest. It's an anxious time, I've got to say, and yet it's rather nice to see all of

London pulling together: wardens, shopkeepers, council men, housewives alike, smothering the city in darkness. Streetlamps hooded. Kerbstones painted white so we can spot them. Even Dad's butcher's window has had to be draped in black. Although Dad, as usual, has been quiet about it all. George and I made sure his home was blackout-ready for the practice; he just sat at the kitchen table, head buried in the paper, worry in his eyes. It's as though he wants no part of it. None of us do, really - but what choice have we got?

The little ones from next door, Rita and James, came over to help. For them, it's all very exciting, like building a camp indoors. They soon got too boisterous, though, and Dad ended up smacking his hand on the table in a temper, so I ferried them back home.

'Thank the Lord for that,' George muttered, nodding at Dad, a strange thing to say for a man who's so set on having children of his own.

They've even been testing the sirens. That sound makes your heart drop into your boots - eerie, mournful - and with it, the whole city seems to hold its breath and vanish into the night. And this is just a practice. I can't imagine what it'll feel like if war is really declared.

I can tell the mood is changing. Mrs Miller quickly gathers us round before another shift at Lyons, her face like thunder - though that's nothing new. Lazy Lorraine is late, but Miller lets it pass. Maybe she should be Late Lorraine now. Or Lazy Late Lorraine. Bit of a mouthful, that. Useless Lorraine, perhaps; less alliteration but a fair summary.

Anyway, Mrs Miller informs us that despite 'what is going on out there', as she points, quite literally, outside - nothing will change in here.

'There might be a war, but people will always need tea,' she says optimistically, like it's a line straight from head office. She's not wrong, though. Tea might just be the thing that keeps us going.

Afterwards we scatter to start work. Sheila is quick to sidle over.

'Feels real now, doesn't it? I didn't think it would actually happen,' she says, worry in her tone.

I shrug, trying not to dwell on it or panic Sheila. She's usually so carefree; it unsettles me seeing her like this.

'What will be, will be. We'll get through it,' I tell her, mustering my most reassuring look.

Later we learn from a customer that the blackout becomes mandatory tomorrow at sunset. So all that practice is for something. Esther won't be pleased - she hates covering the windows, says it makes her feel trapped in a cage.

At the end of the shift, Sheila and I leave together. She's eager to pop to the shops. I tell her to be quick - I've George's tea to see to. She doesn't even notice what I say, just keeps going on about her love interest, Samuel.

'Here, Vera, there's something I've got to tell you about him,' she begins.

'Go on…' I prompt, but before she can continue, a loud voice screeches above the hum of the high street.

'Blimey, that's our Pat,' Sheila exclaims.

We hurry forward to see Pat standing there, flyers and papers clutched in her hands.

'Talk to Hitler! Avoid the slaughter! Peace, not war!' she shouts, her voice echoing through the street.

'Pat, why are you doing this!' Sheila barks, almost offended.

'Trying to stop a bloody war, Sheila! While you serve tea and look pretty, they're preparing to slaughter our men, our brothers, for nothing!' Pat is fierce, consumed by anger. She shoves a flyer from the Peace Pledge Union into my hand. 'These moments are crucial,' she says with blazing eyes. 'If we don't stop this now, we'll all be brown bread. It's the working people they sacrifice.'

'You need to go home, Pat. Dad will be mortified,' Sheila says, her cheeks burning red, but Pat ignores her.

'Reject the lies! Demand peace!' she cries again - until a man in a long coat barges past so roughly she stumbles and falls. We quickly help her up as she brushes herself down, her flyers littering the pavement, some whisked away by the wind.

'We should go,' Sheila urges me, dread in her voice. 'My dad will lose it when he finds out.'

In truth, both sisters are petrified. They just show it differently. Pat's fear comes out fierce, a desperate need to stop it, a deep suspicion of those in charge. Sheila just wants to hide under a blanket and hope it all sorts itself out, pray that God might be listening. I'm more like Sheila, really. What can a girl like me from Turner Street do to stop this madness? Nothing. Besides, we've got little Nadine at home, and I feel like I'm doing my bit keeping the tea poured and making sure the German girl isn't bothered by anyone.

When I get home, I'm surprised to find Violet inside, talking to Esther. Violet wears her ARP armband, clutching a bundle of flyers and leaflets, while Esther stands with a heavy drape in her hands, tears glinting in her eyes. In the doorway, Nadine lingers, too fearful to come closer.

'Everything all right?' I ask, stepping in.

'Just explaining the mandatory blackout to Esther,' Violet replies, calm, matter-of-fact. 'From sunset tomorrow. Making sure she's got what she needs.'

'This is not all,' Esther says, using the drapes to wipe away a stray tear.

'I know it's a lot. None of us wants to do this,' I tell her gently, rubbing her shoulder for comfort.

'No… no… She wants Nadine to go. To leave!' Esther bursts out, her voice sharp with desperation. Violet tries to steady the moment with her soft, even tone.

'No… no,' she says. 'I did say it's voluntary. But it is something the government are actively encouraging.'

Esther drops the drapes and waves her hand dismissively, pulling her cardigan tighter with purpose.

'Voluntary,' she scoffs, hugging herself, her eyes brimming.

Violet hands me an information booklet. The cover reads: *Government Evacuation Scheme. Important to Parents and Guardians. Children First! Are Your Children Ready for Evacuation?* The words chill me. I've seen the posters around town, of course, but there's so much to take in you hardly register it. This makes it real. They want Nadine to leave, and she's only been here six months.

'She's safe here with me, with her family!' Esther cries, her voice cracking with pain. 'This is already a strange land and now you want to send her away, a refugee again!'

'I don't want any of this, Esther,' Violet says softly. 'I just have to tell you what the advice is.'

I step in, not wanting Nadine to leave, knowing what that would do to Esther and how lost Nadine would be. She's welcome here, to a point, if she keeps her head down, sticks with us. God knows where she'd end up otherwise - some bleak little village, a German girl with barely a word of English, foisted on strangers already struggling to feed themselves. The thought turns my stomach.

'She should stay, Violet,' I say firmly. 'For now, at least. And besides, you've got the little ones, Rita and James, and they're still at home.'

But the moment I say it, Violet's face changes. Her composure cracks; worry, pain, and dread rise in her eyes, and she presses her lips together to stop them trembling.

'What is it, Violet?' I ask.

'They go tomorrow afternoon,' she whispers. 'I have to take them to Waterloo.'

'Going where?' I cry, though my voice catches halfway.

'I don't know. Somewhere safe. Away from here. It's what we're told we must do. They say the Germans could strike at any moment. I've tried to make it sound like a little holiday… but - ' Violet's tears fall freely now, and she makes no effort to stop them. I stand frozen, my heart heavy, my tongue useless. I adore those children. I can't imagine this street without them.

'When were you going to tell me?' I murmur, blinking back my own tears.

'I've been meaning to, Vera... It's just, these last few days, trying to get everything sorted, my own family too. It's a lot. I must take them tomorrow. My poor Stanley won't get to say goodbye, stuck at sea. I don't even know if he agrees with it, yet I have to do it, it has to be done.'

She seems so small then, so crushed by the weight of it all. I pull her into a tight hug.

'I'll come,' I say. 'Tomorrow. I'm not working. I'll come with you to wave them off.'

Her breath catches, and she nods.

'I'd like that, Vera. I'd like that very much.'

And then, perhaps cheekily of me, I ask if I might pop round to see them both before bed, give them one of my bedtime stories they're so fond of.

'That would be lovely,' Violet says softly, managing a small smile. 'They'd be made up, Vera.'

So I leave with her, letting George fend for himself for the evening. There are, occasionally, more important things than cooking his tea.

When we arrive at Violet's, little James and Rita are overjoyed to see me. In their bedroom, James refuses to sit still, clambering over the furniture, pretending to be a soldier, his arms out like wings. At last, I manage to settle him with one of my elaborate tales.

'This,' I begin, leaning closer, lowering my voice, 'is the story of the magical train. So marvellous it can travel anywhere in the world. Nobody knows quite where it goes, only that it's always somewhere safe, and exciting, and new. Sometimes it feels scary at first, because it's all so strange, but the braver you are, the more magical it becomes. And the braver you are… the bigger the present waiting for you when you get home.'

I spin them a story of mythical lands and ancient cities, places full of colour and wonder. James and Rita sit cross-legged, eyes wide, completely lost in the tale, smiles beaming, their innocence unbroken for a little while longer.

I wish I could climb aboard that magical train with them. But no. There's a desperate lack of magic now.

Soon the city will crawl into darkness, and Rita and James leaving is just another light extinguished. The street won't be the same. I won't be the same.

# 5 Pied Piper

The next day I'm round Dad's place very early, just as the sun lifts itself over the rooftops. For months he's had the fragments of an Anderson shelter scattered about his tiny garden, refusing to put it up, insisting it wasn't needed. Ignoring orders like a stubborn fool. Well, the chances are it will be needed, so that morning Henry and George finally get on with it, frantically working to piece the thing together: a few curved sheets of corrugated iron, some steel plates, nuts and bolts, like some grim Meccano set.

The men get stuck in, shirts already off, George with a cigarette clamped between his lips. Henry is quick to tease.

'You been feeding him, Vera? He's a bag of bones,' he says with a grin.

'She didn't do me tea last night, that's for sure,' George mutters, shooting me a glare as Henry only laughs it off.

The process of erecting this shelter is no easy feat, despite what the authorities might say. First comes the digging: a hellish trench, three feet deep and wide enough to take the curved panels. Then they'll have to climb in and bolt it all together. The real backbreaker will be heaping the earth back over the top, fifteen inches thick, until the whole thing is just a dark hump swallowing the modest garden, promising safety.

'We're digging our graves,' Dad mutters, shaking his head, puffing on a pipe he rarely smokes, before retreating inside.

'I'll stay in the shop. The basement. This is pointless,' he adds, still smoking away as he disappears through the back door.

'Well, the shop won't be much good in the middle of the night when you're in bed, will it, Dad?' I call after him. 'They could strike at any time.'

'So they keep saying,' he replies, his voice heavy with sarcasm. 'It's like they want this bloody war. All this prepping, sirens, shelters, gas masks, posters everywhere. It's like they've talked themselves into it now.'

I can't help but nod in agreement as I watch Henry's shovel bite into the earth once again.

'It's good to be ready,' I say.

'Nothing prepares you for war, Vera,' Dad replies, his voice lower now, thoughtful, with a note of regret I rarely hear. 'No posters. No drills. No training. Nothing can prepare you for it.' He brushes the side of his scarred face and takes a sip of his tea, until suddenly Doris appears, as she always does, cake tin in hand.

'I brought a cake for the hard-working men,' she trills, already fussing about George's physique as though she owns it. Then she looks at me and her smile falters. She stares me up and down, her displeasure undisguised.

'You not got things to do in your nice little house up the posh end?' she says sharply.

'No,' I reply evenly, 'I'm helping Dad.'

'So I see,' she says, glancing pointedly at the cup of tea in my hand. Then, her tone hardening: 'That Jerry still with you?'

'Her name's Nadine,' I say flatly.

'I wouldn't trust her,' she says with a little sniff.

'Oh, you and all,' I mutter, feeling my patience fray.

'They're crafty, the Germans,' she says, almost gleeful.

'She's a Jew,' I fire back sharply.

'Even more crafty, then,' she cackles, as though she's made some grand joke.

It's remarkable how the mood changes so dramatically when Doris turns up. Luckily, I don't have to stay long, as I must join Violet to make the trip to Waterloo.

'I'll be back soon, George,' I call on my way out, nodding towards the half-assembled shelter.

He walks over slowly, wipes his hands on his trousers, kisses me on the cheek, and speaks low enough for just me to hear.

'Maybe, with those kids gone, you can focus on having one of your own.'

And with that, he turns back to Henry, sticks a cigarette between his lips, and carries on as though nothing at all has been said. He always manages that - say things, do things that none of the family would ever pick up on.

With George's words echoing in my ears, I head towards my old school, St Mary's, which has been turned into an assembly point. The playground hums with noise and movement: children with their parents, familiar faces from the neighbourhood, gathering under a thin late summer sun. There's a strange kind of buzz, a mix of excitement and dread, parents trying their best to hold it all together while the little ones bounce between nerves and curiosity.

At last, I spot Violet in the distance, walking towards me. Little Rita clutches her teddy, her gas mask box swinging against her hip, and a large brown luggage tag - her name and the school scrawled across it - pinned firmly to her coat. James is all elbows and restless energy, fiddling with his own tag, undoing the string and retying it again and again.

Violet's face is set, serious but calm. She's the parent here, not the air raid warden, though even now she can't help but play that part, pointing others in the right direction. When we hug, her grip is so tight it tells me everything.

Then Mrs Henderson emerges briskly from the school doorway, the teacher now doubling as organiser, clipboard in hand, bun immaculate, her expression set to "orderly."

'What are you doing here? You're far too old to be evacuated,' she calls towards me, half-joking.

'Supporting Violet,' I say with a small smile, as though I need permission to be present. 'You're not going yourself, then?'

'No. A few of the younger teachers are, but I'm staying to teach whoever's left, if there are any,' she says drily, before turning back to usher the children in.

What follows is slow and painstaking: a methodical process of lining up the children, checking names off, pinning tags straight. Violet is forced to sign her children over to the care of strangers. One by one, the little ones become numbers, shuffled into some strange, chaotic order that no one quite seems to understand.

There are tears and bursts of laughter, parents stooping to press last-minute instructions into their children's ears, teachers barking names above the din. The sheer ordinariness of it all, the neat queues, the polite smiles, makes it feel surreal - almost like a game.

Mothers cling, fathers swallow hard. Mrs Henderson disrupts it all with a whistle.

'Group C, single file!' she bellows, and the line shuffles forward. Soon the kids disappear, swept into a sea of small uniforms and flapping name tags.

Eventually, the children are shepherded onto specially designated buses bound for Waterloo. We're allowed to follow on another bus of our own, permitted one final goodbye at the station before they're sent away for who knows how long.

On the bus I grip Violet's hand. She manages a faint smile.

'Won't be forever,' I tell her.

She keeps nodding, the kind of nod you do when you're trying to convince yourself.

'The Butlers at the posh end, they're not sending off their girls…' Violet says.

'Lillian and… Elizabeth, isn't it?' I recall.

'That's them. Little Lillian's six I think, and Liz is eight, sweet things. I'm not being over-cautious, am I, Vera? I'm doing the right thing?' she begs.

'I'm sure you are, Violet. I'm sure you are,' I say convincingly, though what do I know? It's hard to imagine being in her shoes.

'Are you thinking of volunteering, Vera?' Violet asks after a short pause. 'They want to recruit even more wardens.'

I consider her question. Perhaps she finds the role lonely, or feels I should do more, having not had to sacrifice anything, really.

'Lyons wants us for every hour we can give them. I won't have the time,' I say, feeling slightly inadequate.

We arrive at Waterloo station. It isn't just busy; it's a roaring, echoing cathedral of goodbyes.

The vast concourse shudders under the shuffle of thousands of feet, the sharp hoot of whistles, the drone of announcers, and a thousand tiny, choked sobs. Khaki uniforms blend with ARP grey and the bright splashes of children's coats. The air tastes of steam, fear, and even excitement.

We don't know where Rita and James are going - not even most of the teachers seem to know. *Somewhere safe*, they say. It's the mantra everyone clings to, a thin comfort against the vastness of the unknown.

I kiss them both on the cheek, feeling the warmth of their small faces. Violet hugs them long and hard, crouching so she can look Rita in the eye.

'Take James's hand,' she whispers. 'You look after him now. Promise me.'

It's a lot for an eight-year-old to carry, but Rita nods solemnly and squeezes her brother's fingers. Then James turns to the train and points.

'The magical train, like the one in your story, Aunt Vera,' he says with a smile I wish I could bottle up and keep forever.

'That's right, sweetheart, you're going on an adventure,' I say with as much enthusiasm as I can muster.

The authorities keep us behind a little gate - more of a flimsy barrier really - designed to keep the parents back as the children are hurried onto the train. I can't take my eyes off Rita and James. They're not even my own, but still I watch and watch until suddenly they're swallowed by the crowd, their little heads disappearing into the stream of children, lost in the movement.

And then, before we've really grasped it, the train lurches forward with a groan, chugging away down the track. Hands wave from windows, smiles and kisses are thrown into the smoky air.

'See you soon! Be polite! Mind your manners!'

All those cheery cries float out across the platform, trying to mask the sound of hearts breaking quietly in the silence between whistles.

When we finally step outside into the sharp London air, Violet breaks. She sobs openly, her front crumbling at last. I pull her into a hug and cry too, unable to stop myself.

'They'll be home soon, won't they, Vera?' she whispers, her voice childlike now.

'Of course they will,' I tell her. 'In no time.'

But inside, I can't begin to imagine how she feels. And yet this devastating goodbye leaves me hollow. Makes me wonder why I can't have a goodbye like that with a child of my own. And then, quietly, the panic sets in at the thought that perhaps I never really will.

We make our way back to Battersea slowly. Though it isn't yet dark, everywhere already feels dimmer somehow - quiet, hollowed out by the absence of children playing. Any child we do pass stands out like a sore thumb. Nadine will draw even more attention now, poor thing. It's a lot for a ten-year-old to bear, vilified for both her faith and the country she came from.

And yet I can't deny the contempt in me, simmering under the surface. Not for Nadine, never her - but for the Germans. They put Hitler where he is. They wanted him to lead them, to burn the rest of Europe. All of this, every goodbye, feels like revenge for the last war. That useless, senseless war has a lot to answer for.

As we turn into Turner Street, a commotion rises from the far end. The shouting grows clearer as we approach, and then Pat comes stumbling out of the doorway, shoved hard by her old man, Bill, a stocky man with a grey beard, balding head, and thick-rimmed glasses. I've never had much time for Bill; he's always abrupt, very old-fashioned. How the bright and warm Sheila and Pat came from him is a bit of a mystery.

'Go on, get out! And take your bloody propaganda with you!' he bellows, hurling a fistful of leaflets and posters after her. They scatter across the pavement like startled birds.

'I'm only trying to stop the end of the world!' Pat shouts back, her voice cracking as Bill throws a bag - presumably her things - down at her feet.

Anne, her mother, stands just inside the doorway, thin and silent, her hands clutched together.

'You gonna let him do that, Ma?' Pat cries, glaring at Anne, desperate for her to intervene. But Anne only lowers her gaze, staring at the ground.

Bill slams the door so hard it rattles the windows and echoes down the whole street.

Violet and I just stand there, our jaws slack, the air thick with shock.

'Bastard,' Pat mutters, blinking back tears. 'What is it with people? It's like they want a war. They want people to die. Have we learnt nothing?' Then she turns on Violet, her voice sharp now, full of bitterness. 'You - you must like it, eh? Swanning about in your armband. Makes you feel wanted, does it?'

Violet squares her shoulders, her cheeks flushing red.

'I've just sent my children away, if you must know,' she fires back. 'Don't you dare tell me this is what I want. None of us with any sense wants this. But what bloody choice do we have?' She marches up to Pat, their faces inches apart now, her voice dropping to a furious hiss. 'So go on then. Tell me. What am I supposed to do, Patricia? What the bloody hell am I supposed to do? Tell me! Say something!' Her voice rises into a shout, rage trembling in it as Pat remains silent. 'What's the matter, eh? Cat got your tongue?'

Pat swallows but does not utter a word. She just shakes her head, turns sharply, and begins gathering her scattered papers, her hands trembling but determined.

The tension still hums in the air as Violet strides away, shoulders stiff, and heads for home. I continue towards the posh end. The blackout preparations are already visible: curtains drawn tight, some windows painted black, the whole street dim and subdued though the sun hasn't yet gone.

Then I see him.

In the distance, near Number 80, where Eve Morris lives, a tall gentleman stands on the pavement, lingering like he belongs and yet doesn't.

As I approach, he turns slightly. Even in the faint light I can see his striking features, a film - star kind of handsome, with a well-defined jaw, dark eyes, and hair the colour of warm sand, ruffled by the breeze.

He drops a key, perhaps startled by me, and stoops to pick it up, then meets my gaze again.

'Good evening,' I murmur as I pass, my voice coming out quieter than I mean it to.

He nods and then says,

'Careful. It'll be dark soon. Darker than ever.'

I give him a faint smile, returning the nod.

He watches me for a moment longer, then turns into the doorway.

I keep walking, but just before I reach the house I glance back and there he still is, framed in the doorway of Number 80, half in shadow, watching me. When he realises I've caught him looking, he dips his head quickly and shuts the door.

I don't know who he is. But I wish I did.

# 6 War

It's just gone eleven on Sunday morning, and remarkably Mrs Miller has allowed the wireless to be turned up full whack for everyone to hear. We're all waiting for the formal announcement from Chamberlain, though it feels more like confirmation of something we already know.

Then, amongst the crackle and hiss, his nervous voice cuts through:

*"This morning the British Ambassador in Berlin handed the German Government a final note stating that unless we heard from them by eleven o'clock that they were prepared at once to withdraw their troops from Poland, a state of war would exist between us. I have to tell you now that no such undertaking has been received, and that consequently this country is at war with Germany."*

And that was that.

We all just went back to it, nipping from table to table, carrying on as though nothing had changed. We're at war now, but the moment feels no different from the one before.

It's different for me, of course, still working, same customers, same gossip. But it must feel different for people like poor Violet, listening to the news while her children are away in some unknown place. Readying herself for a role that will be so demanding.

Sheila, meanwhile, seems flustered about everything.

'Pat's gone AWOL,' she mutters, her voice tight with worry.

'Your old man kicked her out,' I reply. 'I saw it with my own eyes.'

'Yes, but she always comes back. Not this time. She could be anywhere. And during a blinking war.' She shakes her head. 'She worries me, she really does. She thinks I told Father about her ramblings, but I didn't utter a word. He always finds out about everything. She should know by now'.

'You reckon he'll find out about this Samuel of yours?' I ask, trying to get more information about this slightly mythical love interest of hers.

'Eventually,' she sighs. 'Actually I've been meaning to tell you...'

Mrs Miller's booming voice cuts across the room before Sheila can finish.

'Ladies! Enough nattering. To work!'

We scatter quickly, slipping back into our tasks, the air still thick with unspoken questions.

But our rush to serve customers soon turns into a scramble to reach the basement as the air-raid siren wails, only minutes after the announcement of war.

'Blimey, that was quick,' I call out, thundering down the steps with Sheila close behind. 'They don't mess about, do they?'

Oddly, some customers join us, while others just scurry out of the shop altogether.

'They'd better come back to pay the bill,' Mrs Miller grumbles, glaring after them, as Lazy Lorraine saunters down at the very last moment.

And then we stand there, all of us, waiting, holding our breath, bracing ourselves as the first siren of the war howls above us. We listen, pray, hope…

But nothing happens.

The siren fades and then the all clear sounds. A false alarm, apparently. Or maybe just a practice, to wake us all up to the reality we'll now be living with.

We head back upstairs and slip straight into the rhythm again, back to work, back to normality, rushed off our feet once more.

I finish work earlier than Sheila and I'm ever so quick to get home, partly to check in on Dad, but also because I don't know when it really begins. Whatever *it* is.

Once I'm on Turner Street I walk briskly towards Dad's, only slowing when I pass Number 80, just in case he, whoever he is, happens to appear again. I really shouldn't - it's inappropriate - but the urge is there all the same, prominent and unsettling for someone who barely got a glance of the man.

When I get to Dad's, Henry answers the door. Joy is with him, standing at the stove, cooking, her sharp red hair tied up. The gramophone plays softly in the corner and, surprisingly, there's a faintly jubilant atmosphere about the place. Dad sits at the table, sipping his pint of bitter. His pipe returns, now a regular feature.

'So… it's happening, then?' I say.

He glances up, gives a small nod, then puts his head back down.

My George emerges from the outside lavatory, zipping his fly.

'Didn't know you were here,' I say to him.

'Joy's cooking,' he adds, with something sharp in his tone. 'Wouldn't miss it. A woman who actually cooks.'

I feel so small, so quickly, so useless.

I excuse myself, saying I need to get out of my uniform and have a wash. All of which is true, but as I walk home it strikes me how… normal everything still feels. Like a declaration of war is no great thing. Perhaps it's just a delayed reaction. Or maybe we're all so used to the tension by now that it really is just another day, we live, and we wait for a siren and react when it comes.

When I get into my place, Esther is sitting with Nadine at the kitchen table, playing cards. Esther leans forward and says,

'Go on, show Vera what you've learned.'

Nadine grins and performs a simple magic trick, making the Ace of Spades all but disappear.

'That's marvellous, that is, Nadine. Really clever.'

'Good teacher,' she says, her English clear and careful.

'She's doing all right,' I say to Esther, who's beaming with pride. 'Are you all right, Nadine? With… you know… what's happening? You must be worried. It's okay, you know.'

Esther quickly translates and Nadine nods.

'I'm okay,' she says with a shy smile.

As I turn to leave, she stands, then in her best English says, very solemnly:

'You are not at war with Germany. You are at war with Hitler.'

I nod and give her a smile.

If only everyone saw it that way.

Of course, the fact Chamberlain himself stood there and declared we're at war with Germany doesn't help. No matter how you phrase it, Germany is the enemy - and here I am, living with a German. A child, yes. A Jewish girl, the Nazis' nightmare. How they could hate something so innocent, so gentle, is beyond me.

That evening I sit and wait for George to come home. As the hours crawl by, I keep glancing at the clock, listening out for the air-raid siren, certain it will wail at any moment. Surely tonight it would happen. The Germans wouldn't wait. But for now, there's just silence, worry, the unknown. I feel like I'm the only person alive worrying, though of course I know I'm not.

When George finally comes in, he's tired, drunk, swaying.

'No Jerries then,' he calls out, holding his arms wide like he's spoiling for a fight. 'Except the one downstairs,' he adds with a laugh that makes my stomach turn. 'Come on, what are they scared of, eh?' he slurs, barely managing to stay upright.

'You an' arf reek of beer, George.'

'Yeah, well, make the most of it, eh?' he mutters, already clambering for another glass. 'This could be it for us, you know. Well, for me. They're bringing in compulsory conscription. Bastards like me, they'll put right at the front. Target practice.'

'Don't say that, George,' I snap, his words genuinely frightening me now.

'Well it's the bloody truth, isn't it?' he shoots back. He slumps into the armchair, clutching his glass. 'This is the end, you know. Us Hopkins. I go, and that's it. No more. I die, an entire bloodline snuffed out. That, Vera… that is failure.'

He gulps at his drink, his temper rising with each mouthful.

'You do talk some rubbish when you've had a drink, George.'

'Rubbish? What's rubbish about it?' he sneers. 'It's true, isn't it? You won't give me a baby. You don't love me enough.' There is a wildness in his eyes then, a look I didn't recognise, and it chilled me more than his words but before I can properly process it, he rises slowly, swaying, and starts towards me. 'Why won't you give me that baby, Vera? What have I done to you?' His fingers fumble at his trousers, the other hand tugging at the tie of my housecoat.

'Not now, George,' I say firmly, though my voice betrays me, thinner than I'd like. His breath stinks of beer and cigarettes, but he's persistent, determined even.

He pushes me down onto the sofa, so forceful I let out a gasp.

'George, you're scaring me!'

'Shut up,' he spits, now on top of me, his full weight pressing down. 'You'll give me that baby, Vera. You hear me?'

Then he takes me, though it's not love. Nothing like it. Just this possessive, animal-like determination.

I don't look at him, turning my head away, his hot, angry, pungent breath rasping against my ear.

I let him get on with it.

He goes on, horribly rough, selfish, angry. I lie there, yearning for it to end.

It's amazing really, I think; we're meant to be at war out there, and yet it's eerily quiet outside.

The real war is here, in this room, between these walls.

A battle I never expected to fight. One in which I have to face alone.

# 7 Enough

The next morning, I wake with a dull ache in my chest, though it's nothing compared to the ache in my hips. The night before sits heavy on me still: George's hands, the smell of beer on his breath, the things he muttered in my ear. No bombs, no sirens, no screaming skies. Just his dreadful words and actions.

The morning is quiet, almost too quiet. No air-raid warnings, no distant guns. Just the ordinary shuffle of feet on Turner Street as it slowly rouses itself, life carrying on. So much for this war. Things feel calmer now than they did before it was formally declared.

With the day off and no appetite for spending a minute in George's company - a terrible thing to admit, but my whole body tenses at the thought - I decide to take Nadine into town and treat her to something at Woolies.

As we walk down Turner Street, towards the down end, the whole place feels unchanged, though every window still wears its blackout curtain like a badge of grim resolve.

Then, suddenly, he appears again. The handsome man.

He steps outside just ahead of us, this time wearing a steel helmet, rubber boots, trousers, and a heavy woollen jacket. He doesn't see me, just walks on, his heavy boots echoing through the street.

'Fireman?' Nadine murmurs, half-question, half-practice of her English.

'Yes,' I say, smiling faintly. 'I think he is. He's new to the street, like you.'

As we approach the down end, Bill Warner - Sheila's dad - is leaning on the doorframe, cigarette in his mouth, cleaning his glasses.

'Watcha, Bill,' I say, keeping it quiet.

He tuts, eyes narrowing on Nadine.

'You've got a bloody nerve, haven't you?' he says, voice harsh, at her, or perhaps at both of us. 'Walking round here like you own the place.'

'Give it a rest, Bill,' I snap back, but he carries on.

'All the young 'uns gone, and yet here's a German one, bold as brass. You couldn't make it up. I'd keep my mouth shut round her, Vera. She's not to be trusted.'

'She's a Jew, Bill.'

'Yeah,' he snorts, dismissive, taking another long draw on his cigarette. 'Good cover, that.'

I grip Nadine's hand tighter and keep walking. I hope she doesn't understand much of it, but I have a sinking feeling she understands enough.

When we eventually get to Woolies, the world feels softer. Nadine is mesmerised by it, all the colours, the counters, the smell of sugar and polish.

She lingers by the stationery aisle, fingers hovering over a small notepad and a set of coloured pencils.

'Go on,' I tell her. 'Treat yourself.'

She looks up at me and whispers, careful with her words:

'I will draw… mein haus… order house,' she corrects herself, smiling shyly, 'so you can see it.' I smile back, though my heart twists a little.

Across the shop, I'm distracted by the sound of other children clattering round the sweet counter. And there she is, Mrs Butler from Number 110, with Lillian and Elizabeth in tow. The girls are shrieking, laughing, climbing over each other.

Mrs Butler, professional as ever, stands in her fashionable coat and neat little hat, casting a watchful eye over them. She glances my way, gives me a knowing, gentle wave, then turns back to scolding the girls with quiet authority. I know very little about her. Her husband, Mr Butler, is even more of a mystery, working for the government, which no doubt means he's busier than ever. The children calm down, but the cheeky giggles remain between them.

When we get home, Esther comes rushing towards us, her face alight with hope, tears glittering in her eyes. She clutches a letter tightly in her hand, saying something in French, quick, enthusiastic, too fast for me to catch a single word.

But Nadine understands perfectly. She grabs the letter and literally jumps for joy, clutching it to her chest. Esther turns to me, her voice trembling.

'It's David, my brother. He has reached France.'

'Oh, that's marvellous,' I say.

'He hopes Nadine will be able to join them soon. And perhaps… perhaps I can even go. He's in Lille.'

'Well, thank the Lord he's out of Germany, eh?'

Esther then draws me aside as Nadine continues poring over the letter. Esther's expression darkens as she lowers her voice.

'He wrote me another letter. Just for me,' she whispers, slipping a second envelope from her pocket and glancing back at Nadine. 'About… the horror. *Épouvantable*.'

She presses it into my hand.

'See…'

But the page is filled with scrawled French and cramped, barely legible handwriting.

'It's in French, Esther.'

'Oh, yes, right,' she murmurs, snatching it back. She skims it quickly, translating as she goes. 'He says the final days in Germany were… a test. A test of endurance. They would walk through the streets like ghosts, invisible or worse: targets. He was beaten at random. Nobody helped. Some even cheered. The Nazis have taken everything, their livelihoods, all possessions, even their dignity.'

She lets out a long breath and glances at Nadine, who is still smiling softly to herself as she traces the handwriting on her letter.

'You know,' Esther says quietly, 'it was already like that before Nadine got out. She had to live through so much. I'm just glad she doesn't have that here.'

'I wouldn't be so sure,' I mutter under my breath, thinking back to Bill and his foul mouth.

That poor love can't catch a break.

In the afternoon, I go round to Dad's. Joy is cooking again because, well, she's perfect at everything. Dad is clearly warming to her. She's made a stew, rich thing it is, too filling, but you don't complain. Henry is his usual scatty self but seems more on edge this time. It's understandable; there's so much talk about conscription. George sits beside me. We don't make eye contact. He looks defeated. Is it shame? I don't think so. But it's like he doesn't want to be anywhere near me, and I feel much the same.

'You had a row?' Dad finally says, pointing at me and George with his spoon. I shake my head. George does the same, not long after.

'Something's up,' Dad carries on. 'She being difficult?' he asks George, as if I am the one to blame.

'Henry's got some news that he'd like to share,' Joy finally says, turning the attention to them both which is a relief, deliberate perhaps. 'Go on, Henry, tell him.'

There's a noticeable silence for a second as Henry finishes his mouthful, taken aback slightly.

'Well… I thought you'd all like to know. I've voluntarily signed up today for the RASC, you know, the Royal Army Service Corps.'

'I know, I know,' Dad shouts, shock in his voice, gravy down his shirt. I too can't quite believe what he's saying.

'I want to defend my country, Dad,' Henry says, innocently, defensively. 'I need to play my part. Besides, I'll be called up anyhow. This way I get a bit of control, you know?'

Dad is now speechless. George noticeably nods in agreement, like he already knows.

'So what's that then?' I'm quick to ask. 'Driving lorries or what not?'

'Yeah, some of that,' Henry says, confidence growing. 'But it's more than just driving. It's… logistics, they call it. Making sure the lads at the front get their grub, their fuel, their ammunition. All the stuff they need to keep fighting.'

'I don't believe this,' Dad adds, anger brewing, but Henry keeps going.

'They're taking livestock too, to feed the boys. With my butchery, felt like the right fit, you know?'

'You've never slaughtered an animal in your life,' Dad snaps.

'Well, it's far better than slaughtering people,' Joy chimes in.

'He'll end up doing both or become the slaughtered,' Dad says, a real sadness now taking hold.

'Thought you'd be proud, Dad,' Henry says gently, almost childlike. 'You did, didn't you? Volunteered? I want to serve my country like you.'

'We didn't know what we were getting into, son.' He slides his stew away, unable to eat any more.

'I'm not a boy, Dad. I can hack it. I'm a man,' Henry says, then glances over to George.

'What, and I'm not?' George bites, aggressively, dropping his spoon in his bowl. It clatters and rings around the room.

'Nah, I'm just saying… country first.'

'They'll call me up anyhow. It's just a matter of time,' George says dismissively.

'Well, you could come with me. Same regiment. Dad served with his best mates.'

'And none of 'em came back,' Dad says slowly, every word landing cold.

'This war is different, Dad,' Henry says. 'Look, listen, it's probably a lot of commotion for nothing. I won't even hear a gun being fired. But at least I can say, in the moment I was needed, I stepped up.'

Joy grabs his hand to support him while Dad drops his head.

I don't know what to say. I don't want Henry to go to war, but like he says, at least he's had a say. Determined how he will serve rather than being thrown anywhere. And maybe he's right. Maybe this war will be different to the last one. So far, all is quiet. They might not even need Henry. I've got to stay positive. Upbeat. It's all you can do.

'You'll be brilliant, Henry. They'll be lucky to have you,' I say, forcing the optimism out.

'Thanks, Vera.'

And then George looks at me. Daggers for eyes. Hatred. Vile hatred. I can't put a foot right.

That evening, I just know I'm going to get it from George. What it is, I'm not entirely sure, but it's enough to make me feel on edge. Frightened, even. I think of how our once - loving marriage has deteriorated so dramatically, and I have no idea how to get it back to what it once was.

At home, George sits on the edge of the bed, deep in thought, staring at the floor.

'I'm going to sign up,' he says suddenly. 'Like Henry.'

'I don't think so, George,' I reply carefully.

'So, they're lucky to have Henry but not me?' he shoots back, his voice already rising.

'No… no…' God, I can't win this one. 'I just don't want you to leave, that's all. I want you here.'

He laughs, a cold, dismissive laugh.

'You don't want to know me half the time,' he mutters.

'I just don't want… the worst to happen, that's all. Henry's made up his mind, but I can tell you've no appetite for it.'

'Well, you're wrong,' he snaps. 'I want to serve. To be needed. At least something needs me. You don't think I'm capable.' I choose not to reply. Nothing can draw him back once he's like this. 'You don't think I'm a man, do you?' he goes on bitterly. 'Like what Henry said, you don't think I'm a man, do you, Vera?'

'Yes, George. You're a man,' I say quietly.

He suddenly gets up, dropping his trousers in front of me, exposing himself, sneering. Grabbing his manhood to prove he is indeed a man.

'I'm a man, Vera,' he repeats, stepping towards me, his voice thick and threatening.

I back off into the corner of the bedroom, my breath quickening.

'I'm a man,' he keeps saying, closing the gap between us.

Then I notice her.

Young Nadine. Standing silently in the doorway, clutching a picture she's drawn of her home. She holds it up, so proud of her work, her face innocent and hopeful.

George notices me looking past him and spins round, his eyes locking on her.

'What the hell are you doing, you nosey little bitch!' he roars, charging towards her while pulling up his trousers. He quickly snatches the drawing from her hands and it rips in two.

I rush after him as he raises his hand, this time to hit Nadine.

'How dare you!' he screams. I grab hold of his arm with all my strength, stopping him mid-swing.

He freezes, shocked by my defiance. Nadine, wide-eyed and sobbing now, scurries out of sight. Then he turns on me instead and in one furious motion, he slams me back against the wall and grips me by the throat.

'Who do you think you are, Vera?' he snarls, squeezing tighter.

I try not to show fear, though my tears and trembling lips betray me.

'Eh? Who are you, you bloody cow? Answer me!' he screams, his breath hot and sour against my cheek.

'ENOUGH!'

I hear that word cut through the room like a gunshot, sharp, clean, and unmistakable, coming from the corner of the room. And there Esther stands in the doorway, her back straight, her voice carrying in the clearest, harshest English I've ever heard her speak.

'Enough!' she says again, her eyes fixed on George.

He loosens his grip, staggers back, and storms out of the room without another word.

I slide to the floor, sitting there in the corner, weeping silently, my body trembling. Esther kneels beside me, her arms around my shoulders, whispering softly in French.

'Is Nadine okay?' I manage to choke out, my voice cracked.

I can get through this again, but I just pray she's okay.

# 8 Winter

Not much has been said since that night, not by me, nor Nadine, Esther, and certainly not George. What could be said? What could be done?

I live now with this constant dread, a fear of falling out with the man I'm married to, no, a fear of him altogether.

As the nights draw in and winter falls, the blackout becomes more pronounced. The darkness is like nothing I've ever known, as though London itself has vanished. I wish my thoughts would vanish with it. It's easy enough to black out the streets, but not so easy to black out your mind.

And while everything around me seems to move slowly, the army wastes no time gearing up for the war. I learn quickly enough that George did indeed volunteer his services and so he and Henry are ordered to Aldershot for military training - basic at first, then more specific to their unit. They'll be gone for many weeks, though likely home for Christmas.

When the news came, I felt pulled in two directions; my mind was celebrating, but my stomach was in knots. A relief that I could finally feel safe, away from

George's firing line, yet a fear of the unknown. Worry about how I'm expected to be with his absence.

George's ability to behave so normally, so charmingly, is chilling. When I stood at the bus stop and waved him off to Aldershot, he was all sweetness and gentlemanly, a perfect husband doing his duty for mine and others. It felt like a performance.

But everyone, from strangers to my own nearest and dearest, is so convinced of him, so taken in. Dad even shed a tear for both he and Henry. Nobody would believe there is an uglier side to George Hopkins.

The only person who's glimpsed it is Esther, in that one brief, awkward moment. And ever since, George has gone out of his way to avoid her altogether.

With George gone, even on the darkest of days I hold on to a little light, knowing I can sleep in peace, knowing I won't say the wrong thing and set him off.

But I'm concerned for Dad, who has been left in bits, mentally and physically. His two main workers at the butcher's are gone, and as Christmas looms the weight of it all is crushing him. He's relying on odd help from whoever will offer it. I even saw Doris in the shop the other day, apron on - things must be desperate. And then something even more shocking: Harold in the back, chopping away. Yes, a blind man with a meat cleaver. Needless to say, that was a one-off, after an injury that surprised absolutely nobody.

Henry and George's absence is really felt, and they're not the only ones from Turner Street to be called up. Arthur Henderson, my old teacher's son and once, very briefly, my sweetheart, has also been called up, though reluctantly, not voluntarily. His twin, Ken, remains behind thanks to his reserved role at the power station, a place everyone says will be a target sooner or later.

Sheila's brother Thomas Warner has also been given his orders. He no longer lives on the street, but it still feels close to home. Thomas, apparently, is thrilled about it all, having previously trained in the navy. He's a devoted nationalist, just like their father, Bill. Her older sister, Pat, has still gone AWOL. I think Sheila is more worried about her than about her brother who is destined for combat. Sheila says this war is something that Thomas does not fear, in fact in many ways he embraces it.

One evening, in the darkness of night, I sit on my bed reflecting on where we are. My feet throb from the longest of shifts - Lyons still lively despite so many folk being carted off here, there, and everywhere. I can hear dogs barking in the distance, Clapham Junction clattering as always, a faint whistle, perhaps another train of men being sent off to barracks, off to train, to prepare for whatever the so-called Führer throws at us.

I'm sitting there when Esther gently knocks on my door.

'Come in,' I call.

She enters carrying a little cheese board - is there anything more French? - piled with exotic cheeses, alongside a smell which will no doubt live in my room forever. And with it, of course, a bottle of wine.

'Something to eat? Drink?' I giggle as she sits beside me, laying the feast on the bed between us.

She watches me for a moment, then says carefully, as though weighing up whether she ought to speak at all,

'Are you missing George?'

'I miss the man I married,' I say, after a pause. 'But he left long before he set off on that bus.'

She nods, a faint, knowing smile, then, hesitantly, her accent thicker than usual as she searches for the right words.

'Maurice... was different. So sensitive? Not a fighter. Maybe you say weak.'

'He was a good man,' I tell her, rubbing her leg gently in comfort.

'Yes. But all men... can hurt you. They... let you down. Break your heart. It is what they are destined to do.'

'Did Maurice break your heart?' I ask softly.

'In the end... yes. He hurt me. He...' she falters then, tears springing to her eyes. 'You see... it was no accident. His death.'

Her words slip out into the silence between us.

'What do you mean, like murdered?' I say, too loud, and she quickly shushes me.

'No... not that. No. He could not go on. No work. No hope. But he left me feeling... feeling that I had no purpose. That my love was not enough.'

'He... killed himself?' I ask, making sure I keep my voice low. Esther nods reluctantly. 'That must have been so hard,' I whisper.

'It is... how do you say...' she waves a hand, searching for the word, 'like a shame... a...'

'A taboo?' I offer gently.

'Yes. Perhaps. So… we just say it was this accident. Easier, you see?'

I nod.

'You see, those you love will always hurt you, one way or another. If you love, you will hurt.'

She pours wine into a china cup, a noticeable absence of a proper glass and hands it to me as I try and offer some hope.

'We've just got to stick with it, haven't we? You know… make the best of a bad situation. This war and all that, well, it's changed George. Once it's all over, I reckon he'll be right as rain again.'

Esther gives me a not - terribly - convincing nod, knowing full well I'm clutching at optimism because it's all I really have.

'Have you really not sung since Maurice…' I pause over the word, then finish quietly, '…since he died?'

'No, not really. I don't think I have the strength for that.'

I take a sip from my cup and let her words settle. It strikes me, sitting here in the quiet, how remarkable it is, how we all live with our secrets, our untold truths, hidden away behind these blacked-out windows. And now, with this war pressing in on us, it seems to be spilling everything out.

Soon the Christmas season begins. There's still an attempt to be festive, to hold on to that spirit, but it's not the same. The lack of lights, of decorations, perhaps even of hope.

In the front yard of my old school, St Mary's, stands a beautiful pine tree. Every year the children decorate it with homemade baubles and paper chains, but this year it stands bare, as though it is waiting for the children to come home. Mrs Henderson told me the children who stayed behind, like the Butler girls, were allowed to take their decorations home, but something about keeping up the tradition in the strangest of times felt wrong.

'We can carry on as normal, like they say,' Mrs Henderson murmured, lingering outside her front door. 'But it's not normal, is it? Far from it.' She'd only just seen her Arthur off. You can sense her aching worry.

Violet has understandably refused to acknowledge the festive season, feeling so isolated with both Stanley and the children away from home. Postcards from Rita and James provide mild comfort, but it's no substitute. She also has the reassurance of Stanley's regular letters. His recent one came from some port he wouldn't name. He said the food's cold, the nights colder, and the only music they get is the thrum of the engines. He made a joke of it, but I could hear the fear tucked between his words.

I sat with Violet one evening as we both wrote Christmas cards for the children and packed up a little box of treats. No doubt it will be opened by someone checking the post before it gets anywhere near Rita and James, but we can only hope it reaches them in one piece. Violet seems more frustrated now, all this upheaval and still no real danger. You can imagine her pain, not having the children here when there's nothing to show for it.

On the 22nd of December, the boys return from their military training. Both are surprisingly gleaming, part happiness at being home, part genuine enjoyment of the experience.

Dad is quick to dampen the mood.

'It's all fun and games when you're practising,' he mutters. 'Different story when some Jerry wants you dead.'

Both Henry and George dismiss it with a laugh.

Joy puts on a sort of celebratory spread in the kitchen.

'They've only been gone six weeks,' I tell her, amused.

'I've been worried sick,' she says, laying down scotch eggs. 'You just don't know what's happening, do you?'

'They were in Hampshire, Joy. It's hardly the Somme.' I can't imagine what she'll be like if, heaven forbid, they're sent close to the front line.

'We've got a home telephone put in the flat. I might be able to call Henry on occasion, would be better than relying on letters that take forever,' Joy says gently, with a touch of naivety.

'A home telephone, we are posh, aren't we?' I tease.

Since returning, George has been...peaceful. He sits at the table, sharing stories about his responsibilities, speaking proudly of his much-praised driving skills. Of course, they can't say too much, but it's enough to make me feel Britain is at least somewhat prepared.

There are mutterings of France. Apparently, they'll be heading there before long.

'Oh, you can take Nadine with you then,' I say, trying to keep the conversation light. 'Her dad's in France now.' George shoots me a look and cuts in, sharp as ever.

'Why do you always bring her up? She's got nothing to do with us.'

It silences me immediately. That familiar chill of George, the man I've been fearing all along, creeping back in.

Christmas Day itself starts with a bit of a shock. We're barely through the front door of Dad's when Henry and Joy arrive, flushed with excitement, Joy practically glowing. She's bouncing on her heels, holding out her hand for all to see, and there it is: a modest but pretty ring catching the morning light.

'Henry has asked me to marry him!' she says, barely able to get the words out before tears threaten. Dad gives a knowing smile, and I'm quick to hug her, genuinely chuffed. It reminds me of when George did the same for me on Christmas Day, when I was giddy with happiness.

'Did you ask her father?' George pipes up, directing his question at Henry.

'Of course,' Henry says proudly.

'And he said yes?' George adds, putting on a tone of mock shock.

'Cheeky sod, of course he did!' Henry laughs, nudging George in the ribs.

'Blimey,' George grins, 'you'll be like me, Joy, both of us marrying beneath ourselves.'

The room erupts in laughter, and for a second, it's like everything's normal again. Though I know George is not joking - he never quite is - somehow, he always manages to get the room on his side.

I'm genuinely pleased for Henry and Joy. They make a lovely couple, and in a world full of gloom, the promise of a wedding is something to look forward to.

The announcement truly lifts the spirits, but Dad remains quiet, distant. He usually is, but Christmas is always the exception. After a few ports he's normally up performing his Max Miller impression, blue joke book in hand, making even the shyest of us giggle behind our napkins. But not this year. Not even Christmas can renew his hope or switch him back on. When he does speak, it is more about the war.

'They're going to restrict bacon,' he announces, carving the ham with commitment. 'So enjoy this while you can.'

'There'll be uproar,' Henry grins. 'You can take the kids away, but not our bacon sarnies.' He jokes.

The food looks delicious. There is a sense that this is the last of plenty, and soon a feast will be a thing of the past. This year Joy has taken charge of the cooking instead of me. She has been bustling about the kitchen like she owns it. She's in her element, to say the least, and naturally I feel more redundant than ever. And now, with this engagement, her role in the family will become even more profound.

'You can pour the tea later, Vera,' Henry jokes, already fuelled by port. 'You're an expert at that!'

'She's good at other things,' George mutters under his breath, smirking suggestively.

'Oi, that's my sister,' Henry chuckles. They continue to joke at my expense, and I just sit there, of no help, just a target in so many ways.

That evening, when we get home, George makes love to me, the first time since he's been back. He's at least gentle, for him anyway. But my mind drifts elsewhere, far away. I let him use my body while my thoughts scatter like ash. He senses I'm not present but, as ever, he doesn't understand why. Which says everything about him.

'Something's wrong with you, Vera,' he mutters afterwards. I say nothing. 'That's probably why you can't get pregnant,' he continues, lighting a cigarette. 'Maybe you have to actually be into it to make a baby, you know?'

'There's a lot going on, George,' I say carefully.

'Really? Nothing much going on here,' he scoffs. 'Besides, I'm the one who's gonna have to defend the bloody country. You just have to smile and pour tea.'

'We don't want a baby,' I tell him quietly. 'Not while there's a war on.'

He stiffens, slams his cigarette into the ashtray and stands, pacing, furious.

'Don't tell me what I want, Vera. That's your problem. That's why it hasn't happened. You don't want a baby. Bloody hell, Vera, what other purpose have you got, eh?'

And then he storms out. Gone, swallowed up into the blackout outside.

On Christmas Day. No carols. No festive cheer. Just anger and resentment.

I know now exactly where I stand. What my purpose is supposed to be. And for whatever reason, I can't give it to him.

# *1940*

# 9 Jazz

Not long after Christmas, George and Henry head back to Aldershot to continue their training. It's likely they won't be much longer before coming home again, and then the next call-up will be the real thing - most likely to France.

Still, there are no bombs. The sirens barely sound. The shelters remain cold and empty, and we're all left wondering if this is it, or just the calm before the storm.

However, while the bombs may not be landing, there's little doubt we're at war. A few weeks back, we all received our new ration books - special cards that set limits on how much bacon, butter and sugar we're allowed. With Dad being a butcher, I figured I might be alright, but he's sticking strictly to the rules.

As part of it, we've all had to register with a specific butcher, grocer and sweet shop, so the authorities can plan stock properly. It makes the world feel even smaller somehow, like every step, every sausage, is being monitored. I told Dad I'd registered with Withers Butchers in Putney just to wind him up. You should've seen his face, I was only pulling his leg, his good one.

Needless to say, the whole of Turner Street, and half of Battersea, by the sound of it, have registered with Wright & Sons. It's lovely, in a way, to see such loyalty, but it's put a lot of pressure on Dad. He's working longer hours, dealing with queues out the door, juggling customers and quotas and paperwork he's not used to. These new ways of working don't come easy to men like him. None of it does.

We're all just adjusting. Waiting for the next update, the next rule, the next restriction. Nothing surprises me anymore.

I did, however, get a bit of a shock the other day when Sheila's sister Pat suddenly reappeared after being missing for months. There she was, standing in the middle of the tea room as though nothing had happened. Sheila dropped her tray in shock - the smash made everyone jump. You can tell London is on edge. Sheila ran straight over and gave Pat the most almighty hug. Luckily Mrs Miller was having a rare day off, so she didn't witness the chaos of smashed crockery, wide-eyed faces and emotional reunions.

Weirdly, Mrs Miller's day off happened to coincide with Lazy Lorraine's, so Sheila and I have since spun elaborate stories about a forbidden romance. Well, Sheila has. She could be a novelist with that vivid and rather cheeky imagination of hers.

Sheila was allowed a few minutes with her sister, and when she came back, she told me everything. Pat's been sneaking off to secret meetings and protests, trying to stop the war, a bit late for that, you might say. She's staying in Rotherhithe now, living with their Aunt Ivy. I was told very firmly to keep it a secret, because if her dad, Bill, finds out there'll be another war. Despite

Ivy being Bill's sister, he can't stand the woman, real, genuine hatred. Families are funny old things.

'Dad says Aunt Ivy's got a screw loose,' Sheila reveals.

'Well… has she?' I ask.

'No. She's just a socialist.'

'Right… does your father like anyone?'

'Not really,' Sheila says bluntly.

Later, on the way home, the late December darkness covered us like a thick black blanket, our dimmed torches barely lighting our feet. Sheila stopped halfway down Archer Way and tugged me into a narrow alley. I could just about make out her face in the gloom.

'I might have to run off to Aunt Ivy's too,' she says quietly.

'Why?' I ask.

'It's my Samuel,' she whispers.

'Oh, this mystery man. He a socialist as well?'

'No, worse. He's coloured.'

'Sorry? Really?' I try and disguise the shock in my voice.

'Dark as the night sky he is,' Sheila says, her voice low.

'I didn't know you were into coloured men.'

'Neither did I, not till I met Sam,' she giggles 'Dad'll hit the roof,'

'I should say.'

I guess that is why she was so secretive about him, why I'd yet to meet this gentlemen.

Sheila then spends the rest of the walk quietly telling me how wonderful and romantic Samuel is. From

Jamaica, studying medicine at King's, he's clearly got a brain on him.

'New Year's Eve, I'm spending it with him,' Sheila says, all excited 'You should come.'

'No… there's a war on.'

'Is there?'

'Yes. And besides, George is away.'

'He's in Aldershot. No doubt him and the other chaps will have a merry old time. And they say we should keep calm and carry on.'

'Yeah, but not keep calm and carry on with a coloured fella.'

'I'm not asking you to get with one, am I? Just come. It'll be a good night. Promise,' she says, flashing her cheeky smile.

Reluctantly, I nod.

When New Year's Eve arrives, I feel bad even considering celebrating. With everything going on in the world, it's hard to feel upbeat about 1940. But with Sheila's powers of persuasion, I trot along beside her, wearing my favourite bottle-green crepe dress - one I've rarely had the courage to wear. I slip it on with a touch of elegance and a whole lot of guilt.

We head to Soho just as the sun sets and 1940 looms. The thought of going feels both liberating and nerve-racking. I feel like a rebellious teenager, or worse, an undercover spy sneaking about where I shouldn't be. Especially as a married woman. But it's New Year's Eve, and Sheila has promised not to utter a word to anyone. It can't cause any real harm, can it?

When we arrive in Soho, it strikes me that even in blackout, it somehow shines. Then, in a hidden corner off a side street, we find it: a club tucked down a flight of stairs. The music pulses from below, making the pavement thrum underfoot. It's the perfect place during a blackout, no windows in sight, practically a shelter. Only this one has alcohol, dancing and music. Now that's a shelter I could live in.

The sound draws me in before I've even stepped inside. A rich, brassy warmth cuts through the sharp night air. It's not just music; it's a vibrant hum, a rhythm that seems to defy the darkness above. Sheila grabs my hand and we descend into the heat of it.

Light. Sound. Movement. An assault on the senses. The drums strike first, a steady snare brush here, a cymbal shimmer there, setting the pulse. Then a walking bassline, deep and resonant, murmuring beneath everything like a heartbeat. The piano dances on top, quick and bright at first, then softening into something bluesy, tender. It's magical.

And just as I think I've soaked it all in, the trombones slide in, bold and playful, then come the trumpets, loud and boisterous, commanding the room. And at the centre of it all: the silky, masterful saxophone, curling through the noise like smoke. I get lost in it. Completely.

I must look like a fool, standing there still, drinking it all in. But no one cares. No one's watching. They're all moving, dancing, caught up in the same spell I've fallen under.

And the people, I'd been so distracted by the sound, I'd forgotten the people. Crushed together in this tiny underground club, moving in time, shoulder to shoulder. It's as if the entire world is here. Every shape, shade, smile. And for a moment it's overwhelming - the joy, the beauty, the rawness of it all.

I've spent so long reading headlines, convinced the world wants to kill itself. But is that true? No. Not really. The people want to make music. To make love. Hell, even make tea. Anything but war.

Snapping out of my musical trance, I try to spot Sheila in the haze. And there she is, in the corner with her Samuel. A handsome black man, dark as velvet, with wiry hair, eyes like ink and a smile to match.

I dance my way over. He takes my hand and kisses it gently.

'Good to meet you, Miss...'

'Mrs,' Sheila corrects him, grinning. 'She's married. Poor soul.'

'Mrs...'

'Just call me Vera,' I say quickly. Then I turn to Sheila. 'You wanna dance?'

'Of course,' she says, grabbing my hand.

Samuel joins us for a moment as we lose ourselves again in the beat. At one point, I lean into her, shouting over the music:

'I can see why you like him… he's got a lovely face!'

'I know! I think I love him, Vera. I really do.'

We twist and spin like we've been dancing this way all our lives. Hand in hand, laughing, completely untethered. Then, in the chaos of bodies and sound, I'm swept aside, drifting through the crowd - and I spot him.

The firefighter. From number 80. It's him. It has to be. The wavy hair, the imposing height, a face that stays with you forever. He's standing in the corner with a few friends, drinks in hand, watching the scene unfold. I stagger toward him.

'I know you!' I shout.

'Sorry?' he says, leaning in.

'I know you, you live on my street!' I yell, just as a big man climbs up on stage holding a pocket watch.

'Ladies and gentlemen - let us begin the countdown to 1940! Ten… nine… eight…'

We all join in. The fireman stands beside me.

'Three… two… one - Happy New Year!'

He turns and kisses me on the cheek, quick and soft and surprising, then moves along to greet someone else. But the feel of his lips lingers on my skin like a burn. Time seems to slow. And then Sheila's arms are around me, pulling me into a tight hug.

The rest of the night is a blur, dancing, spinning, drinking, laughing. Forgetting the war. Forgetting my husband. I feel alive. I'm not sure I've ever felt this alive.

Fuelled by music and drink and the sheer thrill of pretending I'm someone else, someone from Chelsea, maybe, or Notting Hill, someone who doesn't live on Turner Street.

Eventually, I stumble outside into the cold air, it is January, just. The streets are eerily dark. Quiet. Normally, they'd still be buzzing, especially just a couple of hours into the new year, but the blackout has snuffed it all out, save for the odd defiant pocket like the one we just left.

Sheila's long gone, swept away with Samuel, staying at his place. She offered for me to come, but I couldn't. I have to get home, back to reality, back to my life, back to the woman waiting for a husband she's not sure she wants.

A taxi back feels far too extravagant, I've spent what little money I had, so I start the long walk south. My torch flickers in protest, barely staying lit, like it doesn't want to see 1940 either. I curse at it, bang it, try to coax some life into it. Panic starts to rise in me.

I shouldn't be here. Not now. Not ever. What has Sheila done to me?

And then I hear him - faint, somewhere in the dark. A voice calling out, carried on the hush of the blackout.

'Excuse me… excuse me!'

I can't see anything at first, just a faded light bouncing in the air, like a ghost or something out of this world. And then, finally, he comes into view. Barely, but enough.

It's him. The fireman.

'You're not walking back, are you?' he says, concern written all over his face.

'Yeah, won't take long. Just across the river. I'll be back in no time,' I say, more to reassure myself than him.

'In this dark? At this hour? Let me walk you home.'

My heart skips a beat. I'd love that. But I daren't say it.

'I'm fine,' I insist, lifting my torch. 'I've got me light.' It flickers once, and then dies. Out. Completely. The timing couldn't be better. He raises an eyebrow.

'I'm walking you. We live on the same street.'

He offers me his arm and gestures to his friends, who grin and give him a knowing whistle. He shakes his head at their cheekiness.

'Sorry,' he says with a sheepish smile. 'I don't think they know you're married.'

'How did you know I was?'

'Your ring.'

'Oh. Yeah.' I glance down at it, feeling a bit foolish - and yet strangely comfortable on his arm. 'You're not from round here, are you? Originally, I mean?' I ask him.

'No, country boy really. I was with the Norfolk Fire Brigade, they asked me to come down to London, serve in the Royal Auxiliary. You know, for when the Germans come.' He says it so calmly, like it's a given.

'You sound so certain of it.'

'Yeah. It's not if, it's when. Are you sure you want to stay in London?'

'I don't have much choice. Besides, nothing's come of it yet, has it?'

He just nods, like he's already made peace with it. Like he's ready. It's strangely comforting, that prepared, focused mindset.

We keep walking, occasionally stepping into the glow of a dim, dulled-out streetlamp, which lights his face just long enough for me to catch the handsome shape of it.

I've never felt so safe. So secure. We wander side by side, almost drifting, trusting the roads will take us the right way. Here and there, a few stragglers, drunk and merry, wish us a happy new year.

'I think they think we're a couple,' I say, glancing up at him.

He laughs.

'You don't even know my name, do you?'

God, he's right. I've been so swept up in the feeling, the night, him, I never thought to ask.

'Well… no. What is it then?'

'Eddie. Well, Edward. But Eddie. You're Vera, aren't you?'

'How'd you know that?'

'That girl you were with kept shouting it. Louder than the saxophone.'

'Yeah… she's got a voice on her, our Sheila.'

I giggle.

He smiles.

And we keep walking, into the darkness, into the new year, just two shadows on a quiet London road.

We arrive at Turner Street far too quickly for my liking. He walks me right up to the door.

'Nice place,' he says, eyeing the house.

'Not mine,' I say quickly, letting him know that while I've lived on Turner Street my whole life, my stay at Esther's is fairly new.

'What's it like living with Mrs Morris?' I ask. 'Stern old lady, isn't she? Doesn't say much.' He shakes his head.

'She's gone to Wales until this all blows over, so I wouldn't know.'

'Blimey. Must be lonely, all alone in there,' I tease.

'I'm rarely in, to be honest. But yes… company would be appreciated.'

There's a smile playing at his lips. I think he's flirting. I think I might be flirting back.

'Wonderful to see you, Vera,' he says softly.

I quietly open the front door, the creak of the hinge louder than expected in the still night air.

'Don't be a stranger,' I tell him, glancing back one last time.

Then I close the door behind me, heart thumping in my chest.

This adrenaline, this giddy warmth, what a lovely, charming, kind man. I shouldn't be anywhere near him. But I'll dream of him tonight. That, I'm sure of.

## **10** Escape

I haven't stopped thinking about Edward - Eddie, as he likes to be called. Not in an obsessive, mad sort of way, just in the quiet moments, the in-between bits, when I'm drying dishes or stirring sugar into someone's tea. That New Year's night replays in my head more than I care to admit. His voice, his arm in mine, the way he looked at me like I mattered. It was harmless, a flicker of warmth in a bitter winter. But it lives in me now.

Of course, it couldn't last. That dreamy little world I'd built in my head, full of saxophones and thoughtless dancing, is quickly torn down.

Because George has come home.

This time it's for his final leave before being called up to France. When he arrives, he dumps his kit in the hallway and kisses me on the cheek - without feeling or warmth. A total contrast to Eddie's kiss on New Year's Eve. It was like George only did it because he thought he should. And then, a moment later, he immediately looks down at my tummy.

'Nothing then?' he says. 'You should go and talk to Dr Clarke. Something's not right, Vera. Something really is untoward. I'm worried about you. Your mum died young, didn't she?'

'I've not got TB, George,' I moan back.

'I'm just thinking of you, that's all. I'm gonna be worried sick about you when they cart me off.' He starts pacing, nervous. You can tell the reality is hitting now. Training was one thing, but this… this is real. And I know he's dreading it, even if he refuses to show it.

Later that day, I head over to Dad's in the hope of seeing Henry, but he's yet to arrive, so for now it's just Dad there, and, of course, Doris, fluttering around making his tea.

'You can just tell her to leave, you know, Dad,' I whisper in his ear.

'I heard that,' she calls out from the kitchen. Her miraculous hearing worries me more than anything.

'I like her company,' Dad says, trying to sound casual.

'Does Harold?!' I shoot back, proving my point.

'My Harold is a very understanding man,' Doris chimes in breezily, appearing with a plate of pie for Dad. 'So keep your oar out. You don't see me interfering with you, Vera.'

'Nothing to interfere with,' I reply sweetly.

'Is that right? Does your father know you were in Soho for New Year?' she says, out of nowhere. My body goes rigid.

'How'd you know that?'

'I didn't. But I knew Sheila went 'cause Bill told me. I just assumed you were with her.' She says it with that smugness that makes you want to throw something.

'What you going up there for?' Dad asks, confused.

'Hanging about with negroes,' Doris says, voice full of relish. 'That's what Bill reckons. What would your George think of it?' she adds, stirring the pot.

'We went to a pub, that's all. You just like gossiping, Doris.'

She throws me a dismissive look and disappears back into the kitchen. Dad stares at me, eyebrows high.

'There's a war on, and you're pratting about up in Soho, a married woman and all.'

'Yeah, and you're letting a married woman into your house every bleeding day of the week.'

'She's a friend,' Dad insists.

'To you, maybe. But no one makes steak and kidney pie for "just a friend" without wanting something in return.'

'It's chicken,' he corrects me.

'Same bleeding thing,' I bark back.

The intensity of our confrontation is quickly broken by the arrival of Henry and Joy, more smiles, more optimism. How I envy them.

'Myself and Henry have both decided that we shan't waste any more time,' Joy beams, barely able to contain herself as she hands me an envelope. 'Not with him being sent overseas at any moment.'

I open it slowly, cautiously. Inside is a wedding invitation.

'You having us on?' Dad says, squinting at the paper. 'That's less than two weeks away? I can't shut the shop.'

'You'll sort something out, Dad,' Henry grins, wrapping an arm around Joy's shoulders. I've never seen him look so smitten, so certain.

'I think it's a lovely idea,' I say, smiling at them both. 'Why not, eh? We need a bit of happiness, don't we?'

'Thanks, Vera,' Henry says, soft and genuine.

Meanwhile, Doris stands off to the side, brow furrowed like she's trying to solve a complex riddle.

'I shall need to get a new outfit,' she announces, as if it's a royal engagement.

Henry shifts awkwardly.

'Well, you see Doris… we're keeping it small. Just close family like…'

'I'll be there,' Doris cuts in, firm as anything. 'I know All Saints Church well. The vicar's wife is a dear friend.' She says it with such certainty that there's no room for argument. Henry just nods, resigned. She really is something else.

I decide to leave earlier than planned, to free myself from Doris mainly. I knock next door quickly, hoping to catch Sheila, but no luck. Instead, I get her mother, Anne, at the door. She's a quiet one, Anne - hair always in a net, deep creases in her face that make her look older than her fifty-five years. Not surprising after six kids. The last one nearly did her in during childbirth.

'You'll look out for my Sheila, won't you, Vera?' Anne says, glancing up and down the street, lowering her voice. 'Her father's ever so concerned she'll end up like her older sister… and, well… you're married. My grave concern is Sheila… might disappoint the family.'

'She's fine, Anne. Good as gold,' I say, trying not to cross my fingers behind my back.

Anne offers a tight, grateful smile.

'I'll tell her you dropped by,' she says, closing the door quietly behind her.

Poor Sheila. Falling for Samuel… she's not made life easy for herself.

That evening, I'm unnerved by the fact George isn't home. No doubt he's dropped into the Old Swan again, probably drinking with Henry, celebrating the sudden wedding date, rushing to make Joy his wife before he faces whatever comes next.

I lie in bed, the darkness outside matched only by the darkness in my head. *Best to be asleep, Vera,* I tell myself. Even if I'm wide awake. Best to pretend. Pretend you're resting, pretend nothing's wrong. Some creatures play dead to avoid predators. I think I understand that now.

Eventually, I hear him. The ruffles, the banging. A drunken George, crashing from one side of the room to the other. My heart's thumping so loud you could probably hear it - if he wasn't making such a bloody racket.

'You're not asleep, Vera,' he says, his voice cold and sure.

I turn to him slowly.

'You okay?' I ask, pretending I've just stirred.

He looks at me, straight through me. That look - disgust, disappointment, resentment. It sends a chill straight through to my bones.

'Did you go into town on New Year's Eve?' he asks, quiet but tight.

'What you on about?' I say, playing stupid, keeping my voice groggy.

'Bill was at the pub. Said Sheila went into Soho. Seeing some fella, apparently. Then Doris told him you went with her.'

'Bloody Doris,' I mutter, the frustration slipping out.

'Don't worry about her - answer the sodding question!' George shouts, the rage now properly brewing. The kind of rage that could frighten even the toughest soul.

'She just wanted company. It was a little pub, no bother,' I say, trying to stay calm.

He slams his fist against the wall.

'So while I was away, preparing to defend our country, you were having a jolly old knees-up… or - or was it a leg over, Vera?' he screams.

'Don't be ridiculous, George. It was just a pub. Across the river, that's all.' I get out of bed and move toward him gently. 'I'm sorry. I really am.'

But before I reach him, he strikes me. A heavy slap across the cheek, sharp and brutal, it knocks the air from my lungs and the balance from my legs. I fall back, hand to my face, cheek throbbing and burning.

I cower at the end of the bed, bracing for another. He looks ready. So, without thinking, I bolt - scrambling past him, down the stairs, panic overtaking everything. I just need to get out. Away. Safe.

As I reach the front door, Esther steps out of her living room. George barrels down after me.

'What is happening?' she says, alarmed.

'Stay out of this, you!' George barks.

'*Un morceau de merde,*' I hear her mutter under her breath as I wrench open the door. Cold and darkness slap me like Geroge just did.

'Vera, you've not got a light! Or your gas mask!' he shouts after me, trying to keep his voice down, desperate not to wake the street.

'Leave me alone, George. I just want to be alone.'

'This isn't normal behaviour, Vera. Come here. Now.'

He grabs me by the arm, too tightly, just as the door beside us opens. Number 80. Blimey. It's Eddie.

Eddie steps out, torch in hand, its dim glow catching his handsome face, confusion first, then sharp recognition. He looks at me, then at George, then back again.

'Sorry, madam - is this man bothering you?' he asks, firm but controlled.

'Man!?' George snaps. 'I'm her sodding husband!'

'Doesn't mean you're not bothering her,' Eddie replies coolly, standing his ground.

I jump in, panicked.

'No bother, sorry for the fuss,' I say quickly, trying to calm the air, even though my whole body wants to shake. A part of me wants Eddie to vanish. Another part wants him to save me.

'Keep out of this,' George growls, pointing a finger at Eddie like a threat.

'You're the ones outside my door,' Eddie says plainly, refusing to move.

The tension thickens. George edges closer to him - baiting, itching for a fight. But then, a noise. A vehicle in the distance. First just a faint blue light flickering down the street, barely visible. Slowly, unmistakably, the outline of an ambulance rolls into view.

It stops.

Not far off, just at the down end of Turner Street.

Something lurches in me. Panic. Dread. I move without thinking, walking fast towards it, heart thudding harder than my feet. I forget I haven't got a torch. Forget my lack of gas mask. Forget the sting still burning on my cheek.

George follows behind me. Eddie hovers by his door, watching.

'Get back inside, Vera,' George calls after me, quieter now, a little breathless.

'It could be Dad,' I say, barely turning back. My legs move faster.

As I get closer, the ambulance workers get out but cross the road from Dad's place. I spot Doris, standing in her doorway. Her dressing gown flaps in the cold as she leans forward, gasping in the night air. She shouts at the ambulance drivers as they enter the house.

'You're too blinking late!' she cries out. The words echo painfully down the street.

I cross the road and approach her.

'What's happened, Doris?' I ask softly.

She wipes her face with a crumpled handkerchief.

'My Harold. He's dead.' Her voice cracks as she breaks into a sob.

From across the street, Dad's door opens. Doris rushes over to him, throws her arms around his shoulders. He doesn't push her away. Instead, awkwardly, he places his hands on her back. Not quite sure what to do with them.

'My Harold, my Harold… his heart's given up,' she says, loud enough for the whole street to hear.

And then, behind me again:

'Come home, Vera,' George says. Not a word for Harold. Not a flicker of concern. Just me. Always me. Still trying to pull the strings. 'There's nothing to be done here. Get back to the house.'

I look around. Doris sobbing into Dad. The ambulance. The silence.

And I realise he's right, not about the control, or the blame, or the slap, but about one thing: there's nowhere to run.

Where was I going, really?

This is Turner Street. This is my life. And right now, I'm trapped in it.

So I turn, and follow him home.

# 11 Funeral

All Saints' Church is set to be busy this week. It'll host both Henry and Joy's wedding, and now, dear Harold's funeral. Since his sudden death, Doris has been doing her best to play the grieving widow. She's been dressed head to toe in black, weeping on cue.

'She thinks she's Queen Victoria,' Henry muttered under his breath - and he's quite right, too.

I had to live with them both when Mum was dying, so I know exactly what Doris was like with Harold. She showed little empathy for a man who was blind and lost in more ways than one. Frankly, I'm surprised he clung on this long, all things considered. But now, Doris is determined to present herself as the devoted, heartbroken wife.

The funeral is arranged quickly, just two days before Henry's wedding, in fact.

'She wants him in the ground so she can move on to your father,' Sheila whispers in my ear.

'You can't say that!' I scold her.

'What? Everyone knows she's got a thing for him.'

I worry she's right. And the fact the whole street thinks it unsettles me. It's hard to keep secrets on Turner Street. Impossible to stop the gossip.

At the funeral, Sheila and I sit as far back as we can manage. Dad's been ushered to the front to sit beside Doris, despite his barely-there friendship with Harold. They've known each other for years but never got on. Long ago, Harold accused Dad of exaggerating his time and service on the Somme. He used to say Dad's limp was put on, not that Harold could see it.

'He's blind and bitter,' Dad would often mutter, while Doris would nod along, acting as though she was enduring great hardship. That is, until Harold died. Now, suddenly, he's being remembered as the most wonderful husband a woman could ask for. It's hard to keep up.

The vicar drones on, his voice flat and soporific, while Doris sobs loudly in the front pew. Meanwhile, Sheila and I whisper away like two schoolgirls at the back.

'My George knows about New Year's Eve,' I tell Sheila, my frustration slipping through.

'I didn't tell a soul, honest,' Sheila says, instantly on the defensive.

'Yeah, well... doesn't take a genius to figure out I was with you. I never should've gone.'

'Dad suspects I'm seeing someone he won't approve of,' Sheila admits.

'I know. So does your mum. When are you going to tell them?'

'I dunno. Trying to figure out a way to do it without ending up in one of those,' she says, nodding towards Harold's coffin.

'Is he worth it, Sheila, the hassle?'

'Oh yeah. Oh, *yeah*,' she says with a cheeky moan.

'Oh *yes!*' I repeat, giggling - until we're shushed by at least four people in quick succession. Doris turns around, her face a picture of stone-cold fury.

After the funeral, a small group of us gather back at Doris's. The house hasn't changed a bit since I lived there twelve years ago. Not even the smell. Of course, the furniture is in a different order, but despite its new positioning they are still the same old dark and dirty fixtures. I sit in a crooked chair, trying my best to fade into the dull wallpaper. Sheila's managed to avoid this part of the funeral, lucky girl. I sit there smiling, but not too much. It's a funeral, after all. You don't want to look pleased about the circumstances.

Dr Clarke sits opposite me, chatting away to Dad. They've been close ever since Mum was ill and passed away. Dr Clarke doesn't look too healthy himself these days, he keeps halting the conversation to cough into his handkerchief. A fat chap, too. Always has been. Must be all those free sausages Dad slips him. Not anymore though, not with rationing and more restrictions rumoured to be coming.

Dad's taken on some help at the shop, a young man from India called Mr Sharma. He speaks better English than most of the street, and always has this huge grin and perfect white teeth. It caused a bit of a stir, mind. Not everyone's pleased. He is a skilled butcher, though, and Dad was desperate. Mr Sharma mostly stays in the back when Dad's front of house, but folk still gossip. Bill even threatened to take his custom elsewhere. Trickier now though, what with ration books. If he wants bacon, he'll have to bite his tongue.

Just as I'm wondering if I've sat here long enough to justify leaving, Doris drops into the seat beside me, plonking her large frame into a chair that looks far too fragile.

'He'd have liked to see all these people turn up for him, if he could see,' she says, chomping through something that resembles a bread roll. 'It's tough being a widow,' Doris goes on. 'I can see how your father feels now. Still, at least me and your father have got each other, eh? Two widows, facing this terrible war together.'

She smiles at me, a warm smile by her standards, but it sends a shiver through me all the same.

Poor Dad.

After more than enough time, I leave Doris's. The fresh February air lets me breathe - just slightly. But there's this strange, lingering dread about going home. Not just because George is there, but something deeper, gnawing at the back of my mind like a warning. It's what this nothing - war does to you. You start fearing tomorrow because today's too ordinary, and you think: well, we can't have it this good for long. Sooner or later, it'll be our turn. It's all going to catch up with us.

Turns out my worries were warranted.

When I arrive home, George is sitting on the edge of the bed, his head bowed, staring at the floor. In his hand is a piece of paper.

'I've been called up,' he says after a pause. 'Officially. Full-time, for His Majesty's service. I've got to be at Victoria next week.'

'France?' I ask carefully.

'Doesn't say. Won't. But where else?' He takes a sip from a glass beside him. 'At least you'll be rid of me,' he mutters, downing the rest.

'Don't say that, George. I'll be worried sick.' I urge as George shakes his head, brushing me off. 'Will Henry be the same?' I ask.

He shrugs.

'Dunno. Probably. Poor you, someone you actually care about being sent to fight.'

I wrap my arms around him. I do feel pain, sorrow, fear. I can't help it, I love him, even after everything. I hold him tightly, but his arms stay limp at his sides, his chin tipped up, distant. He lets me hold him for a few seconds before gently pushing me off and reaching for his coat.

'I'm going to The Old Swan,' he says.

'I love you, George,' I say quietly, a tear escaping down my cheek.

'Do you mean that, Vera?'

'On my life, George.'

'Good. I love you too. I love this country as well. I'm doing this for both of the things I love dearly, you understand that, don't you? And for our children, when that day comes.'

I nod.

'I never wanted to hurt you, Vera,' he says, honestly, openly. 'That's not me. This war - this - ' he holds up the letter and shakes it, 'has put me in a spin. You're going to have to accept that.'

I nod again. This is the closest thing I'll get to an apology, and I realise it's a lot, for George.

'I understand. I'm sorry. I've been… well, a terrible wife lately,' I admit.

He nods in agreement.

'You shan't ever run off like that again, Vera. Not in a blackout. Did you see Dr Clarke at the funeral? You should talk to him. I need you well while I'm away.'

He steps forward and wraps his arms around me at last.

'You mean everything to me, Vera darling. But you do worry me. This war worries me. You understand?'

'Yes, George. I understand.'

And then he leaves. And I wait.

This time, I choose not to pretend to be asleep. I stay, waiting, hoping, praying, that George will come home with his senses intact, with the love he insists he still has for me. The hours are long, daunting. There must be so much on his mind: fighting in foreign lands, doing a job he barely understands.

At last, he stumbles in. His breath hits me before he even reaches the bed, beer and cigarettes, thick and sour. He sways slightly, unsteady on his feet. Before he can say whatever's circling in that muddled head of his, I reach out and kiss his warm, wet lips. The taste of beer, smoke, sweat, it lingers, but I push past it.

And we make love. Like we used to. Or at least, we try. Maybe it's all pretend. Maybe it's something real. I can't be sure. But for a moment - a fragile, flickering moment - there's lust. There's want. There's a desperate togetherness that whisks me back to when we were first courting. The war falls away. The pain dissolves. It's almost magical. If only it would last.

Of course, reality keeps trying to claw its way back in. But I hold it off. I think, if I can keep him well, keep him happy, he won't hurt me again. He won't be cruel. He'll go off to war with a smile, knowing I'm here, waiting for him. That's what he needs: something to hold on to. Something solid, certain.

And I need to be that for George.

I need to stop wallowing in my own pain. Stop chasing temptation. I need to make George my priority now.

Afterwards, we lie in bed, side by side, staring up at the greying ceiling. He lights a cigarette, the soft glow of the ember briefly lighting his face.

'Your Henry asked me to be best man,' he says suddenly.

'Oh, marvellous. I thought he might,' I reply, resting my head on his chest. His hair tickles my cheek, soothing the faint bruise still lingering there.

'He got his letter too. Same day as me. Looks like we'll be going together.'

My heart skips. The panic of Henry being called up too, it's a lot to face. And yet, oddly comforting to know they won't be alone.

'You'll be alright, you two. Stick together,' I whisper.

'It's the day after the wedding. Imagine that, just in the nick of time.' He pauses. 'When I go… on that morning, I don't want a fuss. Just a kiss. See me off from here. No parade, no tears. When we make a fuss, it becomes one. I'm just off to work, a longer shift, that's all. You hear me, Vera?'

I nod.

This is the most open George has ever been with me. Maybe it's the drink. Maybe it's the haze left behind after making love. But even though he's not saying it outright, I can hear everything he's too proud to admit. His fear. His worry. That armour all men feel they have to wear, it's cracked, just for now. And in the thump of his heart against my ear, I hear the truth.

George is petrified.

So am I.

What a rotten world.

## 12 Wedding

'They've only gone and booked out the bleeding town hall,' Dad says in disbelief.

'That's her family, Dad. They're very to-do. They've even put a telephone in Joy and Henry's place,' I say, completely unsurprised.

'We'll look like paupers,' he mutters, shaking his head.

'Oh don't be daft,' I try to dismiss his worry, but truth be told, he's got a point. Joy's lot are well regarded. Her father, Mr Williams, works for the council, quite high up, I think. Probably how he got the town hall booked in the first place.

Still, Joy wants to marry our Henry, even if her family aren't all that keen. You can sense their hesitation the moment we arrive at All Saints Church. Her mother's smile is stretched too tight, and her father looks at us like we're from a Dickens novel.

I try to feel comfortable in my new sapphire-blue rayon, its subtle sheen catching the weak winter light, an elegant enough outfit for a big day like this. Joy's sister gives me a look like I've turned up in rags. Snobby cow.

Sheila, at least, looks relieved to be out of her Lyons uniform, comfortable in a well-worn but clean grey frock and sturdy shoes.

Doris is just behind us, in some elaborate hat that hides most of her face, sadly not her mouth. She sits all smiles, itching to be next to Dad.

Henry looks the smartest I've ever seen him. He can't keep still, back and forth like he's got ants in his trousers. George is calm, spending most of the time outside the church having a smoke, staring off into the distance like he's somewhere else entirely. No doubt tomorrow's thoughts are getting in the way. I want to make the most of today, this little pocket of normality and happiness, because I've no idea when George will be back. And the not knowing is agony. Dad feels it too, I can tell. He wants to enjoy the occasion, but the absence of Mum, and the weight of what's ahead, hangs heavy over him. Funny how glee and grief always sit side by side on days like this.

Then the organ swells, and there she is. Joy. A vision in white, her red hair a blazing halo against the satin, looking every inch the society bride her parents probably dreamed of, even if she's marrying Henry Wright, a butcher from Turner Street.

Unfortunately, the vicar's the same one from Harold's funeral, his drone capable of sending folk to sleep even on a day like this.

Before long, we're heading off to the town hall. Henry and Joy - now husband and wife - are carted off in a gorgeous car to make the two-minute journey. Me and Sheila walk instead, while Dad and George accept the offer of a lift from Joy's family. Doris somehow squeezes herself into the car too, her hat flying off as she pushes her way in with determination.

On the way, Sheila turns to me.

'I hope to marry Samuel,' she says.

'Marry a coloured man? Oh Sheila, people will go mad,' I tell her, genuinely concerned.

'Sod 'em.'

'That's easy to say. You'll be targeted. People will say all sorts.'

She stops right there in the street.

'You sound like everyone else, Vera. You've met Sam, he's smashing.'

'People don't see the person, they see the colour,' I say, reluctant but honest.

She pauses, face set with determination.

'I'll bloody well marry him, Vera. One day. You watch me.'

Her fire is something else. I wish I had even a spark of it.

We step through the towering entrance of Battersea Town Hall, and I'm instantly struck by the sheer scale of the place. The main hall yawns out ahead of us, lofty ceilings, and fancy plasterwork, clearly built for crowds far grander than this modest party. The emptiness only amplifies the cold and echo, but no doubt it pleases Joy's family, who wanted grandeur over comfort.

'They think it's a royal bleeding wedding,' Dad mutters, sidling up beside us.

'It's gorgeous,' I say, still taking it all in.

'It's freezing,' Sheila adds.

'Cost an arm and a leg,' George grumbles.

'Can we just be happy for Henry?' I snap, fed up with the moaning.

We take our seats and quickly realise Doris has been planted at our table while Dad's landed himself a spot at the main one.

I sit beside George, who's taken to the wine like a fish to water. Sheila's with us, as is Violet, who managed to make this part of the day in between her ARP duties.

'Still no bombs,' Doris remarks as Violet sits down. 'Your lot must be twiddling your thumbs.'

'Calm before the storm, that's the worry,' Violet replies.

'They wouldn't be sending George and Henry off for no reason, would they?' I add, hoping to shut Doris up.

'It'll be like a holiday,' she retorts. 'Like her kids' - she points at Violet - 'swanning about in the countryside. This is nothing like the last war, believe you me.'

'Can we not talk about it?' George snaps, slamming his fist on the table. 'This is Henry's wedding. Let's not ruin it with talk of war.'

'Quite right,' I say softly, rubbing his arm to steady him.

Sheila looks startled. Violet sits rigid, clearly unsettled by Doris dragging Rita and James into the conversation.

'I wish my Harold were here,' Doris then adds, suddenly sobbing, pulling the attention back onto herself. We all exhale in unison.

George then gets up to do his best man speech. His words are wonderful, so thoughtful, so frank. Watching him perform, I glimpse another part of him. This time it doesn't fill me with dread, but something closer to admiration. I stay where I am, grinning, as he retells funny stories from his footballing days with Henry - like the time Henry forgot his shorts and had to play in his undergarments. It gets a huge laugh, echoing around the lofty ceilings of the town hall.

I sit there, falling for him all over again.

As he takes his seat to a round of applause, I lean in and kiss him on the cheek.

Then Dad gets to his feet, a bundle of nerves, bless him, trying his best to channel his inner Max Miller, though he's more apologetic chap than a cheeky one. It's not easy for him, you can tell. He mentions Mum, how proud she'd have been. I can't help it; I cry. Sheila squeezes my hand in comfort. George turns back to his drink and won't meet my eye. I can already sense the shift in him.

My worries are momentarily drowned out by the swing band striking up. The family's extravagance on full display again: an eight-piece band, no less. I'm almost certain a few of them played at the New Year do, but I daren't say a word.

Violet is straight up, spinning on the dance floor, lost in the music. For a moment, her fears and her crippling loneliness vanish.

'She don't seem to be missing the kids or her husband, does she?' Doris mutters sourly. 'I know what it's like to miss children. Both of mine were taken by the Lord, God bless 'em.' Her voice drops like a cloud over the table. Then, with a glance my way, she adds, 'Surprised you haven't had any yet, Vera.'

The table stays silent, until Doris finally gets up, and I can't help but breathe easier.

'Thank Christ for that,' Sheila says, watching Doris try to pull Dad in for a dance. He obliges at last, his limp making for an awkward display.

'I hate that woman,' I murmur under my breath.

George turns to me.

'Funny. You remind me of Doris,' he says flatly.

Sheila bursts into laughter at the absurdity, but I feel the sting.

'What do you mean?' I ask, trying not to sound offended.

'Dark hair. Speaks her mind. And childless.'

His words strike me like a slap, but I try not to show it. 'Except… she could have children, couldn't she?' he adds.

I stay quiet, but Sheila's face twists, aghast. Before I can stop her, she blurts it out, proud, loud, far too open.

'Well, maybe it's not her. Maybe it's your thing that's no good.' She points at his lap. She tries to laugh it off, to soften the sting, but the damage is done.

George's face twists, humiliated, incensed, and the look he gives me makes my skin crawl. A mix of shame and hatred, as if the whole room's laughing at him and I'm the ringleader.

Later that evening, George insists on speaking to me privately. My body shakes with fear. I didn't say those words, but it doesn't matter. He leads me outside. The sun's long gone, the blackout in full force, a hush fallen over the streets.

He marches me down the side of the imposing town hall.

'Are you trying to embarrass me, Vera?' he says, voice taut, barely containing the fury. 'You think I'm a joke? Like Sheila does? You think I don't work?'

'She's just… sharing a theory,' I say, trying, perhaps foolishly, to defend Sheila.

'So you agree with her?!' he shouts, spit flying from his mouth. 'This what you gossip about? Our private matters? You think I'm not a man?'

'I don't have answers, George, I'm not an expert.' I say which doesn't help in the slightest. I should be brushing over it, saying Sheila was wrong, saying I'm the problem, always have been. Yet I keep digging myself further into a hole I can't escape.

'I'm just a joke to you, aren't I?' His furious eyes gleam in the gloom. 'You're the bloody problem, Vera. This, you - ' And then he slams his fist into my stomach, hard as a wrecking ball. I collapse, gasping, clutching my belly as pain bursts through me. I try and catch my breath, and then, seconds later, out of the shadows, Henry appears.

'Everything all right?' he wonders.

'Vera's being sick, that's all,' George says quickly.

I stay on the ground, curled in on myself, trying to feel human again.

'Blimey, is it the drink?' Henry asks.

'Yeah, and worry. About tomorrow,' George replies, like it's the most natural thing in the world. Henry crouches beside me.

'You'll be alright, sis. I know it's a lot. Joy feels the same. But you'll have each other.' He gently helps me to my feet. I can't meet his eyes. If I do, I fear I might tell him everything without even speaking.

'I need to go home, Henry. I'm sorry. It's been marvellous, but I need to go home.' I say apologetically while grabbing his torch from his hand, his expression falling.

'You can't go,' George says firmly.

'I have to. You stay. You stay here,' I plead as calmly as possible.

I stumble across the road as a car almost hits me, brakes screeching in the blackout.

'Vera, you idiot!' George yells as the driver toots. Then the rain begins, like even god is spitting at me.

'Vera!' George keeps calling.

'She'll be alright,' Henry replies, though I barely hear him. 'You stay here like she said. Come on, let's go in. It's going to chuck it down.'

The rain grows heavier, a storm splashing my face, mingling with tears I can't stop. My stomach aches, my thoughts reel. If he's willing to do that in public, even in the dark, what's he capable of behind blacked-out windows?

He might just kill me.

I walk blindly through the downpour, soaked to the skin, trying to keep my footing on the slick pavement. Turner Street appears through the haze. Thunder cracks overhead. I pass Dad's house, heading for the posher end, when I stop. Suddenly. At number 80.

I don't know why. The quiet street, the noise of the storm, the confusion in my head, it all pushes me to act. I bang on the door, hard.

It opens, and Eddie stands there, his lantern light catching his face, rain flickering at him.

I push past him into the dry, into safety.

'What's the matter, Vera? You're soaked through.'

'I can't go home,' I sob. 'I can't be near him. He's going to kill me, Eddie. I swear on my life, he'll have me dead.'

The rain drums on outside. Eddie doesn't speak at first. He just waits, takes it all in, allows the storm to make the noise. Until finally he asks.

'Has he hurt you?'

I nod, still breathless.

'He leaves tomorrow. I don't want him to go. I don't want him to come back. I love him, Eddie… but I'm petrified of him.'

'Stay here,' Eddie says, pulling me into his arms. 'You can have Mrs Morris's bed. No bother. You're safe here.'

I shouldn't. I know I shouldn't. But I can't be hurt any more.

So, I go upstairs, lie on Mrs Morris's bed, and listen to the storm fade. I just need a rest, a moment, but before I know it the sun begins to rise. I'm sure I didn't sleep, but time must've slipped past me like a ghost.

I sit up in a panic. My heart races. I rush downstairs - and there he is.

Eddie. Already awake, boiling eggs.

'Blimey. What time is it?' I shout.

'Half six. Would you like some breakfast?'

I don't answer. I can't.

'What have I done?' I whisper to myself. 'I shouldn't be here. My George is going to war, and I wasn't even home to see him off.'

'It's not safe, Vera.'

'Nowhere is safe,' I shout back to him as I open the door to the damp street and run as fast as I can. When I reach number 96, I'm met with a terrible sight inside, Esther in tears, Nadine pale beside her, the whole downstairs in chaos. Broken glass, chairs overturned, drawers emptied.

'What the bloody hell has happened?' I cry.

'George...' Esther says, her voice wobbling. 'He was upset you weren't home. I told him I didn't know where you were. He got angry.' She lowers her eyes.

'Did he touch you? Either of you?'

'No. Just... just so angry.'

'Where is he?'

'He left,' Nadine says. 'To help kill my people, he said.'

'He meant Germans, not Jews,' Esther adds gently, trying to soothe her. Not that I think it's much better for poor Nadine.

'He's gone... Oh my God, he's really gone.' The realisation hits me all at once. Gone to war. Without a goodbye. And look at the wreckage he's left behind. What have I done? When he comes back... if he comes back... Gawd knows what he'll do.

## 13 Turning tides

The regret of not seeing George before he was carted off clings to me like a bad rash. I keep scratching at it, reliving the moment, rewriting it in my head, obsessing over what might happen next. None of it ends well.

Some days, I wish it was me who'd been sent to serve. At least then I'd have something else to think about, something to concentrate on.

It's the not knowing that eats away at you. We all assume France, but no one tells us for sure. Where he is, how far, what the boys are doing - it plays on your mind constantly. And while I dread George's return, I find myself aching for Henry's. I never got to say goodbye properly, never even celebrated his wedding day. I ruined it, sneaking off as I did. I've been in a state ever since.

Joy's been spending a lot of time at Dad's. I think she feels less alone there than in her stylish but empty flat in Wandsworth. Henry's absence is thick in the air, always hanging around the edges. To ease her worry and distract herself, Joy has taken up a job with the Ministry of Information, helping distribute posters across the country. Honestly, there's a new one every day telling us what to do.

She brought one home the other afternoon.

'Dig for Victory!' Dad read aloud. 'Where am I supposed to dig? Whole back garden's a bleeding shelter!'

He's got a point. There's barely room to plant a daffodil.

'Sounds like we're digging our own graves,' he went on, darkly.

'That's not the message,' Joy replied, a little defensive. 'It's been very effective.'

'We need a poster that says: Eat Offal,' Dad barked.

'Noted,' Joy said, utterly serious.

He's been going off on one about the new meat rationing, which has made life even more stressful. It's done by price, not weight - we're all allowed one shilling and ten pence worth of meat a week. That means you get more if you choose cheaper cuts. Offal isn't rationed at all, which thrills no one but Dad.

'We've got to be creative, that's all,' he keeps telling everyone. 'Bulk out your stew with a bit of brain. It's good for you!'

It's not going down too well.

Mr Sharma's come up with a new sausage recipe that doesn't need to be rationed. He's loaded it with spices and breadcrumbs, barely any meat in it at all, but it tastes alright, if a little exotic.

'Foreign muck,' Bill muttered, turning his nose up at the sausage. At least, I think he was talking about the sausage and not Mr Sharma personally. With Bill, you can never be too sure.

At home, we've turned rationing into a bit of a game. Me, Esther, and Nadine each have a little saucer with our name on it and our weekly butter allowance. Whoever has the most left at the end of the week wins. I lose every time. You don't realise how much you rely on the stuff until it's limited.

Nadine barely touches hers, she's adaptable, that one. Sounds like the last few months in Germany were beyond anything imaginable, and she learned how to manage with next to nothing. There's a spring in her step these days, though. Her English is magnificent now. I only wish my brain worked like that, picking things up with such ease.

Esther's done a marvellous job with her. Nadine's confidence has grown so much she's started singing, little performances for us, sweet German folk songs, soft and melodic. I've had to ask her to keep her voice down, mind. Not sure the neighbours are in the mood for German ditties just now. Still, it's a beautiful voice, just like her aunts.

I find myself thinking more and more about the people on our street - how war affects each of us so differently. For some, it's business as usual. Ken Henderson's still at the power station. But his twin, Arthur, well... he's been called up. He might be with George and Henry in France, or somewhere else entirely. No one ever tells you anything. You can't help but wonder.

I get the sense Ken feels guilty, lucky, but guilty. His job's reserved, so he's safe. They say twins can feel what the other feels, some kind of telepathic thing.

'He's not in France, Vera. Somewhere else, mark my words,' Ken told me the other day when I bumped into him on the street. Said it with real certainty. Not that it helps much, just adds to the guessing.

That nagging worry of this war is briefly lifted when I receive a postcard and some photographs from Rita and James. It's a comfort, knowing they're happy down in Cornwall.

'Maybe they won't want to come home,' Violet says to me. She can't win, bless her, sad if they're unhappy, sad if they're having a lovely time. Just sad, really.

Amidst all that's going on, I haven't given much thought to Eddie. Not properly, anyway. Despite how desperate I'd been that night - to knock on his door, to stay with him - now that I've a clearer head, I know it's best to keep my distance.

He hasn't come by the house, which is wise. We haven't bumped into each other either, not even in passing. Sometimes I slow down when I walk past his place on the way to Dad's, but nothing obvious. And still - nothing. I worry he might be going back home. There are no air raids, so maybe his local brigade have called him back. And perhaps that's for the best. You could argue that Eddie off the street is exactly what I need, for the sake of my mind and my muddled heart.

But things shift again when I'm at Lyons. It's a normal day, same old clatter of plates and hum of chatter, until word begins to spread, Germany has invaded Denmark and Norway.

'He's closing in,' one customer mutters, hunched over a teacake. 'We're a global embarrassment.'

There's a new edge in the air. Sourness. Towards the war. Towards Chamberlain himself. You can feel it in people's voices. I don't reckon he'll last much longer.

And that unsettled feeling only deepens when Eddie walks into the tearoom. Just when I'd convinced myself he was gone, there he was, that familiar, glaring smile. A metal helmet hiding his lovely hair. He's in his full firefighting kit, and beside him stands another man - taller, older, with a pencil moustache and the look of someone who's seen a thing or two. My heart skips a beat, then races to catch up. I try to play it calm.

'You see the handsome fireman?' Sheila notices straight away. 'Is that the one who lives on our street?'

'I wouldn't know,' I reply, cool as anything, playing it down.

'It's the one you danced with on New Year's Eve, ain't it? I'm sure of it,' she insists. But I shake my head, dismissing her, walking gradually towards them - smiling, calm, desperately calm.

'Vera!' Eddie grins with real warmth and affection. 'I didn't know it was this place you worked at.'

'Well you do now. Shall I show you to a table?'

I lead them through, hand them menus though I can barely see what I'm passing them. My breath's short, chest tight. I'm struggling to hold it all in.

When I pour their tea, I notice Eddie watching me with that familiar look - admiration, fondness - but he doesn't say much. Just polite thank yous. Pleasant. Proper. Controlled. Then his colleague excuses himself to the gents, leaving Eddie alone at the table.

As I pour him more tea, he leans in ever so slightly, and speaks in a low voice.

'My place is safe, Vera.'

'Sorry - what?' I say, a little confused.

'You said nowhere is safe. You're safe with me. I can promise you that.'

I smile, small, grateful - but I don't say a word. I can feel Mrs Miller's eyes burning holes through the back of my head.

Eddie's presence has rattled me. His calm, his kindness, it only adds to the storm inside. And while the way he makes me feel is something I thought I'd buried long ago, something I'd only ever felt for George in the early days, it's a feeling I have no business feeling now. I have a husband. A marriage I must repair when he returns. I know I'll face consequences when George comes home. But still, I pray - somewhere in his heart - he might find it in him to forgive me.

A few days later, I gather the nerve to knock on Eddie's door. He looks delighted to see me. I step inside quickly, before any prying eyes can catch a glimpse and start wagging tongues. The wireless plays in the background, crackling out another loop of dreadful news.

'Germany has invaded the Low Countries,' Eddie says, concern etched across his face.

'I know. Terrible, isn't it?'

'It feels close. War's coming, Vera. Coming here, for real this time.' He pauses, voice quieter. 'Life's… fragile. Unpredictable. Funny old thing, eh?' He reaches out, gently rubbing my arms, but I flinch away.

'Eddie, I've come to say something. And I don't mean to be rude or unkind, but I would very much appreciate it if you kept your distance from me from now on.'

He looks confused. Genuinely.

'Why?' he asks.

'Well… it's not appropriate, is it? I'm a married woman, and I shouldn't be having conversations with the likes of you, shouldn't be walked home, shouldn't be staying in Mrs Morris's bed. I know I played my part in all that, and I'm not blaming you. But from here on, I want to be clear: your smiles and pleasantries are not welcomed.'

'I'm sorry… for being… polite?'

'Well, thank you for being sorry for being polite,' I say, with a stiffness that even I can hear.

He laughs, gently, shaking his head at the absurdity of it all. And I suppose he is right.

'I am sorry, Vera. Truly. I know you're married. It's just… not often you come across someone so beautiful like you. But I understand. This isn't my place.'

I stay rigid, careful with my words.

'I'm sure a charming man like yourself has no shortage of beautiful women - more agreeable than me - to talk to and… frolic with.'

'None like you, Vera. But… maybe I'll find someone who makes me feel like you do,' he says softly.

'You barely know me,' I reply.

'I know enough. I know your pain. Your hurt. Your courage. Your beauty. I know… and you know.'

'You know this can't be,' I assert.

He reluctantly nods his head.

'I do, Vera love. I do. But that doesn't change how I feel.'

I nod with him, trying to steady myself.

'Then this is it,' I tell him. He continues to nod with a sense of regret.

'This is all it can be. But you deserve better, Vera. So much better.'

I can't reply. My throat closes. I think I'm ready to leave, until the voice on the wireless makes him turn up the volume.

The unmistakable voice of Chamberlain barks through the speaker:

*'I have this evening tendered my resignation to His Majesty the King, and it has been accepted. The gravity of the situation in Norway and the profound events unfolding on the Continent have made it clear that a new administration, enjoying the full confidence of all parties in Parliament, is required to prosecute the war with the utmost vigour. His Majesty has entrusted Mr Winston Churchill with the task of forming this new government…'*

'Blimey,' Eddie says. 'A new Prime Minister.'

'Everything's changing,' I whisper.

'Yeah. He knew it was time. Must've been hard. Takes courage to accept that. Accept a new reality.'

I don't know if he's talking about Chamberlain, or me personally.

I move to leave. But Eddie calls after me.

'Vera.'

'Yes?'

'If you ever change your mind… I'll be waiting.'

I should tell him not to. Wait for what? We've both just said this can't happen. But the words don't come.

Instead, I give him the faintest smile, something vague and unreadable, the kind of smile a person could mistake for hope. And what frightens me is maybe I want him too.

# 14 News

I've not heard a word from George since he's been gone, not one letter, despite him being away for several weeks now. Joy received one from Henry almost straight away. It's all very romantic, full of dreams of their future, brighter days ahead, and their new life as husband and wife. He also writes of the boredom, the waiting, the endless drills. He says he'd rather be home chopping up a loin than stuck waiting for a war that keeps creeping forward.

But the absence of any letter from George panics me. Not just because of what it might mean, but because soon people will start to notice. I've been telling them he has written, but that it's a private matter. Only that adds to the tower of lies I seem to be building around myself. It feels like he's already given up on me because I, regretfully, gave up on him.

As the weeks drag on, the news from overseas only worsens, something made painfully clear in Henry's more frantic letters. There are words of chaos, of lightning-quick advances, of demands for strength and resolve that no amount of training could prepare them for. And still, nothing from George. The silence is deafening.

Dad's become glued to the news, newspapers spread out across the counter, the wireless always on. He's trying to make sense of it all as the Germans move into France. The butcher's shop has slipped in priority. Mr Sharma has taken charge, bringing in a few friends from the community to help. Some of the customers treat it like another invasion, their mutterings louder by the day.

'Wright & Sons isn't Wright & Sons if my son isn't here,' Dad keeps saying, trying to justify his absence, though it hasn't stopped the locals from grumbling as they queue up for their meagre meat rations.

Despite the headlines, Joy insists I come over for supper. She's made one of Dad's "creative" suggestions, a meat pit pie with heavy pastry and various animal parts that no one dares ask too much about. Still, Joy's a marvellous cook. It smells divine.

Doris, naturally, is there. She's part of the furniture these days.

'They're trapped,' Dad declares, stabbing his pie with the side of his fork. 'Trapped in France. Sitting ducks.'

I can barely eat. Neither can Dad who pushes his plate away in frustration. Doris, meanwhile, chews away, unfazed.

'You think Henry and George are stuck?' Doris questions.

'They all are!' Dad shouts. I place a hand on his arm, trying to calm him. Joy looks startled. It's not that he's wrong, it's just the force of it.

'They're talking about an evacuation,' I say quickly, trying to inject some hope into the room. 'Getting the boys back over. I read about it in the paper.'

'Yes, quite right,' Joy adds gently. 'We've got to keep calm and carry on.'

Dad turns to her with a scowl.

'Is that another one of your posters? We can't "carry on" if we've no men left. We'll be giving the right-hand salute before you know it. Not even Churchill can save us now.'

'One must remain hopeful,' Joy says, and then deliberately she rests a hand on her stomach.

'Is the pie giving you jip?' Doris asks, completely misreading the moment.

'No,' Joy says quietly. 'I'm with child. Henry's going to be a father. You're going to be a grandfather, Bertie.'

Dad's face drops. For a moment, he smiles. Then comes the worry, raw and real. His scarred face looking more pronounced than usual.

'Well, isn't that marvellous,' I say, standing to hug Joy, trying to lift the moment.

'How far gone are you?' Doris asks, as nosy as ever.

'Four months already,' Joy replies, beaming.

'Well, that explains the wedding then,' Doris mutters.

'No, I believe it was on the wedding day actually,' Joy says, trying to play along. Probably too much information than we need.

'Sure it was, love,' Doris says, her sarcasm cutting through the air.

'Does it matter?' I say sharply. 'It's something good, something hopeful. He'll be over the moon when he hears.'

Dad exhales, rubbing the back of his neck.

'You'll need to help her, Vera,' he says, eyes suddenly serious. 'Bringing a baby into the world right now... it's dangerous. But I'm pleased. I am. For you both.'

Later, we listen to Churchill on the wireless. He speaks of never surrendering - how we'll fight them on the beaches, whatever it takes, whatever the cost. So resolute, so unshakable. Even Dad, usually so cynical and worn down by it all, seems stirred by it.

'We'll win this, like last time,' he says, a flicker of confidence breaking through for the first time in ages. 'We just need our boys home. Any minute now... any minute, our boys will walk through that door.' He urges it like he's willing it into existence, trying to bend fate with sheer determination. And, by some miracle, he's right.

Esther and I are putting together a little tea party for Nadine, who's turning eleven. It's modest, of course, but we do what we can. We manage a cake of sorts, cobbled together from powdered egg and stale flour, and I bring her some more pencils and paints to add to her growing art collection. Her face lights up when she sees them, and for just a moment, everything feels almost normal.

Mrs Henderson pops in too. She's been giving Nadine extra lessons in English and science, says she's a bright one, that girl, and it's clear she means it. The party starts light-hearted, but as always, conversation drifts to the war. It's impossible to avoid. Mrs Henderson tells us her son Arthur is in Norway, not France after all. Seems his twin Ken was right to trust his instincts. A mother's pride mixed with quiet dread flickers across her face.

Esther, meanwhile, is rigid with fear. Her brother thought France would be safe from the Nazis. But now, with the rapid German advance, that feels like a false fantasy. Hope turns to fear so quickly these days.

There's talk on the street of the miracle evacuation, hundreds of small boats crossing the Channel, plucking boys from the beaches. But talk is all it is. We've had no word. Not yet.

And then, as Nadine leans over to blow out her candles, we hear it.

The front door creaks open. I turn, my heart stopping, and there he is.

George.

He's standing in the doorway, clothes dishevelled, face gaunt and grey, hair soaked with sweat and salt. His eyes are hollow, far-off, like they've seen something no one should. He looks like a ghost. But he's real. He's here. He's alive.

He looks straight at me, eyes cold and unreadable. The room goes silent.

'Hello, stranger,' he says.

## **15** Evacuated

George kicks off his boots, and they land with a thud beside the sofa. He slumps down heavily, taking in the comfort of our modest settee - but his face barely moves. Blank. Worn. Haunted.

I hover nearby, uncertain. Not sure whether to sit, to speak, or to simply disappear into the wallpaper.

'You're alive then,' he mutters, voice bitter as coal smoke.

'Shouldn't I be the one asking that?' I reply, trying to keep it light, but my voice falters.

'You care then?' he says with a rawness to it. 'Quite a few of us didn't make it.'

There's pain in his voice, the kind that sits just beneath the skin.

'Tell us what happened George.'

'No.' His tone rises sharply, echoing off the walls. 'No, I bleeding well won't. Where the hell were you, Vera? After the wedding? Where were you?'

I brace myself. I've played this moment in my head a dozen times.

'I slept in the shelter outside,' I say softly.

'What!?' His face twists, part disbelief, part resentment.

'I was frightened, George. You... you hurt me,' I say, voice shrinking. 'I didn't know what else to do. So I went to the shelter. Put my head down. I was out like a light.'

'You didn't hear me come home that night? I hit the bloody roof when I saw you weren't here. Thought you might have been dead in a ditch somewhere.'

'I wish I had heard you. Truly. But those shelters, turns out they might not be completely bomb-proof, but they're good at keeping out a racket.'

He looks at me, uncertain now. Suspicious. And I suppose he's got reason to be. It's the best explanation I can offer, a lie but then nothing happened at Eddie's. But George would never believe that.

'You hid in a shelter... like I'm the enemy. Like I'm the bloody bomb. I'm your husband, Vera. Your sodding husband. How dare you. I left thinking I didn't have a wife anymore. I'll never forgive you for that. Not as long as I live.'

His anger is pure. Raw and undiluted, I try to hold it together.

'What can I do, George?'

He sparks a cigarette. Takes a long drag.

'There's nothing you can do. You know that.'

So we both sit in silence, thick and choking.

I wait, until I can't bare the silence any longer.

'Tell me about France. About the evacuation.'

His head snaps towards me, eyes narrow.

'Fuck off, Vera. Just... fuck off.'

The sound of his words burn.

I turn and leave quietly the tears already in my eyes. Fear swelling in my chest.

I wish I could change it all.

I stagger outside and make my way to Dad's, hoping Henry might be there, hoping that Joy's news will shine a little light on all this constant darkness. But then it hits me. The news of the pregnancy might be the very thing to push George over the edge.

Inside, I find Henry sitting in Dad's armchair, Joy knelt beside him, gently holding his hand.

'Welcome home, Henry,' I say softly. 'And... congratulations.'

He looks up at me and offers the faintest smile. He looks shattered. Not just tired - truly traumatised.

'Henry was just telling us what happened,' Dad says, realising I've walked in halfway through something. 'Has our George said much?'

'Nothing. I think he needs space,' I reply, instantly trying to justify myself. Always justifying myself.

Henry clears his throat. His voice is low, almost distant.

'We abandoned everything. Trucks. Supplies. Just left it all. Orders came, we moved. Just walked. One foot in front of the other. Like a dream. A nightmare, really.'

He speaks slowly. Each word carefully measured, as if pulling it from the depths. 'On the beach... there were just men. Thousands of them. I've never seen so many people. No sand, just men. Waiting. And the sky was never quiet. The buzz, the scream... then men just dropped. Gone. You waited, either to be saved or to die. Just... waiting. I never want to wait for anything again.'

His head bows. Joy strokes his hand.

'You're home now, Henry. Safe. No war here,' I say, trying to offer something. Anything.

'It'll be here soon enough, Vera,' he says, lifting his eyes. 'We've been told to prepare for invasion. Could be any day now.'

His words hang heavy in the room. Even the air feels still. I can hear Dad's breathing, slow and heavy.

Henry turns to Joy.

'You must get out of London. You're with our child. You have to leave,' Henry begs.

Joy straightens up.

'London is our home, Henry. I'm not going anywhere. No flipping German is going to frighten me away, let me tell you.'

She speaks with a determined spirit I haven't seen from her before.

I decide to leave them, Henry still hollow-eyed, Joy fierce in her refusal. But as I leave the house, I hear another storm brewing. Bill's defiant voice bellowing from next door, and then I see Sheila, falling out through the front door, landing hard on the pavement. An echo of her sister who had been kicked out not long before. A battered bag follows, hitting the ground with a crack.

'Get out! Sling your bleeding hook!' Bill roars from the doorway, his face beetroot red, spit clinging to his lips.

'I don't want to be at home anyway!' Sheila screams back.

'Until you come to your senses and stop mucking about with Negroes, I don't want to know you!'

'I'm in love, Dad!'

'Get away with it, love? You need your head checked, just like your bloody sister!'

I rush to Sheila's side, helping her gather her things.

'Did you know about this?' Bill shouts at me. 'About her and this Sam from Africa, or wherever these darkies come from?'

'He's a nice chap,' I say, trying to stay calm. 'Very charming.'

'Jesus Christ. You an' all?' Bill barks. He's about to slam the door when I, without thinking, shout,

'You do realise the fascists are the baddies, Bill?'

He freezes. Opens the door again and stomps back outside, chest puffed.

'What did you just say to me?' His spit hits my cheek.

'He's not worth it, Vera,' Sheila yells.

She's right. I've said enough, so we walk away, Sheila holding onto my arm, both of us escaping Bill's rage.

'I told him,' Sheila says as we hurry on.

'Oh really,' I say, the sarcasm clear.

'Can I come in with you?'

'I can't. My George is home.'

'He is?' Her eyes widen. 'Well, that's... nice. Is he all right?'

'Yes and no,' I say, forcing a smile. 'Yes and no.'

## 16 It begins

Over the coming days, George can barely utter a word to me. At least he isn't being violent or rotten - just... absent. Isn't it something? You wait all that time for them to come home, and when they finally do, they're not really here at all.

Not everyone's taken recent events the way George - or even Henry - has. Arthur Henderson came back not long after, from Norway rather than France, and despite it being a right shambles, he's more determined than ever to go back and give the Germans what for.

'I think it's given him a sense of purpose,' Mrs Henderson said, though I could hear the worry in her voice.

So, for a few days George lingered on Turner Street, ghostlike, barely saying a word. And then the summons came, pulling him back to Aldershot. Henry alongside him. Both will still be on home soil, thankfully, but once again away from Turner Street. Word is they're in full preparation mode now - for the invasion. It sends a chill down my spine.

Even at Lyons, the usual natter's been replaced by a heavy silence. There's a sense in the air, like things aren't going the way we'd hoped. We're all trying to stay resilient, but it's not easy.

And with Sheila gone, I feel like I've lost my right arm. She's moved east to Rotherhithe to stay with her aunt, joining her sister Pat. Christ, I miss her. The commute was too much for Sheila to keep working at Lyons, but she writes to me often. Her absence is felt down to the bones on Turner Street, that is for certain.

Sheila's father Bill has now joined the Local Defence Volunteers - Churchill's now renamed them the Home Guard. He likes to strut about like he's the most important man on the street, always going on about sabotage and defending London like it's already been lost. We've not spoken since I called him a fascist. Still not sure what came over me. This war does strange things to a person.

The rapid fall of France has startled everyone. Nobody imagined a country so mighty would succumb to the Nazis so quickly. And now, there's a creeping fear that we might be next.

But still, there's that British spirit - that deep, stubborn determination - that refuses to believe we'll meet the same fate.

News of France's fall troubles Esther deeply, especially now that her brother David is living there. It's hard to see the light in any of this.

For Britain, though, the war has taken firmly to the skies. Our boys battle the Luftwaffe over the Channel and the southern coast, fighting to hold them back. Their courage is beyond anything I can fathom - young lads soaring into the clouds with nothing but grit and steel, their lives on the line, our freedom hanging by a thread.

Amidst the darkness, there are still little glimmers of light - moments you cling to, however small. Like Stanley returning to land, for a short spell on leave. It brings a sense of life back to Violet. They also both got the chance to travel down to Cornwall to see Rita and James. Can you imagine it? Almost a year without seeing your children. Their faces changing, new interests forming, new worries settling in. Violet was beside herself with nerves, terrified they wouldn't recognise her - or worse, wouldn't want to see her. But it was nothing like that. She told me it was the most magical weekend of her life.

Their foster carers, she said, were kind and gentle - more like doting grandparents than some poor substitute for Mum and Dad. She brought them the books I'd picked out, and a few packets of seeds they could plant in the garden - something to grow, something to look forward to. Of course, coming home wasn't easy for Violet or Stanley. Bittersweet, as ever. But they were grateful just to have had that chance.

'They asked about you, Vera,' Stanley said to me afterwards. 'They're missing you, their aunt.'

I couldn't find the words to answer him. My bottom lip just wobbled. Truth is, I think I might miss them most of all. That's all I seem to be doing - missing people, missing the children, Sheila, Henry, missing who George was. I'm even missing Eddie, despite the fact I hardly know him and have rarely seen him.

I did catch a glimpse of him, one summer's evening, walking down Turner Street. He stepped out of his house. Our eyes met. I smiled. I ached. And we moved on. There's something forbidden between us now. We've said what we've said. We are where we are. What more can we do? So we both exist - wanting, but never having. So close, yet painfully far apart.

And so the summer of 1940 on Turner Street feels horrendously quiet. No bombs. But no love either. And it isn't long before Stanley returns for another voyage to the unknown, Violet feeling lost and desperate once again. The street feeling even more lifeless. We just carry on. Cope with the quietness.

But then, one evening, on my way home from Lyons, the quietness ends. I am startled by the unmistakable wail of the air raid siren. That sound turns your stomach to stone. I freeze, heart hammering, then bolt for the nearest communal shelter. They've built one now beside All Saints Church, the entrance disappearing into its basement.

As I arrive, I see Violet directing people in.

'Is it a drill, Violet?' I ask, breathless.

'I don't think so, Vera,' she says, eyes wide with panic.

I clamber inside. The place is already filling up - familiar faces and strangers packed shoulder to shoulder. And then we hear it: the low, thundering drone of planes overhead. So many. We all fall silent, save for a few cries from frightened children.

'It's them. It's started,' says a man in the corner.

A cold dread rushes through me. And though I'm surrounded by people, I've never felt so alone. It's as if the war has singled me out. We don't hear bombs falling, just the hideous drone of the enemy overhead, seeking its prey. But while these close surroundings aren't yet a victim, other parts of London have been struck, pulverised to the ground, fires raging across the city. Smoke engulfs us all.

It's real now.

The war has finally come home.

## 17 Balham

It's gone from nothing to everything. All at once. Every day now, the bombs drop from the sky - hundreds of German planes doing their damnedest to wipe us off the map. The first time I heard one fall - felt the pressure shift, then that deafening crack of impact, the crunch of crumbling bricks - you never forget that. It gets under your skin. You find yourself holding your breath, counting the seconds, wondering how close it was. Whose house. Who was in it. Whose life has changed forever.

Since September, we've been living our lives in air raid shelters. Every single bleeding night. All night. No sleep. No peace. Sometimes I wonder if the all-clear siren will ever sound again. We've gone from a strange, eerie quiet to an unrelenting onslaught. London's under siege.

I've been staying most nights in Esther's Anderson shelter - proper job, built from bricks and metal, tucked at the back of her garden. It's a bit roomier than Dad's, enough space for Nadine to create a little corner to feel private, personal - pencils and paper, a torch, a stack of books. She's taken to sketching by candlelight, wide-eyed and silent. But none of us can sleep. Not properly. You just lie there, waiting.

Dad's been alternating between his Anderson shelter and the basement of the butcher's, curled up beside hanging carcasses. He's often caught out by the sirens after closing up.

We haven't been hit as badly as the East End or central London - at least not yet. Here, it's more sporadic. One house gone, then three untouched. A row of shops obliterated, the one in the middle still standing. There's no rhyme or reason to it. I don't think there's a plan anymore. They just want us broken. Beaten. Surrendered. Or dead.

I worry for Sheila constantly - she's right in the thick of it. The East End has been torn apart. Whole streets flattened. I've heard of families gone in a flash, trapped in their homes, buried alive. We try to talk every Thursday, same time, at the payphone near work. I wait in the cold, clutching my coins, and sometimes the other girls gather round too, desperate for word from her. We all beg her to come back to the south - safer, quieter, at least for now.

'I can't,' she says, voice cracking through the line. 'I need to be with Pat. I'd rather be bombed than face Father again.'

I can't believe how badly things have soured between them. I tell her I'll come see her soon - she's not far - but with the raids and the shifts and the constant state of exhaustion, it's near impossible to find a free hour. Even breathing feels like effort some days. Your body runs on borrowed time, jangled nerves, and weak tea. You start living for those strange, golden moments of silence - no sirens, no drones overhead. Just quiet. The kind of quiet I complained about all summer. I'd trade anything to go back to those empty, nothing days. I'd take a hundred afternoons of boredom over this autumn of hell.

And as the nights stretch on, the bombs fall heavier, and the list of the missing grows. It's not long before you start hearing familiar names. Old acquaintances. School friends. Regular customers who just stop showing up. You try not to ask. It's just the way things are now. And yet Turner Street is untouched - for now at least.

I keep telling Joy she must get out of London - her bump now more rounded - but she's stubborn as ever, determined to stay put, committed to her work at the Ministry of Information. She believes in the cause. But no pamphlet, no rallying speech, no words on paper can prepare you for this relentless nightmare.

We've pinned all our hope on the anti-aircraft guns scattered across the city and the barrage balloons bobbing above us like bloated ghosts. That's it. That's our defence. What's meant to stop us from slipping into the abyss.

At first, people were angry - furious, even. It felt like nothing was being done. We were sitting ducks. Now they fire every bullet they have into the sky, every night without fail. Dad questions how much good it's doing.

'Might just be for show,' he says. 'Bit of theatre to keep us from losing it altogether.'

Truth is, people have started taking matters into their own hands. You have to. It's survival now. The government said we weren't to shelter in the

Underground stations, but people started doing it anyway - buying train tickets and bedding down on the platforms. It caught on fast. The stations filled up night after night. Violet told me she was physically having to hold people back from barging in. People wouldn't have it. Pushing, shoving - it shows you what people are really made of when the fear takes hold.

If we had a deep-level Underground near Turner Street, I'd be tempted too. No shame in it. Especially when you hear of flimsy shelters collapsing, people crushed in the rubble. It puts the fear of God into you.

Eventually the authorities gave in. A handful of stations are now officially open for sheltering. But they're unbearable - hot, packed, reeking of sweat and fear. Still, they're safer. That's what matters. I'll be honest, I'm curious to go in one. Part of me wants to see it for myself. Mad, isn't it? But we all know we're living through history. Uncertain of what's to come, but certain it'll never be forgotten.

Most of our intel comes via Chatterbox Catherine at work - who, true to her name, won't shut up about it. She lives in Balham, and Balham station has become her second home. She tells us how people are curling up on the tracks, making little beds out of old coats, or trying to grab a few minutes' sleep hunched on an escalator. It's quite unbelievable.

She loves to describe the smell - says it's like being buried alive with five thousand strangers who haven't washed in months. And still, at the bottom of the pit, occasionally people will start to sing. Whole platforms full of voices, just to drown out the bombs. A sort of resistance, I suppose. That strange British thing - laugh or sing, even as the world falls in.

But Balham station would soon be etched in my mind for a different reason.

In the early morning of the 15th of October, I head out just after the all-clear is given. There's barely a hint of sun, just a faint drizzle misting my cheeks as I make my way to work. Every morning feels the same - disoriented, sleep - deprived, never knowing what you'll find when you come up from shelter. There's a strange eeriness to the streets now, a silence too still, too heavy, often broken by sirens or distant shouting. Always too close.

But this morning, something feels different. Heavier. Like the day itself is mourning.

Then I see Eddie. He's in the distance, still in his firefighting uniform, his face blackened with soot, his eyes wide and hollow. He looks like he's walking in slow motion, staggering almost. The way his body hangs - it reminds me of George and Henry when they came home from Dunkirk. Haunted.

I know we're not supposed to talk. Not anymore. We made our choices, drew our lines. But I can't ignore him. Not like this. So I rush towards him.

'You okay, Eddie?'

He looks at me, slowly removes his helmet, and then just collapses to the ground. He weeps - loud, guttural sobs, completely unguarded. I've never seen a man cry like that before. I look around, hoping someone - anyone - might help, but the street is empty.

I sit beside him and place my hand gently on his knee.

'What's happened, Eddie?' I ask quietly.

His breathing is ragged as he tries to find the words between sobs.

'Balham… I had to go to Balham station.'

He chokes on the words, burying his face into his arms.

'They hit the road above it - it caved in. People were sheltering below. Hundreds. Women, children... The whole road just collapsed. You couldn't imagine it, Vera. There was a double-decker bus right in the middle of it. Smashed into the crater. I can't get it out of my head.'

My mind races at what he's just had to endure, the chaos unfolding only a few miles away.

'It was carnage. Bedlam. People buried alive… and then the water came. The mains burst, flooded the tunnel completely. The Underground was engulfed in water, sewage, Vera. People dying like that. In the middle of Balham. Drowning.'

He's trembling, completely spent.

'Come on, let's get you in,' I whisper. 'Let me make you a cuppa.'

I help him into his home, the horror of his story playing on a loop in my mind. And of course I think of Catherine at work, who may have been caught up in the disaster.

I hand Eddie a hot cup of tea. His hands shake so violently I have to steady the saucer.

'So... you reckon a lot of people have died?'

He nods, hollow.

'Could be hundreds. It's a nightmare. Worse. They'll hush it up - don't want to scare people off sheltering underground, see.'

He takes a sip of tea. I sit beside him, wrapping my arms gently around his shoulders.

'I'm scared, Vera,' he says softly. 'I shouldn't be. But I am. Is that awful to admit?'

I shake my head and hold him tighter. 'We're all scared, Eddie. Every one of us.'

After a while, I reluctantly have to leave - work is waiting and the tea room stops for no disaster. I'm so worried I won't see Catherine there. As I step outside of Number 80, Doris is already by Eddie's front door, eyeing me suspiciously.

'What you in there for?' she asks, her face riddled with judgement.

'There's been a disaster at Balham,' I tell her, flat and honest.

'There's disasters everywhere,' she gripes back.

'Yeah, but this is something else. That gentleman was a firefighter, first on scene - poor soul's traumatised.'

'Well he better toughen up, hadn't he?' she snaps. 'No need for you to go pandering to another man, is there, Vera?'

I shake my head and walk on, ignoring her venom. But it rattles me. Her nosiness. Her constant suspicion. Despite nothing ever happening between me and Eddie, she always senses something. Another reason why it simply cannot be.

When I finally make it to work, I wait for Catherine. She doesn't show. My stomach sinks - was she there? Crushed? Drowned? No one knows anything for sure.

The news of the disaster begins to filter through. We've all become used to tragedy, but this feels different. Bigger. More brutal. So close to home.

The next day, Catherine walks into work. White as a ghost. She's alive. She was there. She got out.

But she doesn't speak. Not a word. Chatterbox Catherine, always with a story or a moan, suddenly silenced. That says it all.

# 18 Flames

It doesn't stop - the bombings or my endless feelings for Eddie. If anything, they grow stronger with every moment I spend in his company, especially now I've seen him so raw, so vulnerable. Women aren't supposed to find men who cry attractive. We're told it's a weakness. Unmanly. But with Eddie... that unguarded grief, that pure, open sorrow - there was something in it that drew me in even more.

Relentless, unthinkable thoughts.

I want to protect him. Hold him. And I want him to do the same to me. Maybe it's just my mind playing silly buggers amidst all this hell unfolding around us. But what I feel has such clarity - such frightening certainty - it shakes me.

My George isn't even overseas. He's still in Aldershot, preparing for the invasion, ready to be sent wherever they need him. He could be home any second now, given leave or called in to help battle the fires tearing through this city. And yet... the thought of that feels like an inconvenience. A terrible thing to say. A fantastically cruel thing to feel. But it's true. Deep down, I don't want him home.

And that - that - is what really distracts me. Not the bombs. Not the sleepless nights or rationing or grief.

It's my own mind. This aching, burning desire I can't put out. That's what startles me most.

It's hell here, no mistake about that, but nothing compared to what poor Violet must endure. Her role as an ARP warden has turned into everything we feared. It wasn't so long ago she was teaching me how to strap on a gas mask without fogging it up, rattling off the rules about blackouts and where to shelter, all of it feeling like a drill, precautions you hoped you'd never need. Now it's real, and the job's near impossible.

She goes out every night into the dust and the fire, picking through rubble where homes once stood, ticking names off lists, sometimes pulling out bodies she recognises - neighbours, old school friends, faces she'd smiled at only days before. She says the hardest part isn't the strangers, it's the familiar ones, the shock of seeing someone's life snuffed out on a street you walk every day. Her voice shakes when she tells me of it, of the silence after the bombs, broken only by the moans of the trapped. She shoulders it all, keeps her helmet on, her torch steady, but I can see in her eyes the weight she carries, heavier than any brick or beam she's had to lift.

And yet she talks often about the need for more help, more wardens on patrol. Perhaps she's hinting at me, but I don't think I have the strength. Not in any way.

There is some positive news amongst the smoke and ember. Joy has decided to leave London and stay with a relative in Canterbury. It's a massive relief, she's safer there. Her bump's more pronounced now, and I keep telling her she should get out before it's too late.

She even asked me to go with her - just for a bit. But my home, my dad, my job… and, well, Eddie - they're all here. I couldn't leave, not yet.

Work's gotten harder, of course. With the war as it is, everything's rationed - even differently for businesses - and we've had to change the menu to reflect what we can actually get our hands on. The endless top-ups of tea are a thing of the past. We're confused, the customers are confused. Lazy Lorraine keeps forgetting about the new rule, and Mrs Miller, quick as ever, lets it slide. Rumours about the two of them still swirl - people love a scandal.

And now, with tea so strictly rationed, Lyons has become a haven for those desperate for a proper cuppa. It's funny, really. Of all things, tea. But it makes sense, doesn't it? A hot cup, a familiar taste - it's a comfort. In times like these, it's everything.

Winter is coming. The bombs don't end, and to make matters worse Dad has caught a nasty cough that's stopping him working. The cough reminds me of my mother's before she deteriorated - how fast it all happened. Dad's chest has never been the strongest, and this bout is knocking him flat. Doris has taken to playing nurse, and I think she's basically moved in, despite living just across the road.

His absence from the shop hasn't gone unnoticed. Some customers were so worried they started spreading all sorts - one even said he'd been buried under the rubble. Mr Sharma had to put a sign in the window:

*"Mr Bertie Wright has the flu. Safe and sound. Please stop asking."*

Still, rumours fly. Some say Mr Sharma poisoned Dad to take over the business. That led to whispers about sausages laced with rat poison. Honestly, the nonsense people come up with. I suppose gossip's all we've got left - some distraction from the fires and the death.

'You needn't be here, Vera,' Doris moans when I visit to see Dad as she dabs his forehead with a flannel. 'I've got it under control.'

I ignore her and go to make some food - though I know it'll never be as good as Joy's marvellous creations.

That is, until the air raid siren goes off - far earlier than usual. The sun's barely set.

'They're bloody keen tonight,' I mutter under my breath.

I help Dad up quickly as Doris scrambles for her handbag - and her Bible, which she now drags everywhere like it's some kind of holy shield.

We squash into Dad's Anderson shelter. I'm not prepared. I'd hoped to be home by now - I've got nothing here. If this raid goes on as long as they usually do, it'll be a nightmare.

Dad's shelter is basic but stocked: tins of corned beef, bottles of water, a blanket or two. A set of dominoes to play with. Doris sits too close to him, fussing and muttering prayers as he tries to get comfortable, his cough rattling the steel walls.

I sit and wait, hoping it might, just might, be a false alarm. I sit, cold, unsettled. Wondering where Eddie is. What nightmare he must endure now. My mind drifts to him, to the thought of me offering comfort - before a brutal, wheezy cough from Dad drags me back.

'You should see Dr Clarke,' I tell him.

'I've seen him. Not much he can do. Anyway, I'm fine. I've got my medicine,' Dad says, revealing a flask of something strong and taking a swig.

Doris shifts uncomfortably, clearly bothered by my presence.

'Strange having you in here. Usually, it's just me and your father,' she says.

'Why don't you use your own shelter?' I ask, as the unmistakable hum of planes begins to rumble overhead and gunfire rattles around us. We're so used to it now, it just fades into the background.

'Would you stay in a shelter built by a blind man?' she shouts. Fair point, I suppose. 'Besides, me and your father like to keep each other company.'

And that's when I see it - her hand resting on his leg. She gives him a nod, and he doesn't say a word. He doesn't move it.

She goes on:

'You see, me and your father... we have - how should I put it? A widow's agreement.'

'A what?'

'It's times like this, Vera. People need companionship. Love. And as widows, well... we don't have that. So we depend on each other to fulfil those needs.'

'What's she saying, Dad?' I ask, confused, eyes on him.

'Me and your father are... amicable lovers,' Doris says proudly.

I stare straight at Dad, but he won't meet my eye.

'You don't need to do that, Dad,' I say, serious now.

'It's what he wants,' Doris snaps.

I try to laugh it off - before we're interrupted by the almightiest bang. The whole shelter shakes. The ground moves underneath us.

'Blimey, that was close,' Dad says. 'Really bloody close.'

'Dad, we were talking about you and Doris... you know... doing God knows what,' I say, trying to drag him back to the subject. Ignoring the rain above us.

'Never mind that. That could've hit this street. Or it might have been the shop.'

'Dad - is that what you want? Doris?'

Another bang, louder this time. But I stay with it.

'Dad, answer me.'

'YES, Vera. That's what I want! Now mind your own bleeding business!' he barks, the words sharp as anything. Then he coughs, loud and painful, like he's torn something in his chest.

Doris looks at me, smug, her face twisted with pride.

'Mum'll be turning in her grave,' I say. It's spiteful, but it's true. 'She hated you, Doris.'

'She hated me because I knew what she was up to,' Doris snaps back, and Dad huffs - like he knows what's coming.

'What are you on about?' I demand.

'Oh, don't pretend you don't know. Your mother had a thing for the men, Vera. *The tart of Turner Street* she was called. It was no sodding secret.'

'You bitch,' I spit, the word tearing out of me.

'I beg your pardon!' Doris cries, clutching her Bible. 'It's the truth - as God is my witness.'

'Says you, who's now messing around with my father.'

'I'm a widow! This is what the Lord wants. Our destiny. My Harold would've approved. I remained faithful to him till the very end - even if he wouldn't have seen anything. More faithful than your mother, that's for sure. And when I saw you creeping out of that firefighter's house the other week, well, like mother, like daughter I suppose.'

I'm raging. The audacity. The filth pouring out of her mouth. And Dad just sits there, taking it all in, and by the look on his face, agreeing with her.

'She's made you believe Mum was something she wasn't - just so she could have her way with you, Dad. It's plain as day. So you don't feel guilty,' I cry.

'Don't listen to her, Bertie,' Doris says.

And I can't take it anymore. I can't stay in this tiny metal shell with this monster and this coward. The war outside might be raining bombs, but the war inside here is worse. It's unbearable.

So I leave.

'Vera!' Dad calls after me, his voice cutting through the dark. 'Vera, get back in here now!'

But I keep walking. Determined. The sky above me bruised and angry, planes disappearing into the clouds. Gunfire and screams swallowing the sound of my father's desperate voice.

I walk onto Turner Street, alarmed by the stench of burning. Then a sea of smoke casts around me. Above, I can just make out the flickering fire reflecting off the night sky. The noise of engines, of shouting, of water against flames - it's close. This raid is very close. I think the next street has been hit. I should get to a shelter, I know I should, but I'm drawn to it, thinking - perhaps... maybe... Eddie is there.

So I take the alley that slices through Turner Street, leading onto Rogers Road. I turn the corner and I can already feel it - the heat. This illuminated, mighty heat that punches through the darkness.

One of the houses - like the ones at the posh end of Turner Street - is ablaze. A mountainous bonfire. There's a frantic effort from all sides - bodies, fire hoses, commands being barked. The power, the chaos, the determination. Shouts. Screams. The fire is angry, not cackling but roaring, and the whole road is basking in its light. Ash flutters into the sky like snow.

And I keep walking, like a moth to flame. The destruction is so vast, so real - not a photograph, not a headline, but something alive. Burning me. So very real.

And then I see him.

A silhouette carved out by the sharp firelight behind, Eddie is there. Like an angel who's stumbled through hell. He sees me and pauses.

'Vera! What the bloody hell are you doing out here?'

He rushes over, grabs my arm. His face is bright red.

'Vera - we need to get you to a shelter, now.'

I glance back at the fire, then into his eyes. His beautiful, kind eyes.

'Come on! Come on!' he urges.

We move quickly back down the alleyway, but I stop. Sudden. Deliberate.

The darkness closes in around us. The fire flickers at the alley's edges, lighting our faces in glowing orange.

And I look at him.

And I kiss him.

Gently. Firmly.

And he kisses me back.

Amongst the fire, the flames, the fumes - our lips meet. Planes rumble overhead. Guns scream into the night. Panic rages all around. But in that moment - just us two.

Lovers kissing.

So real. So right.

Until we stop.

He looks at me. A smile breaks through the soot.

We say nothing. I leave him there in the alley so he can retreat to the fire, and I head for the shelter at home.

No words. Just a dreamy kiss - surrounded by a nightmare.

This... *this* cannot be.

But it *must.*

# 19 Selfridges

There are times we do things we can't explain, so wildly out of character it feels as though we've been momentarily possessed by someone else. Just for a second. Just long enough.

This war has done something to me. Twisted my thoughts. Troubled my spirit. And George - his absence, and even worse, his violent presence - has pushed me to a place I never thought I'd go.

And yet here I am, dreaming of Eddie. In sleep, in waking. Even while pouring tea, I drift off, picturing him - remembering the kiss, the way I felt, the way he made me feel. His silhouette cutting through the flames like something from the pictures. A forbidden romance that still smoulders.

No words have passed between us since. And yet I'm convinced he's thinking of me too. We're merely doors apart, both battling our own wars, both pretending nothing's changed.

But fantasies are safer than reality. That kiss amidst the wreckage was a moment of madness. Beautiful, dangerous madness. Two fools in the fire.

How could I do it? Let myself fall like that? Yes, George is far from perfect - his cruelty and flaws more exposed than ever - but he is my husband. My commitment should be unshakeable. And yet I've betrayed him, practically on the doorstep, while he prepares for whatever fresh horror this relentless war has in store.

So I must, with all my strength, silence the part of me that longs for Eddie. I must put aside that roaring, aching desire. It's an impossible task, but it must be done.

It shouldn't be hard to keep my mind occupied. The war rages on, and Dad remains unwell. His cough has turned into an infection, no doubt worsened by the constant damp in the shelter. Worry for him has reached a point where Joy has come to visit from Canterbury.

Joy is over eight months along now, her belly blooming beneath her coat. She looks radiant, and I try not to envy her.

'You shouldn't be here. It's hell on earth,' I tell her - not to scold, but to show I care.

'I had to see dear Bertie,' she says, 'and I'm so horrendously bored in Canterbury, Vera. Forever uncomfortable. Nobody to gossip with.'

'You mustn't stay long. You don't want a night in a shelter in your condition.'

She waves me off.

'I'm sure Henry will be home soon. They ought to let him go before the baby arrives - decent folk would.'

I don't say what I'm thinking, that her pregnancy is unlikely to be anyone's priority right now - least of all the corporal's. But I admire her hope.

Despite Dad still being under the weather, he's determined to keep up with the war and all the goings - on at the shop. Queues are longer than ever now - folk standing about with sour faces, waiting for bits of this and that. It's no fault of Mr Sharma's, of course. Rationing's made it so we queue for anything and everything, no matter what it is.

Dad's health has picked up a bit, though, and Dr Clarke reckons he'll be back on his feet within days. Doris, naturally, is taking all the credit - says it's her tender care that's done the trick. I let her rabbit on. No use arguing with Doris. She'll talk herself into sainthood if you give her half a chance. We've barely said a word to each other since that row in the Anderson shelter, save for Dad muttering about my stupidity in walking out during a raid.

I refuse to acknowledge Doris's rude and unwarranted characterisation of my dear mother. How cruel and manipulative of her - and I'm certain she's convinced Dad that Mum was something she clearly was not. But with Dad's illness, I choose not to revisit the matter. Not yet. Not until he is well enough to be reminded of the truth.

While at Dad's I can't help but feel exhausted, bone tired from work, running on barely any sleep, and with Eddie stuck in my head like a bad song. Joy clocks me straight away, thinking it's the bombings or George being away from home. She tries to lift the mood - lets me rest my hand on her bump to feel for a kick. And for a moment, I do feel something. A flicker of happiness. Then envy creeps back in, like it always does.

She checks her watch, and suddenly her eyes light up - like she's had an idea she's not supposed to say out loud.

'Let's go to Selfridges,' she whispers, like it's a big secret.

I shake my head.

'Don't be daft.'

But Joy's not letting it go. Says she's still got a bit of money from her mum to spend on baby things. She's a good talker, is Joy - could sell snow to a snowman. Think it's her posher accent that does it. And truth be told, I'm tempted to go. I've only ever been to Selfridges once, and that was just to look, not touch. The idea of going there to actually shop? That's something else. Feels daring. Feels… needed.

Still, I tell her no. I try to be sensible - until Doris plonks herself down with a grunt and breaks wind, loud enough to rattle the windows. We all feel like we need to run for the shelter.

'Let's go,' I tell Joy, getting to my feet.

She jumps up too, though it takes her a bit longer these days with her bump. Doris looks horrified. Reckless, she calls us - two young women heading into central London when the sirens could go off any minute.

But the shop's open for a reason. Life doesn't just stop because the sky's falling in. We have to be normal, although shopping at Selfridges isn't exactly my usual activity. But having a middle-class sister-in-law with a university education must come with some perks, and it's about time I made the most of them.

So off we go. Into town. To see what's left of the world.

It's hard to ignore the rubble along Oxford Street. Some shops have vanished altogether, just scorched gaps where they used to be. Signs hang stubbornly from battered doorways, insisting they're still open for business. One shop's even got a giant *OPEN* sign on its front despite having no roof. Me and Joy nearly giggle at it. You've got to admire the spirit of them, really - the shopkeepers still getting on with it.

Selfridges hasn't come through untouched either. It took a massive hit a couple of months back. Now the famous window displays are gone, boarded up with brick and timber like they're bracing for another wallop. But even with the dust and broken paving stones, shoppers keep on. And here and there, there's the faintest hint of Christmas - a sad little tree, a bit of tinsel, nothing like the usual, but still something. A sign the festive season is upon us.

The moment we step inside Selfridges, the world shifts. The smell hits me first - not smoke or soot or petrol like outside, but something warm and strange: perfume, beeswax, leather, and cloth. It's like stepping into a dream. The ceilings stretch so high they make me dizzy, and the light bounces off glass counters, catching on rows of beads and buttons. It doesn't feel like a shop but a different world entirely.

Joy grabs my hand, grinning, and pulls me along like a kid. She knows exactly where she's going - past the cosmetics, straight into women's wear, weaving between mannequins in silk frocks and rails of winter coats I'd never afford in a month of Sundays. We giggle like fools, trying on hats far too posh for me. Joy even gasps at the price tags. We dare each other to stroke the fur collars like we belong here.

In the baby section, Joy melts. Her fingers drift over tiny cardigans and crocheted bonnets, lace-trimmed blankets that look like they're spun from clouds.

Time disappears. The war, the sirens, the ration books - all of it fades. For a little while, it's just us, wrapped in warmth and light and wool and perfume.

Then a shop assistant passes by and says quietly,

'Closing soon - four o'clock sharp.'

We scramble to the tills. Joy pays for her things, telling the girl they're from me for the baby, even though I haven't put a penny towards them. Then she places a pair of heels on the counter, ones I had only just tried on but could never afford. Ridiculous price, really.

They're a soft oxblood leather, with a rounded toe and a modest two-inch heel. A stitched bow sits at the front, finished with just a hint of sparkle - enough to make you feel special, maybe even a little posh, without going overboard.

'I want to get these as well,' Joy smiles. 'They're for you, Vera. A little treat.'

I insist I can't possibly accept, but Joy doesn't listen. Thirty-two shillings and sixpence, they cost. I don't think I'll ever have the courage to wear them.

Just as we're about to leave, she says she needs the ladies. I nod, and while she goes off, I wander through women's wear again, eyeing the nightgowns. One catches my eye - cream silk, low-cut. I imagine wearing it. Not for George. For Eddie. *Unspeakable thoughts.*

Joy is taking quite a while. I check the time - the sun's starting to dip. That blue-grey light is creeping in, the kind that makes you hold your breath. I call for her, but she doesn't answer. A staff member starts to usher me gently towards the exit. Finally, Joy appears, pale and slow on her feet.

Something's off. She looks almost traumatised. I try to hurry her along, but she can't move quick - her body won't let her. Each step considered, an effort. She's breathing funny too. My heart's starting to race.

We step out into the street and the doors of Selfridges shut behind us. Oxford Street looks different now - darker, but still frantic as everyone heads for home, to safety. We shouldn't be out this late. I can feel it. The sky's turning, and I know the Germans will be over before long.

'Come on,' I whisper, trying to move Joy along.

She shakes her head, then stops me dead. I fumble for my torch as the light fades fast and Joy takes a moment to breathe. She grabs both my hands.

'I think the baby's coming, Vera,' she says, her voice low and trembling. Her eyes are wide and alert, and her fingers shake against mine.

'What - now? Are you sure? You've got weeks yet, haven't you?' I ask, but she doesn't answer. Just moves her hands to clutch her stomach.

'I think it must be.' She moans.

Panic floods in. What do I do - flag someone down, find a warden, get her to a hospital? A hundred thoughts crash into each other in my head, and then the air raid siren goes.

That rising wail slices through the air like a knife, and my breath catches. My heart races like never before.

'Oh, bleeding hell,' I cry.

The sound brings its own kind of terror. Bombs. Darkness. Fear. I look at Joy - she's breathing fast, trying to stay calm, but her hands still shake. The pain in her face is clear to see.

'It's alright,' I say, though my voice is shaky. 'Stay calm. We need to get to shelter.'

'Quickly' an air raid warden shouts, ushering us towards Oxford Circus station, where we're caught up in a swarm of people all heading below ground, seeking safety.

'We mustn't cause a fuss, Vera,' Joy says, squeezing my hand tight. How we're not meant to cause a fuss considering the circumstances is beyond me.

'It might wear off, no bother' she mutters - just before crying out in pain.

We start making our way down the stairs, the siren still howling in the distance. I keep hold of Joy as more people appear from nowhere, most of them clearly regulars with their usual spots, blankets rolled under arms, faces set to routine.

'We'll need to get you some help, Joy.'

'No… let's just wait and see what happens,' she says through gritted teeth, too proud to admit how much it hurts. Doesn't want to make a scene - not even in the middle of one.

I glance around at the crowd pressing past us, the sound of trains still echoing down the tunnels, the place alive with movement and tension as everyone scrambles to survive during a raid that's inconveniently hit earlier than usual. I'm not looking for anyone in particular - just somebody who might know what to do.

And then I spot her - a woman wearing a steel helmet marked with a big black *W*. A warden. Thank God. I tell Joy to stay put, guiding her to a corner where she braces herself against the wall, both hands flat, breathing hard, tears starting to spill.

I hurry over.

'Excuse me, miss-' I call, trying to get the young warden's attention through the noise. She can't be much older than me. 'We might have an issue..'

'What's the problem, mam?' she asks.

'My friend - well, sister-in-law, she's pregnant. And… we think the baby might be coming.'

The warden's face shifts, a flicker of panic as she looks over to Joy, who's doubled over now.

'Right…' she says, clearly unsure, because no training prepares you for this sort of thing in the middle of a bloody air raid.

'Is it her first?'

I nod.

She rushes over to Joy and I step back, watching them speak, though I can't catch a word of it over the crowd. Voices, footsteps, distant rumbles of trains and planes - it all blurs. Then suddenly the warden raises her voice with a power I didn't know such a small woman could carry.

'We require medical attention! Is there a nurse here, please?!'

Joy hides her face, sobbing from both pain and sheer embarrassment. The shelter quiets slightly, just a low rumble overhead now. Then, pushing through the crowd, comes a St John Ambulance volunteer - an older man in his sixties, with balding grey hair, he clings on to a first aid bag like it is precious cargo. He must be stationed here because of the numbers packed into these shelters, though I doubt delivering babies was high on his list of expected duties. And judging by Joy's face, a man is the last person she wants right now.

'Are there any women too?' the warden calls out again, knowingly.

'Well, I've had seven of me own!' a woman calls, stepping forward with her hand raised. She's got the look of someone who's seen everything and isn't scared of any of it.

I rush back to Joy, who's crying loudly now while the first aider starts barking instructions.

'We'll need space, towels, and - if anyone's got it - a curtain for modesty!'

'I can't have my baby here, Vera. Not in a bleeding tube station!' she cries.

'I don't think you've got much choice.'

The woman with the seven children is already beside her, rubbing her arm with surprising tenderness.

'You're alright, luvvie. Safest place to be right now, believe it or not. You're in good hands, I promise.'

'I can't… I just can't…' Joy sobs.

'Yes, you can. And yes, you will,' the woman says firmly.

The old man from St John's reappears, clutching a pile of towels and a face that looks slightly out of his depth. But we're in it now. No turning back.

'We're going to have to take a look at what's going on down there, sweetheart,' the woman says, finally introducing herself as Mabel. I press a cold towel to Joy's forehead, one arm wrapped around her shoulders as she tries to breathe through it, pain shaking through her in violent waves.

'Blimey,' Mabel mutters, her eyes lifting from between Joy's legs. 'You've done well, girl. Baby will be here soon.'

Mabel quickly takes charge, while the St John's man seems to shift into more of a crowd-control role, ushering away curious glances and making sure no one's watching too closely. A few other women gather nearby offering help - blankets, scarves - one of which Joy bites down on now, the pain starting to consume her.

Then an almighty thud reverberates through the shelter, followed by a low, trembling rumble. The ground shakes, dust drifts from the curved ceiling, and it lands softly on Joy's belly and knees.

'That sounded like it was right above us,' I cry.

'Don't you worry about that,' Mabel says firmly. 'Worry about her. She's going to need to give me one hell of a push.'

I try to soothe Joy, tell her I'm with her, that she's doing so well. But she looks dazed now, trapped in a trance of pain and panic, her knuckles white as she grips the sides of the blanket. Around us, the shelter murmurs with nervous voices, a mix of gossip, prayers and tension, all swallowed up by the hum of distant planes and the rattle of falling bombs.

Joy then screams - an enormous, guttural cry that seems to rise up from somewhere deep and raw - and pushes with all she has. In that one moment, her voice fills the underground, drowning out the war above, silencing the entire shelter. A kind of suspended stillness follows.

Until a baby appears.

Mabel catches this little life, slick with blood and warm with heat, wrapping it in a towel donated by a stranger. She rubs the baby firmly - not cruelly, but with urgency - until finally, mercifully, a cry erupts from the tiny mouth. A proper, healthy cry. Around us, you can feel it - the wave of relief. It ripples like a current through every huddled stranger. Passing like the trains in these tunnels.

'Got yourself a beautiful girl, luvvie,' Mabel says,

There's a soft clap from the old St John's man, quickly followed by more - gentle applause echoing quietly through the shelter, warm and respectful. It's oddly moving. People need this. We all do.

'You did it, Joy,' I say, crouching beside her, my eyes burning. 'She's perfect.'

It isn't a convenient place, or a safe one. Joy lies in a mix of blood, dust, and strangers' footsteps, half - hidden by a makeshift curtain rail. But none of that matters. In this impossible setting, something extraordinary has arrived. Life in the ruins. A defiant, beautiful cry in the face of destruction.

'I shall call her Mary,' Joy says softly, and then looks to me, 'after your mother. Her grandmother.'

My tears come without warning. What a beautiful gesture. I glance down at this tiny, perfect child - still warm against Joy's chest, her fingers twitching, her face calm. We've no idea what kind of world she's been born into, no clue what the future holds, only that it's uncertain. But right now, in this moment, I wish it were me. I'd give birth in a shelter, in a trench, in a bombed - out ruin, if it meant having that chance.

The trouble is... I don't want the child to be George's.

## 20 Breathe

Perhaps surprisingly, Henry is granted leave so he can see Joy and their new baby daughter. But instead of coming home, he goes straight to Canterbury, where Joy has returned after her Oxford Circus ordeal. We agree we'll all meet once Dad's health has improved. Perhaps at Christmas.

George, however, is yet to come home. Though I fear he will, any minute now. There have been plenty of chances for him to take the train to London, but instead, he's lingered in Aldershot, waiting for a longer leave period. You'd think he'd do everything he could to be with me, but not now. And I must admit, I feel a sense of relief. Alongside that, though, is a curious envy. What exactly is he getting up to when he has his time off?

Unlike before, he has sent the occasional letter, though they're void of any romance. Just matter-of-fact updates: relentless training drills, a shortage of kit, lads wearing odd boots or uniforms that look like they were made for children. I write back as normally as I can - love and kisses and the like. It's what you have to do.

When a letter does come through the door, Esther's face lights up. She's always hopeful it might be from her brother in France - now firmly under Nazi occupation. But still, no letter has come. Just silence. And it's the not knowing that eats away at you.

I've been keeping up calls with Sheila from the telephone box. Even in the bitter cold, I'll take my time. I was so keen to tell her what happened at Oxford Circus she could hardly believe it. Oh, how I miss her company, her spirit. She sounds so exhausted with it all. The East End continues to be bombarded, and there's a life in her voice that now feels absent. As always, I beg her to come home. But she fears Bill - and I can't blame her. We promise that in the new year, we'll meet in person, somewhere halfway. Maybe Kennington.

It's hard to believe it's been nearly a year since I first properly met Eddie at that jazz club. That long walk home will stay with me forever. We haven't seen much of each other since the kiss. His work is relentless every night, facing fire and tragedy minute by minute, while I remain rushed off my feet at the tearoom.

Part of me yearns to do something more, something that feels like I'm contributing to the war - like Violet. Something I can say mattered. She keeps encouraging me, but then I'm reminded how important it is to carry on as normal. And most vitally, to serve British folk a cup of tea. The medicine for the masses.

Dad's health continues to worry me. He's so up and down, always teetering between recovery and collapse, held back by this endless cycle of damp nights in the shelter. One minute he's up and trotting about - even down at the shop, inspecting inventories - the next, he's in bed again, coughing up his guts. Dr Clarke keeps telling him off for rushing back too soon. But Dad's always been restless.

It's mid - December when I rush home, and as I enter the bedroom I nearly jump out of my skin. George is there, lying on the bed, cigarette gripped between his lips. The room is thick with smoke, heavy with unease. I don't want to be here.

Still, I put on a brave face, force a smile. He doesn't move. Doesn't look at me. Just stares at the ceiling.

I hover, uncertain, before perching on the edge of the bed. Eventually, I lie down beside him - close but not touching.

'I've missed you, George. Something terrible,' I whisper.

Silence.

At last, he sits up, leans across me to stub out his cigarette, then finally looks at me - properly - for the first time. His eyes lock onto mine, unreadable. Then, like it pains him, he forces the faintest smile before his hand slides to my thigh, creeping higher. His intention is clear. And I just let him carry on.

No hello. No tenderness. He knows what he wants, and he takes it. He's aggressive, greedy - not cruel exactly, but careless. When it's over, he straightens up, slowly turns, and mutters:

'I'm going to The Old Swan.'

My heart drags heavy in my chest. My body aches with exhaustion.

'You'll be home before dark?' I call after him. 'We've had it terrible here, George. It's been a nightmare.'

For a moment, it looks like he's listening. Like he might care.

'We'll need to sort out the shelter situation,' he says flatly. 'I can't stay in a place like that with that German girl.'

'Where else is there?' I ask, weary.

'I don't know. But how are we supposed to be husband and wife in such a situation?'

'What do you mean?'

'Private moments, Vera.'

'Is that all you can think about, George?'

He laughs me off, grabs his coat, and slams the door.

As expected, George does not come home that night. I spent the evening with Nadine and Esther, half - worrying he'd been caught in the bombing. As much as I resent him, he's still my husband. I love him. I *have* to love him. And I would never wish him harm - only that he might be different.

In the morning, on my way to work, I see Eddie in the distance. His uniform, his walk - it steadies me. I feel calm, delighted even.

'Morning,' I say gently. Then quieter: 'He's home. not that I know where he is.'

But Eddie doesn't answer. He only flicks his eyes behind me. I turn. George is staggering up the street, still drunk.

'Who needs a shelter!' he roars, arms flung wide, staring at the sky in defiance.

'Have you..been out all night?' I ask.

'And still standing,' he chuckles. His coat hangs open, his face pale, eyes bloodshot, yet he brims with pride. 'Those bloody Germans don't give up, do they?' he mutters, swaying. 'But they'll have to try harder with me.'

He smirks, then fixes his eyes on me.

'We need to talk, Vera.'

'I'm off to work, George.'

'I said we need to talk!'

He grabs my hand, his grip is rough, too tight, he drags me inside the house as Eddie stays watching from afar and I try and act as normal as possible despite George's determination.

'What is it, George?' I ask, bracing.

'I love you and I'm sorry,' he says, voice trembling.

'Sorry for what?'

'For being rotten. I'm going to get better now. Be better. I've been awful. You'll forgive me, won't you, Vera?'

'Yes, George. Of course.'

He kisses me - hard, sharp, sour - then staggers upstairs, leaving me shaken, lips burning.

When I step back outside, Eddie's still there. Silent. Watching. His jaw tight, his eyes full of quiet concern. A look that says: *I won't say anything. But I see everything.*

But what can he do? What can anyone do?

This is my life. My mess. My battle.

All I can do is hold onto George's words - the flimsy promise to be better. An acknowledgement. Maybe even hope.

For a few days, that hope feels real. George stays home, avoids the pub, talks to me like he used to. Ordinary things, memories from when life felt simple. We even laugh. I'm grateful for the effort.

His mood lifts even more when Esther announces she's been invited to spend Christmas with an old friend in Barnstaple. Not that Esther and Nadine celebrate the occasion, but the chance to escape to the countryside - no bombs, clean air - is too good to pass up. With the house empty, George is lighter, easier.

And then one night during a raid, he makes good on his talk about "private moments." I never thought I'd find myself doing that in a freezing corrugated shelter, bombs falling from the sky, but then again - I've seen a baby born down there. Why not make one too? That's George's reasoning. His desperation for me to fall pregnant is stronger than ever.

It only grows worse on Christmas Day.

We're all at Dad's. Henry and Joy arrive with baby Mary, this tiny, perfect creature who softens even the sharpest corners of the room. Dad perks up just holding her. Doris, of course, is more interested in the shoes Joy bought me.

'What a show-off,' she mutters. 'Who you tryin' to impress?' she keeps asking with suspicion but I just ignore her.

When Henry offers George a hold of the baby, he hesitates. But Joy insists. Carefully, awkwardly, he takes her. For a second, his eyes flicker with warmth. Then it's gone - replaced by something darker. He remembers she's not his. You can see it all over him. He shuts down, retreating inside himself. Barely speaks another word.

It should be a happy day. Christmas. A new baby. Even the bombs seem to have taken a break - a strange gift from the Germans. But George's silence hangs over everything. I feel sick with it. Something's building.

Later that night, back home in the quiet, I try to keep it festive. George pours whisky, a gift from Dad, and he drinks it straight from the bottle.

'Our time will come,' I say gently. 'Shall we put some music on, while it's still quiet out there?'

'It won't come.' George says, standing still. Staring at me. 'Because something's wrong. With you.'

He jabs a finger at my head.

'Up here.'

Then lower, to my stomach.

'Or maybe it's there.'

Then lower still.

I flinch, shove him away.

'So much for being better,' I snap, voice shaking. 'You're just the bloody same, George.'

His eyes darken.

'How dare you!'

'I'm sorry, but it's true. When you're here, I feel like I can't breathe.'

He charges. Knocks me to the floor. Air bursts from my lungs. Then he's on me, straddling, clamping a hand over my mouth. His face twisted with rage. I can't make a sound. Can't breathe.

'You can't breathe?' he snarls. 'This is what it feels like. Like drowning. Like getting shot from the sky while submerged in the sea, knowing you're gonna die but not knowing how.'

His free hand pinches my nose shut.

I thrash, legs kicking, arms flailing. My lungs scream. Vision darkens.

'This is what they teach us,' he says coldly. 'If you've got no weapon - this is how you might do it. Easy. Quiet. Simple.'

My chest is on fire. The world closing in.

Then suddenly, he lets go.

Air floods me, ragged and desperate. My body convulses, heart pounding everywhere at once.

He stares like he doesn't know me. Or himself. Then without a word, he rises, walks out into the night.

No air raid sirens. No bombs. Just a deadly, unnatural quiet.

The enemy is not always in the sky. Sometimes, he sleeps beside you.

# *1941*

## 21 Live

'I'm sorry, Vera,' George says, stroking my back the next morning. I don't move. Don't look at him. I stare at the darkened wall and wish I was anywhere else. 'I was angry… I'm fed up, that's all.' Still, I don't move. I feel hollow, like something in me's been scraped out. 'I wouldn't have really hurt you or anything, I was messing about. Went too far, I'm sorry. Don't be in a mood.'

He says it like we were playing. Like it was a joke. And for a second, I wonder if I've got it wrong - if maybe I'm overreacting. But no. I know what happened. I felt it. George could have killed me. A few seconds more and he might have done.

That wasn't a game.

My body still feels like ice. My mind numb. And so, for the days that follow, we barely say a word to each other. He grows more restless by the hour. When I don't respond to his attempts at normality, he starts throwing things, raging at the furniture instead of me. Slamming doors. Kicking chairs. All because I didn't fall for his apology.

Eventually, he starts blaming me for that too.

'You're being cruel now,' he snaps, like I'm the one who crossed a line.

And just like that, 1941 begins. George returns to Aldershot, more bitter than ever.

'You hate me, don't you?' he says as he's leaving. 'Real hate.'

'I hate some of the things you do, George. I really do,' I say quietly.

'I won't do it again. You've got my word,' he says, leaning in to kiss my cheek.

But I've had his word before. They mean nothing now.

Through the darkest parts of my life, I've always managed to find a flicker of light. A sliver of something to hold on to. But now - even that's gone.

I try to ring Sheila. Her familiar voice might comfort me for a second. But we don't connect. Maybe the phone box she used got bombed. I stare at the Christmas card she sent, with her Aunt Ivy's address scribbled inside. Maybe I should go. I need to talk to her. I need someone.

When Esther returns from Barnstaple, she notices the change in me straight away. I'm quieter. Emptier. Like I'm just passing time.

'I worry about you, Vera,' she says. Of course, Esther is one to talk, still mourning Maurice. But there's a different energy to her now, since Nadine came, since she's had someone to care for again. A reason to get out of bed. 'I've learned we've got to live,' she says. 'Live like tomorrow might not come.'

A fair thing to say, living in a bombed-out city, a Jewish woman fearing that the Nazis will soon be on the doorstep.

But what does living mean? Really? Work. Rationing. Scraps of money. Judgement from strangers with nothing better to do. There's what I want - what I dream of - but I can't have it. And even if I could, I shouldn't.

Esther keeps at it though. Like she knows. Like she's guessed the things I'd never say out loud.

'You must live, Vera. It's all we have.'

I look at her, blank. I don't feel alive. I feel like a ghost.

'I won't live long,' I tell her, voice soft, honest, a bit scared. 'I know that. I can't picture myself old. Never could. Can't see me as a little old lady, sitting in a chair with a blanket on me knees. It's not there. Not in my future. I shall die young like my mother.'

She stares at me, stricken. Like I've confessed everything without saying a word. She pulls me close, holding me tightly like she could keep me here by force.

'You don't get to decide that,' she whispers. 'None of us do.'

'Maurice did.'

'I won't forgive him for that,' she says. 'But maybe Adonai will.'

Adonai - I think that's the Lord. She often uses words I don't quite recognise, French or something Jewish.

Esther looks at me again, more determined now.

'We don't get to choose these matters. Life is cruel. Unfair. But while we're still breathing, we've got to make it ours. Live on our terms. Don't let them - any of them - decide what your life gets to be.'

I think, I fear, she might be right.

I keep having this dream that when this darkness is over, me and Eddie are lying in the rings of the sun.

But it is just a dream. But how determined I am to make it real. Tonight perhaps? I have settled with this inconvenient truth, I must follow my restless, imperfect heart.

So, on a cold, crisp January morning, I knock on Eddie's door. I check Turner Street is quiet - no twitching curtains, no gossiping mouths. I close my eyes. Take a breath. Pray he's home.

I have to live.

The door creaks slowly open. I step inside. He quickly closes the door.

My temperature soars. My heart thunders. My body trembles. He looks at me - he knows. He knows why I've come.

'Vera…' he says, so delicately.

'I'm sorry, Eddie,' I whisper. 'I'm a flawed woman, and Lord knows I don't pray near enough - but I think you might be the answer to every prayer I ever said.'

He smiles. We kiss. Gently. Deliberately. A kiss that says everything. His arms wrap around me, safe and sure. There's no turning back now.

There are no flames this time, no buildings on fire, no smoke rising, but still the cold wind hammers the door like it's trying to interrupt. And yet here we are, lighting a fuse. None of this is right. It's all wrapped in wrong. But Eddie begins to pull me from the frying pan and into the fire. Hearts on fire. It burns. We boil over.

He takes total charge - stripping me bare. Not just my clothes, but my worries, my fear, my shame. George will kill me if he finds out. He might just kill me anyway. There's nothing left to lose.

So, I let Eddie take me. And I take him.

Oh, what a mess. A passionate, bothersome mess.

I've never known love like it. To be wanted this much. To be needed so deeply. I give him everything and he gives me more.

Two desperate, lost souls finding each other in the most human way.

And for a moment… the war disappears. The winter fades.

Oh, to be loved like this. It feels so selfish. And yet - I want more.

My body trembles, but this time not from fear. My breath catches, but not from suffocation. Only pleasure. Unending. Unapologetic.

This *cannot* be.

But it is.

# 22 East

Have you ever had one of those smiles you just can't shift? That lingering sort of joy that betrays you even when you try to dampen it down. I've got one now, and it won't leave me. My body still echoes with him, like an aftershock of pleasure. I know I shouldn't go back. But I will. I must.

George still looms somewhere in the distance, a storm cloud that won't clear. What am I meant to do with all this? How do I keep going? Still, I can't resist Eddie. I've had a taste, and now I want more.

Between my shifts and Eddie's endless nights hauling bricks and bodies from this burnt - out city, we're lucky to catch even a glimpse of each other, let alone more. It's as if the war itself is stepping between us, some kind of divine intervention. Perhaps the Lord is trying to stop me, but I don't think even he could turn me from Eddie.

Maybe it's George that's driven me here - his violence, his rage, his constant boiling fury. He's pushed me to the very edge, and I think I've already fallen. But if I'm falling, I'll fall with my eyes wide open.

I live now with a strange kind of clarity. Esther's always saying it: we must live, while we can. A bomb could drop at any second. The shelter could give way. Or George could snap and finish the job himself.

I don't think this war will ever end. And I don't think George will ever change.

Still, my smile doesn't last long. Doris comes knocking with news - Dr Clarke's decided Dad is to be hospitalised down in Worthing. Pneumonia, he says, and Dad won't recover properly unless he's out of London. The air, the bombs, the endless stress - it's too much. And even hospitals aren't safe anymore. We've all seen what this Luftwaffe can do.

So Dad is to be carted off. I worry, of course I do, but truthfully, I think it's for the best. He's a stubborn old soul - anyone else would be pushing up daisies by now. But not Dad. He keeps going. Keeps bloody going.

I promise myself I'll visit once the weather turns. A trip to the coast almost sounds lovely. I'm sure Doris will insist on tagging along, but that's a problem for later. For now, I just want him safe, and Worthing is certainly safer than Turner Street.

His biggest worry, of course, is the butcher's. But it's been ticking along without him, and the locals have grown rather fond of Mr Sharma and his "exotic sausage" - something we all chuckle about. Well, I do anyway.

'You'll write to me, won't you, Dad?' I say, as he's helped into the ambulance. Dr Clarke stands nearby, arms folded, making sure Dad doesn't wriggle his way out of this one.

'I hate writing,' Dad mutters. 'I'll be back in a few days.'

Dr Clarke doesn't look so sure.

And of course, Doris is hovering, all wide-eyed and weepy. She kisses Dad on the cheek with great ceremony.

'I shall do nothing else but pray, Bertie,' she says, full of tragic determination.

I roll my eyes, and she catches it. Of course she does.

With Dad gone, George and Henry back in Aldershot, and Sheila stuck in some bombed-out hellhole, the street feels empty. Eerie.

Except for Eddie.

He's the only light left around here. The thing that keeps me going.

I wave Dad off as the ambulance disappears down Turner Street. When I turn back, Doris is watching me, her hairnet sitting crooked, expression sour, her double chin hanging low like it's tired of holding her face up.

'I shall be accommodating myself at your father's while he's away,' she says, matter-of-fact.

'Why? You've got your own house,' I shoot back.

'Firstly, my shelter is less than adequate. Secondly, I've got a spot of bother with an invasive rodent.'

'I know the feeling,' I mutter under my breath.

'The things make my skin crawl. The house is riddled with mice. The bombs bring them out, you see. Harold used to sort it for me - remarkable senses, that man. Could sniff them out like a dog.'

'There's me thinking he lost all of his senses the day he married you,' I say, half a joke, half the truth.

'What is it with your disdain for me, Vera?' she snaps.

'I've not forgotten what you said about my mother. You dragged her name through the dirt just to get what you want.' She stiffens. I've clearly hit a nerve. 'I know your game, Doris. It won't wash with me.'

Doris gives me a long look, then shrugs.

'Sometimes we choose to remember people how we want to. Not how they really were.'

'My mother was a good woman,' I say, louder now. 'She was no *Tart of Turner Street*, that's for sure.'

Doris laughs - sharp and dismissive, as though I've said something pathetic.

I walk away before she can say another word. With Dad gone, I've no reason to be near her. And that, at least, is a welcome relief.

The following day, I keep my promise to visit Sheila in the East End. We haven't spoken in a while - her phone box must have been taken out by a bomb - so I set off with her crumpled Christmas card in my purse, the one with her revolutionary aunt's address scribbled inside. I worry the place might already be rubble, so I also bring a photograph Violet took of me and Sheila two years ago, both of us grinning on the corner of Turner Street, oblivious to what was coming. I think it might help track her down if she's lodging elsewhere.

It sounds simple enough, five miles from south to east, but nothing is simple these days. Streets are blocked, buses on endless diversions, routes altered by fresh craters. With a bit of help from strangers I start to make headway, but all along the journey there are constant reminders of the nightly destruction. For nearly five months - every single, blooming night - the city has been torn apart. Here, a gap where houses used to be; there, a road now impassable to people and traffic. Playgrounds reduced to splinters, churches with no spires, schools with no windows, no children. Sometimes the bus rolls through smoke still hanging in the air, the scent of burning and death catching at the back of your throat.

The further east we go, the less it comes in patches. No more little pockets of wreckage; here, the ruin is everything. Whole streets flattened. The bus can go no further, as if it has given up. I step down and ask my way again, only this time the faces I meet are doubtful, as if the street I'm looking for has been rubbed from the map completely.

The East End I'd known is gone. In its place, a jagged wasteland - houses gutted like tin cans, walls standing without roofs, staircases climbing to nowhere. The air hangs heavy with brick dust and burnt timber. I pick my way along what used to be a street, now a scatter of rubble and glass glinting in the hard sunlight. Washing lines still stretch between broken walls, shirts and vests fluttering like ghostly flags. A pram lies on its side in the gutter, one wheel still turning, as if it hasn't realised the baby is gone. And yet, amid all of it, a woman sweeps her front step, her home standing proud against the odds, and she herself prouder still.

Eventually I find Church Street, the name on the card, with the church itself still standing at the far end, unbowed. But the rest is blackened, charred, the small terraced houses ravaged by fire - terraces of terror now.

At the end, number 2, the place where Sheila is staying, is completely gone. Just rubble and wood. My stomach sinks. Nobody could live here.

I take out the photograph to help me, but the few people I come across shake their heads. At last, an older chap in a dented tin helmet tells me she's likely across the river if she's been bombed out.

'Tilbury,' he says. 'The whole world's there.'

It's about three miles walk across the river to this Tilbury place. When I reach it, it looms up at me - a monstrous hulk, like a working man's Buckingham Palace, only stripped of any sparkle. Towers of brick and iron streaked with soot. The great depot doors yawn open, spilling out damp, sour air that smells of coal, sweat, and far too many bodies crammed together. I gasp when a police officer at the front tells me a ticket is required for entry, like some attraction that must be seen to be believed. I quickly sort myself out with one, not informing him I'm simply looking for someone rather than staying. As you get deep inside you immediately hear the low hum of voices, babies crying somewhere in the belly of the place, the shuffle of tired feet on cold concrete.

And then the people appear - from every corner, coming and going, an endless tide. The further in you go, the more there are, the sounds swelling, echoing off the walls. This isn't a shelter, it's an underground city. Thousands upon thousands crammed together in the damp gloom, lying on bunks, camp beds, or the bare floor. Makeshift canteens tucked into corners. Communal spaces where people sit reading, sewing, trying to amuse the children. The world carries on in this hidden underbelly - a place built for goods, now holding human cargo, and how marvellous they are.

But there's little chance I'll find Sheila here. Among the countless bodies, she could be a few feet away and I'd never know. My worry gnaws at me, heavier with every step.

After a while I give up, certain I'll have no luck. Then, in the corner by the makeshift ladies' lavatories, I spot her - only it isn't Sheila, it's her sister Pat. Her hair's grown matted and wild. I push through the crowd, almost bowling a couple of people over in my haste.

'Patti! Pat!' I call. She turns, her face a picture of shock.

'Christ, what you doing here?'

'Where's our Sheila?' I ask. She pauses. The longest pause I've ever felt. The whole world seems to stop. Even my heart takes a rest. 'No… no… don't tell me she's - '

'Vera!' comes a voice behind me.

I spin round, and there Sheila is. I grab her, adamant, grateful. I've never known relief like it. 'You're daft as a brush coming here,' she says, tears springing to her eyes.

'I thought you were brown bread,' I tell her, still clinging on.

'No, still here, in this pit.'

'Our Aunt Ivy weren't so lucky,' Pat says.

'No,' Sheila confirms quietly. 'No, she weren't.'

I look between them, waiting for more. Sheila exhales.

'Her house got flattened. We were fine, in a nearby shelter, but she went back in the morning, determined to find her cat, Keir. She started digging through the wreckage before the patchers arrived. They told her not to, begged her, threatened her even, but she wouldn't have it. Then suddenly the only wall still standing came down, right on top of her.' Sheila closes her eyes for a moment. 'She just disappeared under bricks and dust. I screamed so loud the whole East End must've heard me.'

'And you wouldn't believe it,' Pat adds, 'a few seconds later the cat trots out the rubble without a scratch.'

'Nine lives. Shame Aunt Ivy didn't have so many. Poor love,' Sheila says.

I'm sickened by the thought of it. But you hear these stories all the time - lives snuffed out in seconds, homes gone. And yet the living carry on, because we must.

Pat and Sheila take me to the little pop - up canteen they've been helping in. Pat rattles on about the government censoring stories, keeping the real human cost from the public to stop panic and keep the Germans from feeling like they're winning.

'It's all sugar-coating,' Pat says fiercely. 'Bring out the royals for a photo shoot, all smiles, lovely jubbly. What a wonderful war. Bastards might as well be standing on Aunt Ivy's buried corpse.'

'The war hasn't changed her much,' Sheila mutters, half a smile.

'She's right though,' I tell her. 'My Eddie said the same about Balham, how they never give you the full picture.'

'*Your* Eddie?' Sheila arches an eyebrow.

I realise what I've said - too casually, too revealing.

'Is that what I said?' I laugh, fumbling.

'Who's Eddie?' Pat asks, narrowing her eyes.

'Isn't he that fireman living at number 80?' Sheila presses. I have to deny it, but I fear my face might give me away.

'Somethin' going on, Vera?' Sheila leans in. I shake my head, brushing it off. As much as I want to tell Sheila, it can't be done here - not in this shelter, with the masses packed in and every word bouncing off the walls.

'What about your Samuel? Seen much of him?' I ask, steering things away from Eddie.

'Hardly,' she sighs. 'He's snowed under with all that's going on, treating people day and night. Even his hospital got bombed. It never ends, does it?'

I nod, glad to have moved on from my slip about Eddie.

'You must come home, Sheila. Turner Street's still standing. It's awful, but it's better than this.'

'She don't want to be near Father,' Pat cuts in, putting a reassuring arm around her. 'Neither of us do. We'd rather live through hell than spend another minute with that sod.'

We continue to chat, catching up desperately, but before I know it the day has run away from us. I'm all too aware I need to head home before the sky dims and the hum of planes swells into that familiar chorus of engines, gunfire and falling bombs. Before I set off, Sheila insists on walking with me part of the way, to Tower Bridge at least, pointing out a quicker route back south. Pat stays behind, already caught up in plans for some meeting with others who share her political leanings. She tries to press a copy of *The Daily Worker* into my hand as I leave, but I shake my head with a polite smile - I've enough on my mind.

Sheila and I leave the shelter arm in arm, pushing against the tide of people shuffling in to claim their night's patch of concrete. The air outside is cool, a damp relief after the closeness of Tilbury's belly. An ARP warden eyes us and calls out a warning about the light fading.

'We're getting some air before we're trapped in!' Sheila fires back. She turns to me, lowering her voice. 'I'm living down there now, Vera. Day and night. They talk about rehousing us but there's too many of us, and Aunt Ivy's place is gone but it weren't ours. People row in there, proper fights sometimes. Debates too, that go round in circles. You couldn't cram another body in if you tried. Toe to toe it is. Oh, and the toilets, if you could call them that - I've not gone properly in a week.'

'Then come home,' I tell her, more firmly this time. 'Dad's place is empty while he's in Worthing. You could stay there.'

She shakes her head.

'Pat wouldn't have it. We've got to stick together.'

We walk on under a sky shading from pale blue to a darker, more ominous hue. In the distance, clouds gather like the planes we know are coming. How I wish she'd come with me, but I know she won't. Rain begins to fall in light patters that match our steps. We round a corner and the Tower of London rises before us - magnificent still, though scarred. Its ancient walls bear fresh wounds from the Luftwaffe's raids, patches blackened, repairs underway after a vicious fire. The place has seen centuries of siege and misery, but even the Tower must be sick of the sight and sound of bombs by now. A barrage balloon tethers beside it, silver in the dim light, straining upward as though it could defend the old fortress. It hasn't done much good.

'Do you like George?' I ask suddenly, without thinking at all.

'He's alright, isn't he?' Sheila replies. I can sense she's curious why I've asked.

'He… he can be…' I hesitate, worry shaking me. Why am I doing this? Why am I even speaking?

'Go on,' Sheila says.

'He can be quite violent.'

Sheila glances at me, frowning.

'What, fighting like?'

'Yes. With me.' I try to keep my voice steady, not to let the emotion spill over, but there's relief in saying it aloud - quickly chased by the fear of having said too much. 'He hurts me, sometimes. You mustn't tell anyone, Sheila. Between us, but… I just needed someone to know. In case you, see? He's not the saint everyone thinks he is.'

Her eyes widen. She weighs her next words.

'Sorry, Vera. Has he been like that all along?' I shake my head.

'It started with arguments - real angry ones - soon after we were married. But it's got worse. Much worse.'

'This war brings out the very best and the very worst in people,' she says with a small tut. I'm not sure she truly grasps what I've told her - or perhaps she does, but after growing up with her own father's rage, the idea of me being married to a violent man doesn't strike her as shocking. More expected than anything.

We walk on in silence for a moment, just the patter of rain joining us. In my mind, I weigh whether to tell her about Eddie. What good would it do? And yet, these secrets feel heavier with each passing day.

'You see, the thing is, Sheila…' I start carefully. She gives me a nod to go on. 'I've become… quite well acquainted with another man.'

She stops mid-stride.

'That fireman, isn't it?'

I nod slowly, as if my head's been bolted in place and is fighting the movement. She sighs, a knowing smile playing on her lips. 'Well, well, Vera. There's me thinking I was the troublemaker.'

'You can't say anything, Sheila.'

'Not a word,' she says, reassuring.

'I don't know what's got into me.'

'Love probably. Bloody nuisance, isn't it?'

'I should say, George will kill me if he finds out. Honest, he will.' I tell her, the worry aching in my voice. Sheila takes my hand as we pass the Tower, its dark bulk seeming to listen in, judging us as it has judged so many before.

'If we win this war, me and Samuel are going to move - out of London, start again,' Sheila says with a trace of enthusiasm.

'I noticed you said "if",' I say, hearing the doubt in her voice.

'You've not thought about what will happen if we don't win?' she asks. I shrug, knowing it'll be dreadful but not wanting to dwell on it. 'We talk about it in the shelter,' she goes on. 'Pat does a lot with her friends - you should be prepared, Vera. People like Pat, with her politics, the Nazis wouldn't hesitate to put her in prison… or worse. Same with Samuel - they don't like black men much either. And then there's you.'

'Me!?' I say, startled.

'You're living with Jews, Vera. And you've got dark hair. They'd think you were one of them. Christ knows what that would mean. You're telling me you've not thought about that?'

'Not really… not like that.'

'Too busy with your handsome fireman,' she says, half teasing, though I'm not entirely sure.

The horrors of the East have settled into her bones. I can see it - this is not the same carefree, cheeky young woman I once knew. She carries the weight of tomorrow like a sack she can't put down.

'You need to come home, Sheila. That place isn't good for you,' I nag.

I sense she wants to, but her loyalties lie with her sister.

As we reach Tower Bridge, we pause before crossing. The great steel arms rise above us, black against the bruised sky that is now unleashing rain, the bridge's rivets just visible in the last of the light. The Thames below is a sheet of dull brown, sluggish and cold, the tide tugging at the shadowed arches. Rain hammers down like the bombs, causing ripples.

We stop and Sheila hugs me tightly, rain soaking in.

'Tell Father I'm all right - not that he'll care much, but Mother might. And Vera… be careful,' she says with the tone of a parent rather than a friend. She heads back to the shelter, her home, a place of apparent safety, lightly jogging as the rain continues.

As I navigate my way back to Turner Street, her words stay with me, circling in my head. What would it mean for all of us if we lost this war? I've been taking each day as it comes - too tired from the bombardment, too worn down by my husband - to think much further ahead. But now… now I can't shake the thought of life without freedom, the cold grip of it wrapping itself around my ribs. It sends a shiver clean down my spine.

We must win.

We have to win.

# 23 Trap

Not long after my visit to the Tilbury shelter, I'm quick to inform miserable Bill that I've seen Sheila and Pat. I catch him at his doorstep, wearing his Home Front uniform - or rather, just a steel helmet, that heavy dome perched awkwardly on his head, its dark green paint chipped and scratched. Why he's wearing it to sit indoors listening to the wireless, I'll never know.

As politely, and briefly, as possible, I tell him that despite the awful conditions and scenes beyond imagination, both Sheila and Patricia are doing well. Resilient. Determined as ever. Bill looks at me like none of it matters.

'Tell Sheila if she rids herself of her lover she can come back home,' he says, helmet tilting to one side.

'And what about Pat?'

'Beyond saving, communist cow,' he says coldly.

'I assume you know about your sister?' I ask, gently. He nods.

'Only good thing the Germans have done,' he replies.

His cruelty still manages to startle me, though it shouldn't. This man enjoys hating, and the war has only sharpened the taste for it.

Just before he shuts the door, I call his name. He opens it again, a flicker of intrigue in his eyes.

'I've been thinking,' I say, trying to sound as confident as possible, 'about an invasion, and what I might have to do to defend myself. My neighbours. My country. That's what the Home Guard's about, isn't it? So... can I join?'

He laughs. Howls, even - a deep, ugly sound I've never heard from him before.

'You're a woman,' he says, almost choking on his own spite. With a condescending look, he slams the door in my face.

Rotten sod.

Violet has shown a woman can do anything in this war, but for every strong, determined Violet there's a Bill or two about the place.

It's spring now, and we've endured nearly seven months of relentless bombing. Imagine that - night after night without let-up. 1941 has been the most god - awful year, and yet in the quiet pockets between the raids, moments with Eddie soothe it all. If I'm truthful, I think he's what's keeping me going.

Our time is painfully limited. He spends his nights battling the fires and his days grabbing a few hours' rest. More often than not I'm rushed off my feet at the tea room, serving meals that seem to shrink with every ration cut.

We've worked out that at dawn - usually just after the all-clear - is the one time we can see each other privately, as he returns from a night's firefighting. It's risky, slipping into his home while the rest of Turner Street is out surveying the latest damage. And it's hardly romantic, meeting when we're both hollow-eyed, filthy, and utterly spent. Yet somehow we're drawn to each other more than ever.

Sometimes I bathe him, washing away the stench of smoke and burning from his skin. I do enjoy it - touching every part of him - and he clearly likes it too. We're making the best of what little we have, mindful and careful, but deeply in love, refusing to let bombs or the clock rob us of what we've found. Every second with Eddie feels like a blessing.

Of course, I cover my tracks. I tell Esther my shifts have been extended because of staff shortages, explaining my early departures that way. I've also let slip my *concern* for the firefighter a few doors down - living through hell, no time to eat - so that occasionally offering him something from our limited reserves feels like charity, not scandal.

The bombs are a fine distraction. Folks are too busy thinking about their own survival to pry into the goings - on in other houses. Mostly, anyway.

Still, I keep my wits about me. George could turn up at any moment. He spends most of his time shuttling between Aldershot and the south coast, readying things for a German invasion. There's a strange irony in it - my father sent to the coast for his health and safety, only for it to become the very front line should the enemy manage to cross the Channel.

Speaking of Dad, his letters are short and to the point. He writes of feeling stronger, ready to come home, though he's convinced Dr Clarke is keeping him down there on purpose. I think it's kindness, but Dad has other ideas - namely that Mr Sharma is slipping him extra cuts of meat, something Dad put a stop to the minute rationing began. He wants me out of the way so Sharma can take over, Dad insists. Honestly, the daft tales people dream up at the butcher's counter. That said, Dr Clarke does look a touch plumper than usual. Rationings meant to have us all losing weight, not piling it on.

I soon learn that Eddie is being granted a full day's rest from his duties - not that there's much rest for anyone these days. By some small miracle, his day off falls on one of mine, as if the stars have finally aligned in our clouded skies.

We decide to make a proper thing of it. Behind the blacked-out windows, before night falls, we'll have each other - longer than we've ever managed before. It's also a chance for me to look my best, instead of the weary, work-worn version he's so used to seeing. Likewise, perhaps for once he won't smell faintly of burnt wood and dust. In many ways it's a date, hidden behind drawn curtains, a secret Turner Street will never know.

To make the most of it, I put on my favourite navy-teal dress, patterned with a scatter of tiny white flowers. The rayon is soft against my skin, still hanging beautifully despite countless washes. On my feet are the oxblood heels Joy bought me from Selfridges. I feel, so special, so wanted.

This occasion, though, isn't only about passion - though that will no doubt be a priority during the short hours we have. It is also a rare gift: a chance to talk, to simply be together, unless the Germans decide an earlier -than-usual raid is what London needs.

And so, we spend our time together, talking, exploring each other figuratively and literally. Eddie tells me about his closeness with his mother, who writes often, and about his father, also a fireman, still working in Norfolk. Eddie is twenty-four - just a year older than me - but speaks with such calm experience I can hardly grasp it. Then, suddenly, he tells me he's twenty-five *today*. I'm furious - no clue, no hint - though I suspect he's not in the mood for celebrating.

We spend much of the afternoon in the bedroom, lying on our backs, staring at the ceiling, giggling. The blackout blinds keep our secret safe, the dimness wrapping round us. We keep our voices low - hard to do when one wants to really let go.

We laugh over the silliest things - private jokes, I beg him to perform his absurdly good Churchill impression. He obliges: face scrunched, double chin forced, voice deep and gravelly. I run my fingers through his sandy hair, softer and cleaner than I've ever seen it. We touch each other endlessly, never tiring. It feels perfect - until the sudden, determined knock at the door.

A jolt of panic shoots through me. I leap up as Eddie scrambles into his trousers, hurriedly smoothing his shirt. I peel back the edge of the blackout drape, I glance down to see Doris planted at the doorstep, surveying Turner Street like a detective. I step away, terrified she might look up. My heart thumps so loudly I'm sure she'll hear it.

Eddie rushes downstairs and opens the door only leaving a crack, his head poking through.

'Good afternoon, sir, sorry to bother you,' Doris calls, her voice unmistakable even at its most *polite*. 'Don't suppose you've a rat trap, have you? The bleeding things have invaded my home like the Jerries.'

'Er… I'm not sure, this is - '

'Yes, yes, I know, Mrs Morris's place. I know her dearly. She always had things like that. I've already got three, but I need one upstairs, you see. It'll be in that messy cupboard of hers - shall I come and look?'

'No… no… I'll see if I can find one.'

Eddie ducks away from the door, leaving it ajar, and glances up at me with a flash of worry. Doris keeps on, voice raised so it carries through the gap.

'You see, my Harold - God rest him - used to deal with pests,' she shouts over the clatter of Eddie rummaging in the cupboard. 'I'd ask my dear friend Bertie Wright, the butcher, but he's taken unwell, gone to the coast to recuperate. You know Bertie?'

She leans in suddenly, and I step back so fast I nearly lose my footing. Eddie reappears quickly, holding an old rat trap, blocking her view.

'You're in luck,' Eddie says with a touch of relief.

'Wonderful. I'll add some cheese before they ration it altogether,' she replies, plodding off down the street.

I let out a long breath, trying to calm the pounding in my chest. Eddie joins me upstairs.

'She had no idea you were here.'

'How can you be so sure?' I ask, sharper than I mean to.

'You're fine, Vera. Honest.'

'I can't do this, Eddie. It's… so wrong. So - '

‘I love you, Vera.’ His voice is steady, his eyes bright with feeling. ‘I mean it, I love you like I’ve never loved anyone.’

I look straight into him.

‘I love you too, Eddie.’

And we cling to each other, trapped here on Turner Street, surrounded by judgemental eyes. I don’t know how this can go on.

# 24 Disgrace

By early evening I am back home - elated, panicked, worried, smitten - a whirlwind of emotions rattling through me like the planes and bullets screaming overhead.

Like clockwork, another raid hits. I sit in the shelter with Esther and Nadine, dazed by everything. Nadine tries to smile, but she's grown up so quickly; her girlish innocence stripped away by this war that drags us all down. My mind won't stop turning over the same problem: how to find a path forward with Eddie. How could this possibly last? How could we carry on when people like Doris circle Turner Street like sharks? What if the rat trap was nothing more than an excuse to poke her head in, to feed her suspicions?

When dawn creeps in, I climb up for air. The spring sun pushes through the haze, smoke still hovering on the horizon. No large bombs have fallen nearby overnight, but other parts of London will have taken a hammering. Our little street south of the river has been spared once again.

Still, bombed wreckages now scar both roads either side of Turner Street. The main one came the night I kissed Eddie among the flames, but Turner Street itself remains untouched - defiant, lucky. Although it feels like it's only a matter of time.

I have a little while to get ready for another shift at Lyons. This morning, though, I won't be visiting Eddie at first light, much to my own disappointment. As I step outside, Mrs Butler and her girls, Lillian and Elizabeth, come skipping past, full of chatter and school - morning energy. Mrs Butler, as ever, gives me her warm smile.

'How are they holding up?' I ask, surprising even myself. We usually stick to nods and smiles.

'They're fine. Adaptable, children are,' she says with a small nod. Then, more sharply, 'This might just be our lives forever, you know. What's one supposed to do - never have children? Only be allowed to procreate if one resides in the countryside?' She scoffs. By now the girls have run off to the far end of Turner Street, free as birds.

'Elizabeth! Lillian!' she calls, her voice straining to stay ladylike as she hurries after them, heels clicking against the pavement.

I turn to continue my own walk to work, but then freeze. Doris is there - only inches away, as if she's materialised from thin air. The morning sun blazes behind her, her face in shadow, eyes fixed on me like bayonets.

'You are a disgrace to your family, Vera Hopkins,' she says sharply, leaning on the word Hopkins. My chest tightens. Panic claws up my throat.

'You… what?' The words stumble out, my voice shaking.

She steps closer, her frame blocking out the light completely. 'I know what you're up to, Vera.' A slow, smug smile curls her lips.

'I've no idea what you're talking about,' I say, trying to sound firm, but it comes out thin.

'You were round the fireman's house. You're an adulterer,' she spits, 'fornicating with a neighbour. A disgraceful woman.'

I shake my head too quickly, trying to dismiss it, but my hands are trembling.

'You're talking nonsense. Utter - '

'The heels!' she snaps, cutting me off. 'Those red shoes. I saw them in the doorway, shining like an angel in the night. Those audacious, pretty heels of yours. I assume the rest of your garments were upstairs, scateered on the floor without care or consideration?'

My breath catches. Those bloody shoes. I can't speak, can't move, my mind scrabbling for something - anything - to say. But Doris barrels on, relentless.

'When your father returns from Worthing, which I believe will be very soon indeed, I'll be telling him of this scandal. Mark my words. And of course, your heroic, devoted husband will also be informed of your affair.' She tuts, the sound sharp and deliberate. 'You're in a spot of bother now, aren't you, Vera? What a shame. A mighty shame.'

She brushes past me, jolting my arm. I steady myself against the wall, heart hammering.

This will end me. Doris is going to destroy me.

I have to stop her.

## 25 Rat

All day I find it impossible to concentrate. Doris's words circle my head like fighter planes. Every time the tearoom door swings open I half expect George to storm through and do God knows what. My hands will not stay steady; trays wobble, orders slip clean out of my mind. I wander between tables, hopeless and distracted. The other girls notice - ask if I'm all right, if I need a moment. But no minute, no break, lifts the terror clawing at me.

By now, surely the whole of Turner Street knows. I can't imagine setting foot home again. The hours drag like the longest I've ever known.

On my way back I keep turning it over: what to do, what to say. Should I deny it all? Admit I was there and twist the conclusion? Be truthful and accept my fate? I have to talk to her before she gets to Father - though perhaps she already has. What words could sway her? What bribe, what bargain could make her change her verdict? Doris is relishing this. She's never liked me, and now she's got the perfect weapon.

When I reach Turner Street I'm burning with determination, though I have no idea what to do.

Instinct takes me. I bang on Eddie's door - he must know, must hear it from me before anyone else. There is no answer. He's already gone, preparing for another night of fire and fury. I don't give up. My feet drive me toward the fire station, ten minutes away, each step sharp with purpose. My shoes bite; my arches ache, but I don't care.

As I turn the corner the scene stops me dead. Both ends of the street are wrecked: shops and houses caved in, rubble spilling across the road. I've seen many bomb sites, but this one feels too close to home. Yet at the far end the fire station stands intact, its great doors flung open, engines lined up like soldiers on parade.

The place is a sea of men - shovelling, hauling, shouting, all moving in strange, precise harmony, like a clockwork machine built for war. And then, there in the corner, I see him. Eddie. Bent to his task, handsome as ever, his shirt damp, brown hair pushed back.

"Eddie!" I call. He turns, startled, colour rising in his face. His friends glance over and smirk knowingly as he strides to me, fast, protective.

"What are you doing here?" he says, real concern in his voice.

I pull him aside, away from their eyes and ears. "Doris… it's Doris. She knows. She knows about us."

The words hang in the air. For a moment he says nothing, just stares at me while hammers and engines fill the silence. Then a voice bellows from across the road from a stranger: "How many sugars does he take, love?" Laughter erupts from the crew.

And then I realise I'm still in my Lyons uniform - my neat dress and apron, the badge pinned clear for all to see. I've come here openly, like a fool, and now I've only poured fuel on the fire. A fire even Eddie might not be able to extinguish.

He pleads with me to make Doris see sense. He grips my arms, worry etched across his face like a man who believes his days are numbered.

'You've got to tell her it's nonsense, Vera. I'll do the same.'

I nod, trying to agree, but the words feel hollow. How could anyone persuade Doris of anything?

'We shouldn't have been so bloody stupid,' Eddie mutters, eyes down. It lands like a blow. For a second I feel myself shrink - no longer the woman he swore he loved, just a mistake, an inconvenience.

'I'll do what I can, Eddie,' I say quietly. 'But you don't know Doris. She's difficult at the best of times.'

He looks past me at his fellow firemen, who are already pointing, laughing. I've made a fool of myself coming here in broad daylight. But he had to know. He had to.

So I turn away, feet carrying me back to the down end of Turner Street - straight to Dad's, where I know Doris has been making herself at home. I hammer at the door, but there is no answer.

I cross the road and head for Doris's house. My frantic knocking echoes until, at last, the door creaks open. Without thinking I push past her, shoving inside. Doris stumbles back, flustered, and I slam the door. She stares, round face set stern, utterly mystified by my nerve.

'Now you listen to me, Doris,' I begin, forcing courage into my voice though it shakes. 'I won't have you spreading unfounded rumours. You'll ruin my good name, my marriage, for nothing but vicious hearsay.' She smirks, scoffing. 'I admit I've become friends with a fireman a few doors down,' I press on, desperate, 'but only to give him support. He's got no family here, no friends. He's living through hell every night. It's been really hard – '

'Oh, really hard,' she laughs, dismissing me with a wave. 'You think I was born yesterday?' She waddles into the kitchen. On the table sits a rat trap. With careful fingers she sets a piece of cheese, lips curled in satisfaction.'I know you, Vera. I know exactly what you've been up to. You ought to be ashamed.' She lifts her head and stares straight into me. 'The *new* tart of Turner Street. Runs in the blood, doesn't it?'

My fists clench. I want to throttle her, silence her forever. She picks up a long stick, slots it into the trap and - SNAP. The jaws spring shut, splintering the wood clean in two. I flinch. Doris smiles, eyes gleaming.

'Imagine your father's face when I tell him,' she says sweetly. 'And your wonderful husband too.' I can't breathe. 'You're in trouble, Vera. Big trouble.'

I take a deep breath, trying to conjure something that might change her mind. Before I can speak, the siren's unmistakable wail splits the air. Too early, too loud, too inconvenient.

I ignore it and press on.

'You've no idea what this will do to me, to my family. All for a misunderstanding – '

'I've misunderstood nothing. Don't take me for a fool,' she snaps, voice rising above the siren.

'You don't know what George is like… what will happen if he – '

'You should've thought of that before spreading your legs for another man!'

Her words sting, sharp and merciless. My temper surges. I throw her own sins back in her face - her cruelty to Harold, her obsession with Dad. It only riles her more. The shouting escalates, our voices tumbling over each other until they're drowned out by the thunder of planes overhead, the distant crump of falling bombs, the rattle of machine - gun fire from the sky.

'We need to get to shelter,' I plead, pushing past her into the garden. She follows, grumbling, and we duck into her Anderson shelter.

The sky above burns with fire and noise, but inside it's colder, darker - a bare tin can that stinks of damp. No blankets, no water, no stores of any kind. The place has never been used.

'We can't stay here,' I say, shuddering as another blast shakes the earth.

But Doris lowers her bulk onto the metal bench, arms folded, lips pursed. 'I'm not staying anywhere with you,' she spits.

I want to leave, to run, but the noise outside pins me there. The danger is too close. And then it comes to me: I'll never shout or argue her into silence. Doris is too stubborn, too cruel. My only chance is to make her understand what George really is, what I've been through.

It's my last roll of the dice.

'I'm sorry, Doris. I've been terrible, said awful things… and I know you mean well. But this is all wrong. A mistake.' My voice cracks. I press my fingertips hard against my eyes, trying to stop the tears from spilling. 'You have to realise what this will mean if George thinks something that just isn't true.'

She sits motionless, arms folded, lips tight. Perhaps - just perhaps - I'm reaching her.

'Doris…' I cough, dragging the courage back up from my throat. 'George is not the man you think he is. He can be cruel. Awfully cruel. Inconsiderate. Violent in ways I can't bear to describe.'

The tears break free now. They run hot down my cheeks as the shelter shudders with a blast outside. Doris stays exactly where she is, unmoved by the war, unmoved by me.

Then suddenly she asks,

'Has he hurt you, Vera?'

I can't speak. My body shakes, but I manage a small nod.

She rises slowly, her eyes fixed on me. For a second I think - hope - that she's softening. Her step is cautious, her face unreadable. She comes closer, searching my eyes like she's looking for proof of my soul.

'He'll kill me if he finds out,' I whisper, voice trembling. I lean into her, head heavy against her shoulder. It's the first time I've ever touched her, and for the briefest moment, her arm settles on my back. It soothes me, almost like a breakthrough, a comfort I've been desperate for.

But then she speaks.

'Is this your game? To dirty the name of your wonderful husband in order to justify your deeds?'

I reel back, stunned, panicked. I shake my head furiously.

'It's the truth!' I sob, my voice cracking into the shadows.

Her face hardens, eyes gleaming with judgement. And then, cold as steel, she says:

'Then if it is true, you deserve everything you've got coming to you.'

The words slice through me. For a moment, I don't even know how I'm still standing. Around us the air raid howls, the earth moves, but nothing feels louder than her cruelty - her pleasure in my suffering.

I hunt for words, but before I can speak Doris suddenly bellows:

'Rat! Rat!'

She jerks her dimmed lantern towards the corner of the shelter where a wet, disoriented creature crouches, fur slick, eyes glinting in the gloom. It too has fled here for safety, another refugee from the bombs.

'Bleeding things in here!' Doris shrieks, stumbling back. With a wobble she bolts out into the garden, terror not for the planes tearing the sky apart but for the rat at her feet.

I follow her into the open air. The heavens roar above us - flames, smoke, tracer fire cutting through clouds. It feels as though we're caught in the very crossfire.

'Where are you going?' I shout, my voice nearly lost in the clamour.

She stands at her back door, wild-eyed.

'To your father's shelter! Don't you dare follow me!'

She sets one foot into her home when it comes - the sound. A screaming whistle that rips the air clean apart, like a banshee shrieking down from the heavens. Time stalls. For an impossible heartbeat there is only the shriek, then an aching silence - before the world ends.

A white flash swallows me whole. Then the blast - roaring, ripping, monstrous. The air itself seems to tear in two. I'm hurled backwards into the shelter, body thrashed like a rag doll. Glass shatters into a thousand icy shards. Doris's home groans like a wounded animal, timbers splintering, bricks collapsing into a boiling orange dust cloud that surges over me, swallowing the light. The entrance to the shelter seals shut under rubble and beams, plunging me into choking blackness.

I lie crumpled, head throbbing, vision blurred. Dust clogs my throat, fills my lungs. The rat skitters frantically across my leg, its claws a frantic patter against my skin. I close my eyes and try to draw breath, each one like swallowing earth. Buried. Broken. Still alive - I think.

Time loses meaning. Each attempt to move is met with agony, as though boots stamp down on my skull. I try to cry out, but no sound escapes. Only the ceaseless thunder of bombs answers me. And so I close my eyes and prepare to die.

But eventually I'm awoken by the noise of shifting rubble. A beam is lifted, a brick pulled free, then another. A thread of light slices through the dark, widening with every scrap removed. Voices seep in, muffled, urgent, echoing against the tin walls I thought would be my coffin.

And then - clear, unmistakable. Eddie.

'Vera! You in there?'

A hand thrusts through the wreckage, fingers clawing for mine. I grip, weak but desperate, and he drags me into the light. I collapse into his arms, coughing, body limp but alive.

For one fleeting second, I manage to lift my eyes to his. His face swims before me, blurred but steady, a glimmer of hope in the ruin. My saviour.

It had to be him.

# 26 Destruction

Once I am freed from the wreckage, Eddie, with a team of hard-working helpers, see me to Battersea Town Hall, now a makeshift hospital for the walking - and the barely walking - wounded. Hard to imagine that not so long ago I'd stood on these very floorboards watching Joy and Henry say their vows. On that occasion, the air had been heavy with white roses and extravagant champagne, the ornate ceiling echoing with laughter. Now that same plasterwork absorbs the groan of generators and the sharp, metallic clang of surgical instruments.

The hall is alive, a grim symphony of chaos that somehow manages to function. My eyes follow the stretcher-bearers weaving through the makeshift wards, their faces blackened with soot, their movements precise as dancers in a macabre ballet. Nurses hurry past, aprons already stained red and brown, their steps quick but controlled. An elderly man sits slumped against the wall, his arm wrapped in a wool blanket, muttering to himself. Children with pale, shocked faces cling to their mothers' skirts, traumatised and silent.

A kind-faced nurse with tired eyes kneels beside me with a basin of warm, soapy water in her hand.

'Right then, let's have a look at these,' she says gently.

The sting in my leg is sharp, but I barely notice it as she dabs at the inflamed skin. Then her hand brushes against the bandaged bump on my head - my souvenir from Doris's shelter - and a fresh jolt of pain shoots through me.

'It's the noise that gets you, isn't it?' she murmurs, as if she can hear my thoughts. And she's right. The crying, the shouting, the wail of sirens, the endless clamour of human distress and mechanical urgency - they're all one endless note. 'You'll be pouring tea in no time,' the nurse says with a smile.

'How did you know I was a tea girl?' I ask.

'You're still in your uniform,' she says, nodding towards my dusty, torn dress.

'I'll need a new one, Mrs Miller will hit the roof.'

'Not if you tell her the roof fell on you.'

'You don't know Mrs Miller,' I tell her, and she giggles, patting my shoulder for comfort.

'You're good to go. The doctor says you're strong, just keep that leg clean. You can head home now. Or... wherever your safe place is'

'Does such a place exist?' I ask her, she smiles, knowing, we're all trying our best to get through it. Of course, I feel lucky, grateful even, and I'm certain that Doris did not have the same fortune. All I can recall is her entering her home and then it imploding with a vicious flash of light.

Before I leave, I glance towards the door, hoping to see Eddie, but he's already gone - vanished back to duty before I could even thank him.

When I finally step outside, the light is fading, and I limp through the streets, slow and unsteady. Every few minutes I have to stop, leaning against a wall or lamppost, the ache in my leg gnawing at me.

As I turn a corner, my eyes catch on a spot near the town hall wall - the very place George had struck me, hard, in the stomach. And here I am again wounded, but despite the ache in my head and leg it does not compare to the agony of that moment with George - blows that don't bruise the skin but scar the soul, wounds that never really heal.

I limp my way back to Turner Street. Battersea has been battered - giant craters puncture the roads, homes reduced to dust. I brace myself for what I might find on our street.

The smoke still clings thick in the air, not from the power station this time, but from the power of a blitz. At first glance, Turner Street seems untouched - but then I look left. Doris's home is gone. Nothing left but rubble and splintered wood, furniture flung and shattered, rearranged for the final time. The neighbouring houses are damaged too, but still standing to some degree.

I turn my head to the right, towards the posh end. Limping a few steps, I see more devastation. Beyond my own house, number 110 - the Butlers' home - has been flattened. Number 112 shares the same fate. Not even the posh end is immune. The grand inside bathroom, once their pride, now gapes open for all the world to see. Beside the Butlers' place, the road itself has been torn apart, a crater gouged deep into the ground, turning Turner Street into a dead end.

I stand there, loitering, taking it in. Relieved, at least, that Dad's house still stands, and mine, and Violet's. Even Bill's. But the street itself is scarred now, stained with war for the first time.

In the distance, Violet comes hurrying towards me. She wraps her arms around me, tight, whispering her relief that I'm still standing - bandaged, bruised, but alive.

'Vera, I'm so sorry to tell you this,' Violet says, pausing, her face grave. 'But Doris is dead.'

It's the news I expected, yet hearing it spoken makes my head swim. Relief floods me, shame follows close behind. Her death means my secret is buried with her, my forbidden love safe - for now. Doris, with her sharp tongue and judging eyes, gone forever. Turned to dust.

How cruel I am to feel it - this relief. Freed from the rubble, freed from her dangerous knowledge. And yet, I do feel sorrow. Dad has lost a friend, a partner, no matter how I struggle to understand it. And Turner Street has lost another soul, another home crumbled.

I can't take it all in. How can one ever get used to such carnage?

Mrs Henderson walks slowly along the road, picking her steps carefully, flustered. Her neat bun is loose, hair straggling, her face pale and lined. She stops when she reaches me.

'Good to see you alive, Vera,' she says, her tone solemn. I glance down the street at her home, still standing, spared for now.

'Bit too close, wasn't it?' I answer. 'Poor Doris, eh?' I add, remembering I should at least show some grief.

'It's tragic. A dear friend. Still, she's with her Harold now.'

'Poor sod,' I mutter, half-joking, but it falls flat. Mrs Henderson shakes her head, folding her hands together as if to comfort herself.

'Half the school's been turned into a rest centre,' she says quietly. 'They'll start relocating people tonight, out of town. Mrs Butler and her girls are there already. Whole streets have been flattened - Howard Road, Marion Street, just like this. It's awful. Luckily for my Ken, the power station hasn't been touched,' she adds with relief.

Then Violet tells me that Sheila is home - swears by it, in fact - saw her slip into Bill's place only minutes ago. I rush down the street, forgetting the ache in my leg and throb in my skull. I bang at his door. It opens, and there stands Anne, with a rare smile on her face.

Before I can even speak, Sheila bursts past her and throws her arms round me. We cling to each other, tears catching in both our eyes.

'You had me frightened,' Sheila whispers, still holding me tight.

'You the same. Welcome home,' I manage, before I see Bill loitering in the doorway.

'I've heard about Doris - God rest her soul,' he says, removing his Home Guard helmet that's practically become part of his head. I give him a grateful smile, but turn quickly back to Sheila.

'You're home now? Properly?' I ask.

She gives me an unconvincing nod.

'I've separated from Samuel. And apologised to Father,' she says, the words unsure in her mouth. Bill holds up a crumpled piece of paper proudly.

'In writing as well,' he adds.

Sheila's eyes search mine. I can see the truth - she's doing this out of duty, not desire. I understand it completely. Still, Turner Street feels no safer than the East End, judging by last night's bombardment. In some ways, it's like she's brought the destruction with her. I feel lighter knowing Sheila is back. Strange, but despite the destruction and death, things almost feel normal again - how they should be. All I need now is for Dad to come home, though he's safer where he is.

I start to limp home, as I pass number 80, I slow down, pretending to watch neighbours picking through the rubble of the Butlers' house a few doors along. In truth, I'm loitering, hoping Eddie might notice me outside. But I can't bring myself to knock. The street is too alive with activity, too many eyes. I imagine Doris's ghost is still watching me.

After a few minutes, I give up my pretence. Surely Eddie knows about Doris's terrible demise by now. Still, what I would give to have even a few minutes alone with him - to steady myself after the terror of these last hours.

I walk on, my bruised legs slowing me down again, when a commotion erupts outside the Butlers' burnt-out wreck. Shouting, screaming - a fight breaking out between three men. I quickly realise one of them is Ken Anderson, fresh from the power station. Two rough - looking men get the better of him, kicking him to the ground before scattering as others rush to intervene. I, along with a few neighbours, help Ken back to his feet. He brushes himself off just as Mrs Henderson hurries over, her face taut with worry.

'Bleeding bastard looters - trying their luck,' Ken mutters, still shaken.

'Looters? I can't believe it,' I say, appalled by the audacity.

'They're everywhere,' Ken adds grimly. 'Some even pickpocketing from the dead. Honest to God.'

'Lynch the looters, I say,' Mrs Henderson barks, her voice suddenly fierce.

'People are terrible,' I sigh.

I make my way back to the solitude of home, where Esther and Nadine greet me with warmth and relief. They've done their best to put together a decent lunch, though rationing makes it near impossible. Still, the worry sits plain on their faces. The war feels closer than ever now - right on our doorstep.

Nadine's silence is striking. No German, no French, no English - just quiet. She's lost in her thoughts, haunted by the absence of letters from her father. No word, nothing. France is now under the full grip of the fascists, a fate that sometimes feels uncomfortably close for us too.

'This is hell,' Esther says, her voice trembling. 'But it's better than the alternative. I feel it. I know it.'

The disaster on Turner Street has changed everything. For many nights now, Esther and Nadine have taken to their Morrison shelter in the living room – a steel cage that seems to have no business being there. It fills the space completely, a hulking slab of industrial might crammed into their home. A cage that looks designed for a dangerous animal rather than a human. Yet it's still warmer, more comfortable than the cold Anderson shelters outside - those damp, airless coffins that even spring can't soften.

But after the recent raids, staying inside feels impossible. After months of relentless attacks, people have carved out their own underground worlds - shelters turned into neighbourhoods with their own rules and routines. Step into one that isn't yours and you're an intruder.

So tonight, we decide on All Saints' Church. Just round the corner, its basement will be our refuge. Perhaps not the safest place from bombs, but less cramped than other deeper shelters, more space to breathe, and filled with familiar faces. These are the constant dilemmas of war: where to sleep, how to be safe, where you might catch a moment's rest.

I'm pleased when Sheila tells me she'll join us - anything to avoid being crammed into an Anderson with her gloating father.

Our luck is in: we manage to secure two bunks side by side, one for Sheila and me, the other for Esther and Nadine. For a few small moments, it feels almost like a girls' night out - a sleepover, of sorts.

We talk lightly, careful not to mention men in case it makes Nadine blush. The steady thuds of war roll above us, dust and grit occasionally trickling down from the ceiling, but it's nothing we haven't grown used to. We laugh, tease Sheila about her dad's obsession with his helmet, pretending he's some great war hero. It's the lightness I need - a scrap of escape, a welcome contrast to the night before, when I'd been inches from being blown apart. They say laughter is the best medicine, and I believe it. For a while, I forget the pain in my leg, the pounding in my head.

But the mood changes when Esther, late into the night, tells me her plans. She means to leave Turner Street. The news is sudden, unexpected - and yet I understand. Her friend in Barnstaple can make room for her and Nadine. She'd turned the offer down before, but after the bombs, she feels she has no choice. At least they'll be together and safe.

I encourage her, though a pang of loss tugs at me. I'll miss them desperately. The house will fall quiet without Esther's laughter drifting up through the floorboards. And I can't help but worry about George - how his temper might flare without her calm to temper it. But it would be selfish, even cruel, to try to talk her out of going.

Nadine, I sense, is less keen. She's only just begun to settle here. Trying to find her feet in England while the war rages has been hard enough. London, for all its chaos, is a mix of everyone - Esther, Mr Sharma, the lot - and here she belongs. In Barnstaple she'll stand out. Still, Nadine is strong. She'll manage. She has to.

I try to sleep, drifting in and out, my mind flickering between the explosion and Eddie's hand pulling me from the wreckage. I can still feel his grip, the strength of it, as if it's imprinted into my skin. How I miss him. It's only been hours, but I miss him so deeply it hurts to breathe.

But sleep won't come. Whispers spread through the shelter - murmurs, cries of alarm. Talk of a hit at St Mary's - my old school, just five minutes away. A serious incident, they say. My stomach twists. Relief comes when I remember the children wouldn't be there at night, but worry claws at me - worry for Mrs Henderson, for Eddie, for anyone caught in it. Then Sheila leans close, whispering,

'The Butlers… weren't they in there?'

Her words hang heavy.

'No,' I say quickly. 'They were being sent to temporary housing - that's what Mrs Henderson said.'

'I hope so,' she murmurs, but dread lodges deep in my chest. That awful weight that tells you something terrible has happened. We live with it almost every night, but this feels different. Stronger. Darker.

I ask around, but there's only confusion. No one knows. No one can leave - the ARP wardens bark the order again and again. We must think of our own safety, even as every instinct screams to run, to help. Their very presence confirms it - something dreadful has happened close by.

The night drags on. Minutes stretch into hours. Faces restless, frightened. Only Nadine sleeps soundly through it all. How lucky she is.

At last, the all-clear sounds. The moment it does, we rush - me, Sheila, Esther, and Nadine - four women on a mission, joined by others from the shelter. Rain lashes down as we walk, sharp against our skin. I search for signs of damage, praying there are none. Perhaps it was only rumour.

But then, the sound - ambulances, fire engines, shouting, boots splashing through puddles. A crowd gathers ahead. Panic in the air. Suits, uniforms, a photographer's flash bursting white against the grey.

And then I see it. St Mary's - what's left of it. The red brick façade I knew so well, reduced to a smouldering ruin. The smell of chalk dust and floor polish replaced by plaster, smoke, scorched cloth. My old school - a tomb. The Christmas pine tree, once covered in tinsel, now blackened ash.

Rescue workers in tin helmets crawl over the wreckage, torches cutting through the gloom. Muffled cries echo from beneath the rubble. Voices shout, desperate, like wounded souls.

I glance to the others. All are silent. On the opposite pavement stands Violet, pale as bone, ARP band loose around her sleeve, eyes fixed on the ruins. The place she used to take Rita and James every morning. Her face is exhaustion and grief carved into skin.

I put my arm around her just as stretchers emerge from the wreck, shapes under cloth, unmistakably human.

'Bloody hell,' I whisper. Violet says nothing. Her eyes don't move.

Then I spot Mrs Henderson slumped near the edge of the rubble. Her face grey with dust, hair wild and streaked, clothes filthy and torn. She looks hollow, like life itself has drained from her. I rush to her side while Sheila stays with Violet, holding her tight.

I crouch beside Mrs Henderson. Her bloodshot eyes meet mine.

'We tried, Vera,' she says, her voice raw. 'We did our best.'

I nod, unsure if she's been buried herself or broken by the effort of digging.

'The Butlers,' she breathes, 'Mrs Baker. Little Lillian and Elizabeth.' Her voice cracks. 'They were in there.'

She collapses into my arms, weeping, and I hold her, trembling. 'The bus to take them to safety didn't come,' she forces out. 'It went to the wrong St Mary's. So they sheltered here. Them and others. When the blast came, I knew. I came straight away. We've been digging for hours. They told me to stop but I can't.'

'They might still be alive,' I whisper, clinging to the words though they taste of ash.

Mrs Henderson shakes her head, eyes red and ruined.

'No. I saw them. With my own eyes. Those little girls are gone. It'll haunt me forever.'

Her words tear through me. The world holds its breath. Even the rain feels still.

Then officials move in, pushing us back, determined to shield the scene - to censor the horror. Esther and I lift Mrs Henderson to her feet and guide her towards Sheila, Violet, and Nadine.

'The Butlers, isn't it?' Sheila asks softly, tears glinting.

'They're gone,' I manage, my throat tight. 'Mrs Butler too.'

We all stand there, hearts breaking.

'There were forty-odd in there,' Violet murmurs. 'They shouldn't have been there. They shouldn't…' Her voice breaks. She's had enough of everything.

And I just stand, staring at the ruin of my childhood, knowing an entire family has been wiped from Turner Street in a single night.

The rain joins our tears, flooding the pavement. So cruel. So horrendous. I think of Mr Butler - what he must be feeling, if he even knows yet.

And then, almost mocking us, the sun breaks through the clouds. The rain eases. The work continues. Men keep digging, faces dark with grief. But there's no sign of Eddie - spared this tragedy only to battle another elsewhere.

Then, across the sky, bright and desperate, a rainbow appears. Crystal clear, stretching over the ruins. For a moment, we all look upward together, silent, united, caught by its impossible beauty. A fragile kindness from the world itself.

And then, to my disbelief, Esther steps forward. Tears streak her face as she begins to sing - her voice trembling but full, carrying through the broken street. People stop. They listen. They hold still, as though her song alone keeps us from falling apart.

She sings *Somewhere Over the Rainbow* – the first song she's sung since Maurice died - her voice rising through the smoke and ruin, conjuring dreams of blue skies and better days.

And for those few minutes, as the rainbow burns against the clouds, it feels like the impossible might be true - that peace, our peace, might one day come.

This must be the worst of it.

We have reached the bottom.

# 27 Grief

How do you find words to describe the horror of what you've seen? The cruelty of it all. The street is scarred for life, its pain embedded in the brick, its tears stained on the pavement. A spirit of sadness swells through every corner, the rubble where the school once stood now a monument to the suffering, we all endure.

I am exhausted with trying to be positive, to find comfort in the chaos. It is a constant darkness now, a grief we all carry in our blood. I've perhaps always been a dreamer, drifting through life with my head in the clouds, but the bombing has stolen even that. No dreams now. No sleep to dream in. No time to think, to believe, to plan. There is no tomorrow, and if there is, you're simply grateful you lived to see it.

How long can we hold out? How much more can our resolve be tested? Our children are dead, our streets trampled. Is this even worth living? And yet we all hunt for a glimmer of hope, something to hold onto. Perhaps it's freedom itself, but for me, it is undoubtedly Eddie. He makes me grateful to be alive. He makes me want to live in every way. Despite the inconvenience of it all, I sometimes wonder if Eddie was sent by God to give me purpose. Without him, I don't think I could muster the strength.

Soon after the St Mary's tragedy, I manage to find a moment with Eddie. He is hollow-eyed, worn thin by exhaustion after one of the most relentless nights of bombing yet. We hold each other as I grieve for the Butlers. I hadn't known them well, but their young, mischievous lives - snatched in the most terrible way - linger with me, lodged in every breath.

Their funeral was a private affair, but still the whole street turned out. Everyone stood at their doors, draped in sombre black, as three hearses rolled past. Sheila linked arms with me, while their father, Mr Butler, stricken with grief, had to be held up by others. His job in government brought dignitaries to the service, and rumours whispered that Churchill himself had written privately to Mr Butler with his personal condolences.

The grandeur and dignity of it all stood in stark contrast to Doris's burial. With coffins in short supply, she was laid in a makeshift cardboard box, with quiet fears it might not sustain her weight. Such are the realities of war - the shortages, the indignities, the silences never spoken about lest morale be shaken. No coffins. No space to bury the dead. Mass graves becoming the norm. At least Doris has her own plot, placed next to Harold who hadn't been there long.

And yet there is something to be grateful for. Dad has returned home, given a clean bill of health. But he has come back to a street smothered in grief, bruised by bombs, choked with smoke. Losing Doris has cut him deeper than I could have imagined. Despite my reservations, he truly valued their friendship - the companionship of two widowed souls. For him, it feels like losing a wife all over again, however much it pains me to admit.

'Not many understood her, but I did,' he says quietly, retreating into himself, refusing to show emotion. Still, it's clear he aches at her loss.

The thought of my secret being buried alongside Doris in her cardboard coffin brings me a quiet solace. A relief Eddie shares too.

'God works in mysterious ways, Vera,' he says, nodding at the turn of events.

'I didn't think you were a religious man, Eddie.'

'I wasn't, until this happened,' he says with a small grin. I shouldn't laugh, but he always manages to make me smile, even in the darkest moments.

Still, the whole atrocity is a stark reminder that complacency is our enemy when it comes to keeping our secret.

That truth is driven home the moment George returns for Doris's funeral, and I'm forced back into the role of the devoted wife. A wife on edge. Terrified of one wrong move. Terrified my secret will come out.

During his time home, George does not mention the tragedy of St Mary's or the deaths of the Butler children. It is as if none of it exists. He barely speaks at all. For him now, there seems only a sense of waiting - wondering where he'll be sent next.

Arthur Henderson has been moved from the icy fjords of Norway to the roasting deserts of Egypt; another worry to add to poor Mrs Henderson's burden, still scarred from the school bombing.

As for George, though it's awful to admit, I find myself wishing he would leave - return to Aldershot so I might have my moments with Eddie again. A dreadful thought, I know, especially as this time he hasn't raised a hand to me. Drunk, yes. Boisterous, yes. But no violence. His hands kept to himself unless he wanted me for his own private gratification.

George's stay is short, perhaps shorter than it should be. I sense he doesn't want to remain in London, though the irony is that the city is far more dangerous than Aldershot. That will change soon enough when he's called up for the next campaign.

And so, once he's gone, I return to my secret routine of intimacy at dawn. Despite the ruins around us, my resolve remains intact.

At the same time, change comes to Turner Street. Esther has finally arranged her move, and she and Nadine are set to leave for Barnstaple. I will miss them dreadfully. Without them, the modest house will feel like a stately mansion - cold and echoing. But I understand it entirely. Esther's determination has hardened since the bombing of the school, where Nadine herself had been doing lessons.

Nadine, though, is tearful at the thought of leaving. She has grown used to the city's bustle and even the nightly terror of the bombs. The beaches and clean air of Devon will feel alien to her.

The night before their departure, we huddle together in the Anderson shelter, playing cards, inventing silly drawing competitions. Nadine has grown so confident, so fluent, her German fading by the day. All of it will serve her well in Devon.

Then suddenly, Esther turns to me and says,

'Come with us, Vera. To Barnstaple.'

I stare at her, stunned.

'I can't leave here.' I wave the thought away.

'Of course you can,' she insists, and Nadine tugs at my arm.

'Please, Vera,' Nadine begs.

'I can't,' I tell them. 'Not with Dad here. My work. My life… no. I appreciate it, but I couldn't possibly.'

'You don't want to leave him,' Nadine blurts suddenly.

'Excuse me?' My heart lurches, panic prickling my skin. 'Do you mean my George?'

A silence settles, broken only by the drone of planes and the thud of gunfire above us.

'Not George,' Esther admits. 'Him.' She tilts her head towards the direction of Eddie's house.

'I don't know what you're talking about,' I snap, heat rushing to my face.

'You go there every morning,' Nadine says quietly as Esther nods in agreement.

I shoot up, pacing the tiny tin box we're caged in. I want to run, to escape. How could they possibly know? Has it been that bleeding obvious?

'It is okay Vera,' Esther says softly. 'We will never say a word.'

'You nosey pair, making up nonsense like that!' I lash out, my voice sharp, hating my own stupidity, my audacity.

'Vera…' Esther rises and takes my arms, steadying me. Nadine sits pale-faced at my outburst. 'We understand. We just want you to be happy.'

I turn away, eyes burning with tears I refuse to let fall. 'We know what George is. How he can be,' Esther continues gently. 'You deserve better.'

'To be loved,' Nadine adds. Still a child at twelve, yet speaking with a wisdom that cuts me to the core.

'If George suspects anything, he'll kill me,' I say flatly.

'You can trust us. Always,' Esther says, drawing me into her arms.

My heart hammers. My mind races. Too many people know now. The net feels as though it's closing in. I go from sadness to relief that they're leaving. Selfishly, it's for the best. If they slip up, it could cost me everything. Their absence will give me cover.

But it's another reminder that this cannot last. Our secret is no longer just ours - it's simply a truth that a few people already know. For now, the right people remain in the dark, but how long can that luck hold? Every stolen moment with Eddie increases the risk, and yet I can't stop. It's like a drug, an addiction - as relentless and unstoppable as the bombers above. Wrong, dangerous, and selfishly, irresistibly gratifying. A dangerous pursuit towards an end I can't yet see.

# 28 Shock

It feels like an unbelievable twist of fate. Since Esther and Nadine left for Barnstaple, the bombs have stopped - at least for now. The raids that once fell nightly have dwindled to the occasional alarm, and even those are often false. On Turner Street there's a strange mix of relief and unease: part gratitude for the quiet, part dread that the Germans are simply rearming, changing tack, biding their time before the next onslaught.

News that Hitler has turned his eyes eastward, driving his forces into the Soviet Union, has taken us all by surprise - none more so than Stalin, it seems. For the moment, London is granted a reprieve. Why Hitler has chosen now to look east is anybody's guess, and quite frankly I struggle to keep track of who's meant to be on whose side.

Still, regardless of the ever-shifting politics, there's pride among us - pride that after endless nights of terror our resolve isn't broken, our spirit not dented. We did not cower before the brutality. That's the story the authorities and the newspapers are eager to tell, a message of defiance to carry far and wide. And while it's true, it cannot erase the grief or the exhaustion etched into our bones, nor the gnawing worry of what comes next.

The nights may be quieter, but the toll of war remains: the absence of our men, the silence of children still scattered in safer towns, the rationing of food now joined by the rationing of clothes. The endless call to make do and mend. And indeed, we do. We make do. We get by.

The house, however, isn't empty for long. Now that Sheila has returned to Turner Street, we've agreed she can stay with me. It's the ideal arrangement - giving her a break from Bill but still keeping her close to home. Unfortunately, Mrs Miller flat-out refused to take her back at Lyons, but luckily Sheila's landed a new position as a maid at the Thameside Hotel, recently reopened after being struck by a bomb. It's only a modest place, a handful of rooms, and despite its name you'd be hard-pressed to find the Thames unless you craned from a certain window - but Sheila is delighted with it. Hard work, of course, though she's no stranger to that.

The best part of Sheila staying with me is that she can continue her shenanigans with Samuel. I knew she'd never really ended things with him; she's far too in love to have put a stop to it. The pair of us feel like schoolgirls again - whispering secrets about our lovers, sneaking off at dawn and dusk to fulfil our romantic desires. We warn each other constantly to be careful, that we're making it too obvious, only to dissolve into giggles and red faces as we gossip about it anyway.

Sheila, though, is far less subtle than me. Her noises carry through the house - better than bombs and gunfire, yes, but still enough to turn the air red.

I prefer to keep my business private, slipping into Eddie's place with as much caution as I can muster. Even then it's risky. Once, Violet caught sight of me just as I was about to knock on his door during her early round. I had no choice but to stop, exchange polite words, and carry on as if I'd been passing by. I missed my time with him that morning, and I was miserable the whole day for it.

When Sheila and Samuel aren't rattling the walls, the three of us often spend our evenings together - the gramophone humming, cards on the table, laughter spilling across the room. It's the most content I've felt in months. We talk about the things we miss: when we can have a normal amount of chocolate again, how Sheila hasn't seen a banana in a year, only for Samuel to follow up with a rude joke - a rather naughty sense of humour that man has. Still, we laugh like we've never laughed before, perhaps because we rarely have these last few months.

Sheila begs me to bring Eddie along to join us, but I always refuse. Even with the bombs easing, he's usually on duty in the evenings - and besides, it would mean Samuel knowing. Enough people know already. I can't risk one more.

Not that I don't trust Samuel. He's a thoroughly decent soul - genuine, with a wicked sense of humour and an outlook so infectious it lifts the whole room. He speaks often of the better days to come, of how certain he is Britain will win now that Hitler has turned on Stalin.

'If the Americans join us, everything will change,' he says, so assured, so knowledgeable. His certainty is like a tonic. I find myself smiling, warmed by his optimism, comforted by the idea that perhaps, one day, he might be right.

The new dynamic in the house changes the moment George returns from Aldershot. The news that Sheila is staying sets him off at once.

'We wait this long for some actual space, time alone, time for ourselves - and she's here,' he barks, his voice far too loud, filling every corner. My stomach knots, fearful of what he might do, especially since I've already told Sheila of his violent ways.

'It's not forever. I didn't know you'd be back,' I say, defensive but calm. 'You know what things are like between her and Bill. I don't want her back in East London.'

'She isn't our bloody responsibility, Vera. She's a grown woman.'

'I'll tell her to make other plans, but give her some time, will you George?' I try to find a middle ground, but he doesn't even acknowledge me. He just lights a cigarette, sulks in silence, muttering about being hungry.

Things get worse when Samuel turns up that evening. I make the effort, polite as possible, and introduce him to George. Samuel offers his hand, but George only stares at it, then flashes him a grin so dismissive it leaves a mark.

'This who you've been knocking about with?' he sneers at Sheila, then tuts, the sound loaded with contempt. I want to sink through the floor with embarrassment.

Later, I tell George he must keep quiet about Samuel - how Sheila has supposedly ended things with him, and if word got out it would help nobody.

'I dunno what she sees in him,' George mutters, ignoring me. 'Wrong, ain't it?'

'George, did you hear what I said?'

'Yes, Vera. It's none of my business. She just needs to leave us alone, the sooner the better.'

His dismissiveness grates. It's unfair, especially as he'll likely be gone soon enough. But I can see he's relishing the idea of the house being just us - quiet, private, no one around to watch or intervene. He hasn't asked a single word about Esther or Nadine, how they're faring in Barnstaple, and I know it's because he's glad they're gone. Does he want the house empty so he can unleash himself unchecked? His cruelty has never needed an audience, but interruptions from Esther or Nadine have rattled him, kept him in line at times. Without them, I feel exposed. Vulnerable. Alone.

I pray his stay is short, that Aldershot calls him back quickly. In the meantime, I whisper to Sheila not to rush off, to stay put no matter how much he hates it. His loathing of the situation might be safer for me than his unvetted comfort ever would be.

But it isn't long before things change. Just twenty-four hours later the front door is banging with such fury I could have sworn the bombers were back again. A desperate hammering.

I open the door to find Bill barging inside, sweeping me aside like I'm dirt. His Home Front uniform clings to him, the steel helmet perched on his head, his face red as fire, a crumpled sheet of paper clenched in his fist.

'Did this letter mean nothing to you, Sheila?' he roars, storming through the house until he finds her. 'Sorry!' he spits, waving the paper at her. 'Not worth the bloody ink it's written in. You deceitful cow!'

I soon realise the paper is Sheila's apology note - her attempt at peace, now turned into fuel for his fury.

'Calm down?' Sheila says with a panic.

'Calm down' Bill screams, his voice breaking with temper, spit flying. 'Carrying on with this man when you promised me it was done with!'

At that moment George appears in the doorway, leaning against the frame with a knowing smirk, enjoying every second of it. That spiteful little grin tells me everything - I swear he's nodding along.

'You're here so you can carry on with your promiscuous, sinful ways,' Bill goes on, words slurred with venom. 'You need to come home, Sheila,' he barks. 'Staying here like a lodger - how embarrassing! Vera and George want peace and quiet, man and wife while he's home, not you skulking about with your shenanigans. Get yourself back home, Sheila Warner. I mean it.'

And perhaps surprisingly, Sheila doesn't fight. She just nods, as if she knows this isn't a battle worth having today. My heart sinks. George's grin widens.

I'm on my own now.

That evening Samuel comes to the back door as usual, peering in with his adorable, hopeful smile - only to be met by George, whose smirk has sharpened.

'She's gone back home,' he drawls. 'Said she's had enough of you.'

'Don't be so cruel, George,' I snap. I step in to explain to Samuel that Bill has discovered the truth of their courting and that he ought to keep low for now, until Sheila finds another arrangement.

Samuel looks George dead in the eye.

'Did you do this?'

George doesn't flinch.

'And what if I did?' he gloats, squaring up, puffing his chest.

The room bristles with danger. I rush forward, hands out, desperate to defuse it, urging Samuel away before fists - or worse - follow.

And so the eerie emptiness of the house returns, only now with a dread beneath it, with George here.

With George home, Henry is usually not far behind. Dad insists we gather for Sunday lunch. He's cheekily set aside some of the unclaimed rationed meat, which is remarkable to think exists at all. Dad has cautiously handed over his dodgy goods to Joy who, as ever, works miracles in the kitchen. She takes everything in her stride - even motherhood. No bags under her eyes, no weariness in her frame. It's hard not to envy her.

An occasion like this is also an excuse to hear what the boys are really up to in Aldershot, and what might be next. George, of course, refuses to say much - whether in person or in his letters. Always vague, always dodging. He'll talk about yesterday or tomorrow but never today. It unsettles him, I think - the present. Perhaps I understand, with the state of the world and the state of our marriage, but still I wish he'd give me more. Some glimpse into his new world. Instead, he remains a closed book, simmering with anger - at me, at everything.

Henry, by contrast, is overflowing. Almost too eager. A natural storyteller, with a lightness that fills a room. There's a bounce to him now, with baby Mary perched on his knee, her sweet eyes fixed on her father with admiration.

'We're basically scavengers these days,' Henry says cheerfully. 'Pulling broken-down lorries from ditches and fields, patching things together after all we lost at Dunkirk. Tell you what though - strangest thing. On a clear night the sky flashes with the bombings in London. Like some grotesque firework display. I kept thinking I should be there, worried sick. Not sure if it meant another raid or a full-blown invasion, like we've been drilled for.'

Even when he speaks of dread, Henry manages to sound warm, almost reassuring.

And then, out of nowhere, George finally chimes in.

'They're preparing us for the desert,' he says flatly.

The room falls silent at his sudden contribution.

'Might be Egypt?' I venture, remembering Arthur Henderson being sent there.

George turns to me with a snigger.

'Look at you, sodding military expert now?' He sneers, the others giggling lightly at my expense.

Before I can be made to feel any smaller, Joy announces that dinner is ready. And what a feast it is - by wartime standards, anyway. The smell alone is enough to trick the senses into believing this is a proper Sunday roast, the kind we used to have before the madness began.

The slices of beef - generous, thanks to Dad's cheek - are the centrepiece, surrounded by a clever spread of vegetables from Joy's family allotment: carrots, cabbages, parsnips, all glistening in their makeshift glory. No Yorkshire puddings, of course; eggs and milk are too precious. Instead Joy has thickened a simple gravy with flour, its rich scent filling the small room with something close to home comfort. Roast potatoes are absent too, replaced with thin slices of fried bread, browned in saved fat, crisp at the edges.

We gather round the table, offering the usual compliments to Joy's marvellous efforts. But George goes further. Much further. He tells her how radiant she looks, how motherhood has only made her more beautiful. Joy blushes noticeably, and George keeps on, praising her, circling her with words as though she were the guest of honour.

'Do you miss your important work, you know - the posters and that?' George asks, leaning towards her, his eyes fixed. She's so flustered she barely touches her food.

'I loved the people,' Joy admits quietly, 'and the feeling of helping…'

'Good as gold, you are,' George interrupts, smiling broadly. 'They must miss an intelligent woman like you. Brains, looks - Henry's the luckiest man alive.'

The room erupts with laughter, Henry beaming, Joy turning crimson like the hair on her head. And me? I feel like the only person really hearing it. Each word feels sharpened, a deliberate effort to raise her up while grinding me down.

Then George turns to me.

'Pour us summink, will you, Vera? Make yourself useful.' He grins, basking in his own charm.

I bite my tongue. This is the most he's spoken in weeks - chatty, cheerful, almost like Henry. But it's all performance. A mask. Every word a little cut meant for me, invisible to the others. It's not physical, but it wounds all the same. And I know if I so much as protest, he'll laugh it off, call me daft. And the others will all agree with him.

But I can't stay silent forever.

Not this time.

That evening I corner George, unable to let it rest. I ask him straight: what is it about Joy that fascinates him so much? Why he insists on showering her with compliments as though she were some shining star. Is it deliberate? Does he mean to wound me?

As expected, he scoffs, says I'm imagining things, reading too much into it. But I press on - cocksure in my persistence, almost reckless with it.

'I'm not going mad, George. You spent the whole afternoon gushing over her,' I snap, my words spilling out, frustrated, flustered.

He pauses, lets out a sharp laugh, then begins pacing the room. My stomach twists. I know the signs - I've overstepped again. Only this time, his pacing doesn't read as fury. It's something else. Restlessness. A weight he's toying with, deciding whether to drop it or not.

'What is it, George?' I ask quietly.

He stops, turns, and for a moment his face is unreadable, shadowed with something heavy.

'We all liked Joy,' he says suddenly, blurting it out like it's nothing. 'All the lads. None more so than me.'

The words punch the air out of me.

'What do you mean?' I ask, voice cracking.

'At football, us boys, we all had a thing for her. I mean, look at her. But Henry - he was relentless. Said he loved her. Wouldn't let it go. Insisted she'd be his. We all wanted a chance, but he was like a man possessed. That's why he pushed me towards you, Vera. His own sister. So he could have Joy all to himself.'

His words crash through me, shaking everything I thought I knew.

'You're telling me… you've got a thing for Joy?' I whisper, barely holding myself together.

'I let Henry get his way,' George shrugs. 'And you weren't half bad. But Joy - let's be honest, Vera - Joy's something else.'

My tears fall before I can stop them.

'What do you mean?' I shout.

'She's beautiful. Clever. From a good family. And still interested in scoundrels like us lads. It was a dream, and Henry got it. But I could have given him a run for his money. I can sense I would have had a chance.'

I stare at him, hollow. Joy - the woman I'd helped bring a baby into the world, the one I'd been building a bond with - she was the one George always wanted. And me? I was the stand - in. The second prize. Perhaps not even that.

'Are you saying you're in love with Joy?' I demand.

George just laughs. A cruel, bitter sound.

'I'm just telling you the truth. Joy's special. She's talented, beautiful, funny. She's got ambition.'

'And I don't?' I cry, cutting across him.

'You pour tea, Vera. You live on this street, you'll die on this street. That's all you'll ever be.'

His words cut like glass.

'And you're just a butcher's assistant,' I fling back, my anger breaking loose.

'I'm defending our country!' George roars, puffed up with self-righteousness, as if a medal should fall at his feet. 'I don't envy Henry but look at him - he's got it all. A wife like Joy. And a child…' He falters, lingering on the last word. 'A baby. She's given him everything. Lucky bastard.'

And with that, he storms out, slamming the door behind him, swallowed by the darkening street. Off to the Swan, no doubt. Leaving me alone, his words echoing like blows.

But tonight, I cannot be alone. Not like this, not when my world feels as though it has splintered to pieces. My mind reels back through every moment I've seen George with Joy, every glance, every laugh, blind to the truth of what lay behind it. I never suspected. I never knew.

In my confused, wounded state I do the unthinkable. I leave, I can't breathe in that house another second. I head straight for Eddie's, knowing I might catch him for a few minutes before his evening shift. My legs carry me faster than my thoughts, until

I'm pounding on his door, frenzy and grief coursing through me like fire.

He answers almost at once. And I fall - literally fall - into his arms. He catches me before I hit the ground, pulling me inside with a speed that speaks of practice, shutting the door behind us. Panic flickers across his face as he checks the street through the corner of his eye, terrified of prying neighbours. Then all his attention comes back to me.

Eddie holds me, tight, steady, as I sob into his chest. I tell him everything in a rush, my words spilling out like a confession I've no control over. And all the while he listens, stroking my hair, his strength a harbour against the storm.

It should comfort me - but instead, guilt floods in. George may long for Joy, may never have loved me the way a husband should, but he has kept faithful as far as I'm aware. And here I am, in the arms of another man. Weeping over the absence of love from one, while clinging to the warmth of the other.

How are we to find a way out of this minefield? How do we carve out a life that belongs to us, when every step feels like it will bring collapse, exposure, ruin? We both crave happiness. We both dream of living beyond this secret in the blackout. But neither of us knows how.

Eddie cups my face, his eyes burning into mine, his voice steady but low.

'We must find a way, Vera. We have to. It can't go on like this. Not in the shadows, not hidden.'

His words slice through my panic. Our love is real. Of that I have no doubt. Perhaps we've been fooling ourselves, waiting for the war to subside, waiting for peace to make it simple. But the stark truth is - this war may never truly end, not for years, perhaps not ever.

We cannot wait for peace to truly love.

# 29 A Plan

Not long after George's revelation, he returns to Aldershot, and I am left with the remains of a marriage hanging by a thread. Knowing how he feels about Joy has shattered me into a thousand pieces. Everything feels different now. I've never felt more inadequate. That knowledge, along with George's behaviour, draws me ever closer to Eddie, fuelling a fierce determination to find a way out.

It has also unsettled me in how I feel about Joy. Through no fault of her own, of course. I'd always been a little envious of her, but knowing George's eyes were always fixed on her makes me harshly resentful. It isn't fair, and I know it, but I can't help it. She's back in her flat now with Mary, the raids easing, and she's eager to spend time with me. I often make excuses. I adore young Mary, but I can't trust myself not to let something slip - not after George's confession.

It all comes to a head when Joy turns up with a bag of clothes. Rationing has tightened - sixty-three coupons a year, gone in no time if you dare buy a coat. We're told to *make do and mend*, to darn and patch, to knit our way through the shortages. I've never been much good with a needle, and Joy knows it. She comes with clothes she no longer wants, all fine quality as you'd expect, and offers them to me kindly.

'You'll look lovely in this,' she says, holding up a navy dress, the fabric catching the light in a gentle shimmer. 'I wore it when I was carrying Mary. It's too big for me now, but it will suit you.'

'Excuse me!?' The words are out before I can stop them, sharp and biting. 'Are you saying I'm overweight?'

'No, no…' Joy stammers, her face flushing. 'You're just a different shape to me, that's all.' She means it innocently - I know she does.

'Oh, well, you're the perfect shape, aren't you, Joy,' I snap, my voice dripping with spite.

Her eyes widen.

'What on earth is that supposed to mean?'

'You're perfect, Joy. Everything about you is perfect. I don't know what your game is - posh girl like you playing at being one of us, marrying Henry. Is it a fantasy? Something to make you feel good? Like charity?'

'Vera… what are you talking about?' Her voice is soft, bewildered.

'You ain't like us, and you know it. You're here to make yourself look better. To make the rest of us feel small. Poor. Ugly. Incapable. We can't cook like you, we can't dress like you, we can't make a baby as perfect as yours.'

Tears pool in her eyes, shock written all over her freckled face. My words hang in the air - cruel, heavy -

and even as I speak them, I know they're twisted by envy.

'Is that what you honestly think?' she whispers, her voice trembling, tears now spilling down her cheeks.

I nod, though the conviction falters the moment I do. She scoops Mary up from where she's tottering between the furniture and holds her close, her face pale with hurt. She looks at me one last time - stricken, wounded - then she's gone, leaving the bag of clothes abandoned on the floor. And I feel like the worst person alive.

This sets up the most awkward and uncomfortable of Christmases. And I thought last year's was bad. But this year, playing at happy families with Joy, who can barely look me in the eye, is unbearable. Everyone senses the tension between us, but nobody has the courage - or the energy - to say a word.

The atmosphere is no easier with Henry and George home, both on embarkation leave before shipping overseas. That takes up most of the conversation, Dad bent over a literal map, tracing what he imagines to be their route - Egypt, most likely, though with detours through safer waters. Talk drifts too to the attack on Pearl Harbor, which happened only weeks ago and has brought America crashing into the war.

'Samuel predicted that,' I say proudly. They look at me bemused - George most of all, his face twisted with disgust at the mere mention of Samuel.

Amid the chatter of strategy, and the strained avoidance of any real conversation with Joy, I sit and wish Christmas away. I dream instead of the day me and Eddie might spend it together - ordinary, as lovers. I picture him now in Norfolk, home for the festive season, sat round the fire with his mother, Heather, who he speaks of so fondly. I imagine her thinking well of me, and us sharing the kind of happiness that belongs on the side of a biscuit tin - where war is a world away and love is all that matters.

My daydreaming is a temporary reprieve from the constant watching and studying of George's behaviour when Joy is near. The smiles he saves for her, the eye contact so generous, the space he gives her to talk about Mary's milestones - things he'd never once cared to hear from me. Despite the confession he made, his behaviour hasn't shifted an inch. Still he lets her shine, and still I am the afterthought.

So for most of Christmas I sit apart, distant, my head full of longing and overthinking, the gnawing question of what I must do next.

For months now, I've quietly explored the unthinkable: divorce. Everything is stacked against me, of course. A woman like me is bound to be branded a failure - unable to keep her husband. But the law does, as far as I understand, allow for divorce in cases of proven cruelty. Proving it - that is the difficult part.

I know, as I conjure a route out, that I cannot reveal Eddie, not at first. Instead, I would build my case, seek the divorce, begin again, and only later, when the dust has settled, reveal the truth of us. It will take time, and I doubt many would accept it. But it's a plan - more than I have ever had before. Eddie listens, accepts, though I see the worry in him. Because even if I could prove George's cruelty, the costs alone might ruin me. What I've tucked away is not nearly enough for a process so long and expensive. Still, I remain determined: to get out, to start again, to be with him.

The greatest obstacle, though, lies closer to home. I will need those dearest to me to see George for what he truly is, to pierce the mask he so carefully wears - the good husband, the dependable man. Before I can take a single real step towards freedom, I must tell them the unthinkable. It feels an impossible task. But if anyone can help, if anyone can see me through this, it will be Henry. It has to begin with him.

He just has to believe me.

# *1942*

## 30 The truth

A few days into 1942 and I've got Henry to myself at last. Every New Year the three of us - me, George and Dad – would take a long walk round Crystal Palace Park, rain or shine, a tradition my mother started. Henry loves it the most, gawping at those stone dinosaurs as if they might lumber off through the trees. He was obsessed as a boy, same as Mum had been. But it won't happen this year. The park's sealed off now, swallowed by the military, rubble piled where the lawns once stretched. A sorry sight.

So, we've come to Richmond instead, where the beasts are gone but, every now and then, a deer flickers through the bracken. The park's so wide it swallows London whole and makes you forget the city sits right outside its gates. Coming here suits us: Dad bows out the moment he hears how far we intend to walk, which was the idea. I need Henry alone. He's shipping out any day, and this is my last chance to tell him the truth I've been choking on.

The thought rattles me. The January air burns our cheeks raw. A majestic, almost ancient fog dusts the park; tears sting at the corners of our eyes and Henry boots at puddles like he's ten again. He talks, laughs, remembers, but I barely hear him. My head goes round in circles, sick with nerves. What if he doesn't believe me? What if he runs straight to George? Is it worth the risk?

But the thought of freedom - real freedom - keeps pulsing through me: to live without George, to love openly, to breathe again. I stop dead on the path, last autumn's leaves still clinging to the ground. The stillness presses in; only the hush of branches shifting overhead.

'I need to tell you something, Henry,' I say, careful.

'I know,' he answers, quick.

My stomach drops.

'You… know?'

'Course I do,' he says.

Panic shoots through me. Does he know about George? About Eddie?

'What do you know?'

He pauses, and for a second the silence is worse than the icy wind.

'I know about your argument with Joy,' he says at last. Relief floods me - too sharp, almost painful.

'Oh. That. I was ever so rude. I had a really bad day.'

'You should apologise,' he says, ever the loyal husband. I nod in agreement.

'Is that what you were going to tell me?'

'No,' I say. 'No, it isn't that.'

We walk a few steps further before I stop again. My chest feels tight; my whole-body trembles, shivering but not just from the cold.

'Henry,' I say, breath catching, 'I know you think the world of George - like a brother - but there's a side of him he doesn't show you.'

Henry's eyes fix on me, gentle, puzzled.

'Go on.'

'He can be cruel. Terribly cruel. In ways I'd never want to describe.' The words pour out and I sob with the release. Henry edges closer, studying my face.

'Cruel to who?'

I can't speak. Tears streak down; my chest heaves.

'Who, Vera?' he presses. Then the realisation lands in his eyes. 'You? He's cruel to you?'

I nod. The heaviest nod of my life. A nod that changes everything.

With it the words spill out. I tell him about the punch on his wedding day. The suffocation. The brutal sex I can't refuse. Every horror I can force myself to speak aloud. Henry stares at me as if the world he knew has been turned inside out. Then he shakes his head, pacing, lost.

'This is unbearable,' he mutters. 'Our George? No. Vera, what's all this?'

'You've got to believe me,' I beg, pleading, spilling more detail, anything to make him see.

'You've wound him up,' Henry snaps. 'He's clipped you round the ear, maybe, but you're making him sound like the devil himself.'

'He is, Henry. He bloody well is!' My voice bursts out into the freezing fog, echoing and startling the birds from their nests. 'As God is my witness, that man is not who you think he is.'

Henry stares, shaking his head, but I see it - the crack forming. He's listening now.

'Bleeding hell,' he whispers. 'Why… why are you telling me this now?' His voice breaks with confusion, sharp in the cold air.

'I can't live like it any longer Henry.'

'And what do you want me to do? Give him a hidin'? You remember that brawl we had one Christmas? He can fight, our George.'

'I know!' I shout, desperate for him to hear me. 'That's what I've been saying - he's dangerous. I just need you to believe me, to stand by me. I'm going to find a way to leave him.'

Henry stares, confusion hardening into anger. His eyes carry doubt - whether about me escaping, or in my words about George; I can't tell. Maybe both. He drops down onto a fallen log, the bark wet and cold biting through, but he doesn't flinch. He sits there, breath clouding in the air and joining the mist, and gathers his thoughts. I lower myself beside him, my heart rattling against my ribs.

'I'm sorry, Vera,' Henry says at last. 'Sorry for what you've gone through. Dad won't believe it.'

'He won't,' I whisper. 'I know.'

Henry clenches his fists.

'I'll kill him.'

'You can't tell him you know,' I cut in, sharp.

'Then why tell me?' He shouts with frustration. 'I'm meant to go to war with him, and now you've laid this on me. How am I supposed to look at that bastard the same way?'

He's right. I've placed this weight on him, heavier than I should, and I hate myself for it.

'I told you because you had to know,' I say, steadying myself. 'When you're away I'll plan my way out. And when you come back, George won't find me at home. You'll know where I am. You'll know I'm safe. Dad might never believe me, but I hope you will. And I hope you might help Dad realise the truth too.'

'We could be gone a long time, Vera,' Henry says quietly. 'Not like before. That's if we come back at all.'

'You will,' I answer, fierce, determined. 'And when you do, you'll understand. I just need you to believe me now.'

Henry turns and looks at me full on. Then, without another word, he wraps his arms around me. His coat smells of damp wool, his warmth pressing through, easing the cold in my bones. My wonderful Henry. I feel dreadful for burdening him, but I've done it - somehow, some way.

'I understand, Vera,' he murmurs against my ear.

Relief surges through me so strong it nearly knocks me flat. For the first time in months, I let myself feel hope.

A few short days later, George and Henry return to Aldershot, soon to head for some port, then across the seas towards war. Their unit is needed desperately now, the fighting growing fiercer. But when George comes back, things will not be the same. Of that I'm certain.

With Henry knowing the truth, I feel lighter, as if a stone's been lifted from my chest. Alongside the relief comes a strange new boldness - riskier, reckless even.

That's how me and Eddie end up slipping out of London on what can only be called an unofficial date. We travel separately, cautious, but meet beyond the smoke and rubble.

Eddie suggests Whipsnade Animal Park. I think he meant it as a joke, but I jump at it. Why not? I've never been, and the very idea of it feels daft, playful, daring. George won't be there, no one we know will be there, and the elephants aren't about to carry tales back to Turner Street.

So off we go - a stolen day, strolling arm in arm through the vast open grounds, watching creatures in their paddocks. The zebras graze, the wind carries their scent, and a calm settles over me. Some animals, like the great panda, have been evacuated here from London - children weren't the only ones shipped to safety. I clutch Eddie's arm tighter, comfort blooming inside me.

I tell him then. About Henry. About how I've spoken the truth at last, and my intention to leave George. Eddie stiffens. His hand fidgets at his side, his eyes dart. I hadn't expected that. We've spoken about this before, more than once, and I thought he'd be glad.

'This is what you want, isn't it, Eddie?' I press.

'I want you away from that maniac, yes,' he says quickly.

'And you want to be with me?'

He hesitates - just a flicker, but I catch it.

'Of course. Of course,' he says, layering on the reassurance. But something in me knots. Perhaps Eddie's more of a dreamer than a doer, but you can't stay a dreamer if you're living in a nightmare.

Even so, the day feels perfect - a small taste of freedom, of what life could be. We wander among animals and craters, the land itself carrying scars from bombs. The holes have been filled with water, turned into ponds for the wildlife, proof that even in war, life resists - in all forms.

Like our journey there, we travel back separately. By the time I turn onto Turner Street the sky has deepened, a heavy dusk pressing down, and I freeze at the sight of someone perched on my doorstep. Dirty hair spilling loose, cheeks raw from the cold, eyes tired, coat crumpled from the road - it takes only a moment to realise. Nadine. She's home.

She's only been gone five months, but the shock of her there, grown, changed, steals my breath. The second she spots me she leaps up, clings to me, arms wound tight with the desperation of someone who's run too far.

'What are you doing here?' I gasp, hugging her back, her grip unyielding. 'Does Esther know you're here?'

'I could not stay there,' she blurts as I hurry her inside, the warmth hitting her at once. 'Everyone is… is… awful.' Her English is steadier now, more certain, though her voice cracks.

'What about your aunt?' I ask gently.

'She won't leave. She does not see it. She is blind, you understand?'

'I know all too well,' I tell her, bitterness sharp at the back of my throat. 'So who is unkind?'

'The girls at school,' Nadine says, clutching at her hair and pulling it aside to reveal a bald patch, raw and jagged. 'They call me Nazi. They cut it.' Her tears spill fast, and I draw her close, my chest aching at the sight of her.

'You mean to tell me you made it all this way on your own? Without Esther knowing?'

She nods, stubborn chin set. My heart pounds. Esther will be frantic.

I rummage for Esther's letters until I find one with a telephone number scrawled inside, then bundle Nadine out with me to the telephone box on the corner. The night air is bitter, her small figure huddled close as I push coins into the slot. When the line finally connects, relief rushes through Esther's voice - only to twist, quick as a whip, into fury.

She bellows down the wire in French, curses so sharp I pull the receiver from my ear. Nadine stiffens beside me but doesn't flinch. Esther demands she return to Barnstaple at once, but Nadine shakes her head fiercely, lips pressed tight. She won't go. She refuses.

How do you force a girl like that onto a train back to a place she hates? But she can't stay here either - not with me, not when my own time on Turner Street is running out.

# 31 Betrayed

Spring creeps in, and Nadine is still here on Turner Street, her stubbornness winning out. Esther quickly gives in, agreeing that Nadine can stay in London with me - unless, she says, the bombers start coming back night after night. I can't blame her. Nadine is desperate to return to school, where she's made friends, she refuses to name - boys, perhaps, though she gives nothing away. More than that, she's itching to work, asking how old she has to be to join Lyons like me. She's only thirteen, but so determined. I've a feeling that when this war is over, she'll want to stay here for good.

The real surprise is Esther. After all her fury at Nadine for running away, she doesn't put up much of a fight in the end. I'd wondered why she was so set on remaining in Barnstaple - until Nadine, sly smile on her lips, tells me Esther's grown close to an American. That's all she'll say, but I hope it's true. Esther finding love again, after Maurice… it would be a blessing.

The bigger change is Sheila. Once more she's had to leave Turner Street - though this time not because her old man threw her out, but because the government has. The new conscription law now pulls in unmarried women, and so Sheila's packed off to Birmingham, ordered to join the ranks of those riveting wings and engines for the fighters overhead. A letter from the Ministry, and that was that - her bags packed before the shock even wore off. She's to stand on a factory line day and night, metal burning her hands till they blister. She dreads every minute, not least because it steals her hours with Samuel. Love rationed as tightly as sugar.

And me? I'm spared all that. Not because I'm lucky. Not because I'm special. Because I'm shackled to George. To the outside world, that counts as a blessing. To me, it's the cruellest joke going.

Still, Bill couldn't be prouder of Sheila - which is some turn of heart. He tells anyone who'll listen that his girl is "doing her bit," puffing out his chest as though she alone is winning the war. One child on the front line, another on the factory line. Bill's children, carrying the weight of it all.

I've had a fair few letters from George, which is remarkable in itself. When he was in Aldershot I'd hardly hear a word, yet now, from the other end of the world, he can't seem to stop writing. His words tell of an agonising journey to Egypt, of chaos in the desert, of plans changing by the minute - driving trucks through the blazing sun while bombs rain down. Brutality. Carnage. Confusion.

Henry's letters are different - lighter, brighter. I can see him shaping his words not to frighten Joy, who grows paler with worry each day. His tone is almost cheerful, though I know better. Their letters don't match. They don't align. I can feel the distance between them widening, as though my confession to Henry has cracked the bond they once shared. They no longer speak as one.

And yet, while George sweats and suffers beneath the desert sun, I move deeper into Eddie. We've fallen into a rhythm now - passionate, euphoric, never tiring, never stale. Everything about him thrills me: strong, dependable, yet gentle too. Vulnerable in ways I never thought men could be. His kindness, his care - they disarm me.

The bombing left scars on us all, but particularly on Eddie. He still speaks of what he saw at Balham, his words carrying images I can hardly bear to picture. But where other men would swallow their grief, Eddie lets it out. He doesn't cling to the stiff upper lip. He feels. He reflects. And in that, I see a strength greater than any fist or medal. Some might call it weakness. To me, it's the truest kind of courage.

So, I live in this dreamy haze - the bombs gone, George gone, Eddie beside me. Our love, relentless and pure. Hidden, yes - love in the blackout - but secrecy has become second nature by now, another habit of wartime life.

With that confidence burning in me, I start making enquiries, quietly gathering what I need to free myself from George. I'm determined. Certain. I tell myself everything will fall into place, that all will align, that contentment is within reach at last.

But that, I'm afraid, is only wishful thinking...

It's a stiflingly hot day, the sun blazing down on my face, sweat trickling across my brow. I can't help thinking how unbearable it must be for Henry and George, somewhere under that foreign sun, their bodies heavy in uniforms and dust.

When I reach work, though, the shock of it near stops me in my tracks - the tearoom is closed.

'No shifts today,' Mrs Miller snaps, annoyed and frustrated. 'No delivery, no sugar, no tea. A tearoom without tea's just a bleeding room.' She mutters on - stock has been a problem for months, and now it seems we've run dry.

So, I turn for home, telling myself I'll enjoy the sunshine while I can. But another thought takes me quick and firm - I'll call on Eddie. Perhaps he's in. Perhaps we can steal a rare hour in daylight.

I knock quickly on his door. It creaks open. And there he is - Eddie. Only his face drops the instant he sees me. A look of shock, panic even, spreads across him, too sudden, too raw to disguise. At first, I think it's only surprise, me appearing at this hour. But no - it's something more, something heavier. His body blocks the doorway, stiff as a soldier on guard. Usually he's quick to usher me in, to keep the neighbours from their twitching curtains, but now he leaves me stranded on the step, the sun burning one side of my face, the silence between us stretching cruelly.

And then I see her.

She lingers in the shadowed hallway behind him until curiosity, or arrogance, pulls her forward. A sweet - looking thing at first glance, no older than me, though her confidence makes her seem taller. Her dark - blonde hair is swept immaculate, not a strand daring to fall out of place even in the heat. Lips painted a fierce red, a green dress light and fine with puffed sleeves that speak of quality, not ration coupons. Pearls gleam at her throat, shoes polished so bright you'd think they'd never touched a London street. She stands beside Eddie as though she owns the ground he walks on, her smile bright, almost dazzling - but edged with something that feels like a challenge.

'Who's this, Edward?' she asks, her voice honeyed.

'A neighbour,' he says at last, the words dragged out slow, heavy with dread. His face is pale now, eyes flicking between us, guilt laid bare in every twitch of his mouth.

'Vera Hopkins,' I manage, my voice steadier than I feel. 'I live a few doors down.'

Her gaze slides over me, settles on the uniform.

'Tea girl?'

I nod.

'I see,' she says, her smile widening. And then, with an easy, casual grace, she adds, 'I'm Beatrice. Edward's fiancée.'

The word lands like a shell-blast.

'Sorry?' I whisper, though my stomach has already turned to stone. My legs buckle beneath me, bile rising as though my body itself rejects the truth.

'Vera - ' Eddie's voice cracks and he stops himself from going on. He half-steps forward, his hand twitching as if to reach for me, then falling back useless at his side. His face is a tangle of regret, shame, desperation - but he doesn't stop her, doesn't correct her. And that silence destroys me.

I stagger into the street, clutching at myself, my body folding with nausea. Tears blur my eyes, but I force them down, call back over my shoulder:

'The sun - I'm not well, far too hot for me.' My voice shakes, but I don't stop.

I keep moving, one foot then the other, refusing to look back - because if I do, I'll collapse into his arms, and I can't, I mustn't. Not now. Not ever.

When I reach my door, I slam it shut behind me and fall hard to the floor. The sobs rip through me, gut - wrenching, uncontrollable, my body shaking until I can hardly breathe. Agony floods me. Real pain, worse than any bruise George ever left.

How could I be so stupid? How did I not see? Everything is ruined. Everything is lost.

And so I fold into myself, a crumpled heap on the floor, my cheek pressed against the wood, the grain cool against my burning face. Tears seep through the cracks in the boards as though I might drown the house in sorrow. I have never felt so foolish, so wrong, so utterly betrayed. Time ceases to exist. I lie there, unmoving, the tears never-ending, my pain refusing to loosen its grip.

The door creaks, and a small figure edges inside - Nadine. She slips past and lowers herself to the floor beside me, lifting my head into her lap, her arms encircling me with a quiet strength. She doesn't speak. She doesn't need to. Her touch is enough - gentle, steady, far older than her years. And that, somehow, makes me weep harder. How is it that a child is the one cradling me? She doesn't ask the source of my grief - perhaps she knows, perhaps not. She chooses silence.

When I next look up, the light has gone. The fierce summer sun has drained from the sky, and the house is cloaked in dusk. I gather some strength and slump at the kitchen table while Nadine fusses with the so called national loaf, its dense grey slab heavy as a storm cloud. She smears margarine across it - thin, tasteless, waxy - and presses it into my hands. I can barely swallow, but the thought alone undoes me: her tender, tentative mothering, more than I deserve, more than she should have to give.

I urge her to bed, though I know I won't sleep myself.

And then come he knock at the door.

My heart jolts, beating wild, reckless. I drag myself to the door, legs weak, and open it.

Eddie stands there. His face is shadowed with sorrow, his eyes carrying pain, remorse - something close to shame.

How I *hate* him. How I *love* him.

I stand torn between both truths, my mind screaming to shut the door in his face, my body aching to let him in. And in the end, I yield. I step aside - because I have to know. I have to hear him say it. Was any of it real? Or has the war gone and fooled me too, making me believe in something that was never there to begin with?

I say nothing, only turn back to the kitchen. He follows behind, slow, considered, nervous - aware that a single wrong word might shatter me altogether.

'I'm sorry, Vera,' he says softly. 'I didn't know she was coming. It was a surprise, I… I'd been meaning to tell you, to find the courage - '

I scoff - a hollow sound that cuts him short. Almost a laugh. I wipe a stray tear but won't look at him.

'Vera, I love you,' he insists. 'I really do. And I've made a huge mistake.'

'Why should I believe a single word out of that mouth of yours?' My voice is steady, though rage trembles through it. 'You've lied from the very start.'

'Beatrice's from my way. We got engaged before I came down to London. I should've told you, or ended it straight off. But my God, I fell for you. I've never fallen like that before.'

'You should have told me,' I cry, lifting my eyes to his at last. 'I was never anything real to you, was I? Just *your* tart of Turner Street, to keep you warm while the rest of the city burned. I've been such a fool.'

'No… no,' he says quickly, defiant. 'I don't want Beatrice. I want you, Vera. I just haven't found the way - the time - to put it right.'

'You're just another unfaithful bastard, like the rest of them.'

'We're both sinners, Vera,' he shoots back, certain - as if that excuses him. Perhaps he believes it. But my betrayal was born of survival, of clawing free from a violent marriage. His? His is comfort. Convenience. Him and that Beatrice - side by side they look the perfect couple. How could I have been so blind?

'I want to be with you,' he says again, tears brimming now. 'I really do, but - '

'But you can't,' I snap, finishing it for him. 'You've got a bloody gorgeous fiancée.' My temper boils over.

'...No. It's just - I've got to go back to Norfolk. Now the raids have stopped, my watch want me back there. I don't want to go, Vera, but I must.'

It's like another bomb has fallen, straight through me. First the lie, and now this. I've lost him twice in the same breath. Maybe it's for the best, so I won't have to see him, won't have to be haunted by what we were - or what I thought we were. But knowing he's leaving, knowing I might never see him again, is pain beyond bearing. My head falls into my hands, and when he reaches for me I push him back with all the strength I have left.

'Then go. Bloody well go!' I scream, my voice rattling the walls, my desperation laid bare for all to see.

He edges towards the door, pauses, turns back. His face is desperate, stricken.

'I love you, Vera,' he says, voice breaking. 'And I'll never stop loving you.'

And then he's gone, swallowed by the night.

My world is changed forever.

Once again.

# *1943*

# LETTERS

***Great Yarmouth, Norfolk***
***2nd January***
*Dearest Vera,*

*I am writing because I feel utterly lost without you. I carry such regret for how things were left. Life up here is not what I want. My tie with Beatrice is built on convenience and old assumptions. We have known each other since childhood. It is not true love, not the love I feel for you.*

*I should have told you, I know, and in keeping silent I have ruined everything. But, Vera, be sure of this, what we had was real, my love. Every moment. You are always on my mind.*

*Now I am back here, feeling inadequate. It is a horrid thing to admit, but I almost wish the bombs would fall again, so that I might return to London and see you once more, though I fear you will not wish it.*

*I have enclosed an address that is safe for you to write back to, if you choose, though I will understand if you do not. I shan't pester you, Vera, but be certain of this, I will never forget. I will never love another as I loved you. I will never know such happiness again.*

*I am sorry for everything.*

*Your Eddie, always*

***Birmingham***
***10th February 1943***

*To Vera,*
*I'm done in here, love. Nothin but hammerin and rivetin all day, wings this side, engines that side, the noise near splits your head. My arms feel like lumps of lead come nighttime. Lyons was a dawdle compared to this, I didn't know I had it so easy. Still, it keeps me goin thinking i'm doin me bit. Some of the girls are lovely, from all over the country, some I can barely understand and they can't understand me. Does make you laugh.*

*I've got leave soon, thank heavens, and I'll be seein you. Can't wait for a sit down with a cup of tea if you're lucky enough to have any. You'll laugh at this, dear Samuel has been up twice already, standing outside waiting for me like he's straight out the pictures. Proper romantic, though I try not to let on too much in front of the girls. Father will be go mad, I don't care really.*
*I'll bring all the chatter when I'm back. You keep yourself safe till then.*

*All my love,*
*Sheila x*

*Barnstaple,*
*2 April 1943*

*Vera,*

*I hope this letter finds you in good health, and that Nadine is well and behaves herself. She writes to me much, which is very good, but you must tell me, please, if she gives you trouble. She is young and stubborn, I know this.*

*If any word comes from my brother David, please tell me as soon as you can. It is now three years and nothing, not a line, not a whisper. I cannot stop hope, but the waiting is heavy. So cruel.*

*Here in Barnstaple, life is quiet and fresh. I am still giving lessons at the school, there are many evacuated children here. They have almost forgotten London. My darling Jacob is with me often. He trains at the assault camp not far from here. I think the Americans have something big planned that may bring an end to all of this. Jacob comes to me whenever he can. His care and his gentleness are so much what I need. And his romance too, even for a French woman, it is making me blush.*

*Write to me soon, Vera. You are in my thoughts always.*

*With love,*
*Esther*

*Tunisia*
*14th May 1943*

*Dear Vera,*

*It's over here now. The Jerries and the Ities are finished, all throwing their hands up yesterday. White flags everywhere - you never heard such a cheer from the lads. After all the dust and long drives and chasing about, it feels strange it's done. Quiet almost, though I don't reckon it will stay that way.*
*They don't tell us much where we go next. Some say back to Egypt, some say further east, names of places we can't even find on a map. All I know is there's still plenty of work left to do. Course we all want to come home, that's all anyone talks about - but it don't look like that's coming soon.*

*I keep thinking on us, Vera. These months drag and it's you that keeps me going. I dream of starting a family when this is all done. I'd love a boy, strong and healthy, growing up in peace, never knowing this sort of thing, only kicking a ball about. That picture stays in my head when the heat near kills us on the road.*

*Please look after yourself. I worry for your health. I'll keep writing as much as I can.*

*Love,*
*George*

*Tunsia*
*21st August 1943*

*My dear Vera,*
*I hope you had a nice 26th Birthday and father atleast remembered, I did remind him in my most recent letter to him. Joy has promised to make a fuss. It has quietened down here now. The runs with the lorries go on, and the dust never leaves you, but after all that happened in the spring it feels strange. Some say we'll be off to Italy next. You always talked of wanting to see that country one day, though not in the way we might.*

*Vera, I must tell you something, though I don't know if it helps or not. Your George and me, we've not been seeing eye to eye. He's changed out here, gone about with a different crowd. I lost my temper and told him straight that I know of his ways with you. He denied it of course, swore I was making it up. Some men even seem to think nothing of his ways, which I find hard to stomach. After that the officers thought it best we be sent to different duties, so we are apart now.*

*I regret letting my words get the better of me, but I could not keep silent. I don't want this to trouble you more, though I thought it right you should know. I am thinking of you often and hope you are keeping yourself safe and sensible. It is not easy being so far away and feeling I can do nothing.*

*Yours,*
*Henry*

**Tunsia**
**1st September 1943**

*My dear Vera,*

*The mood is changing here. We are to be moved soon, within days they say. No one tells us much, but all feel it coming. Who knows what we face next.*

*I do worry about your Henry. He has been acting most strange, saying things that are not true. I think the heat and this life are getting to him, it does that to men. Please let the lovely Joy know I am still looking out for him, even if we are not on the best of terms. I hope she is well, and little Mary too. Anyway, I won't say more, I am mindful of what I write in these letters. Gossiping is the enemy in this war, something you should know.*

*And you, Vera. You must know this above all. I love you beyond words, and I am the luckiest man alive to say you are mine. That is what you are, mine forever. Don't ever forget it. When I come home, I will put all things right. I will make it so. Our love will be stronger than ever because it must be. There is no other way. Our eventual child deserves nothing less. Everything I face out here, I face for that future, for us.*

*Yours always,*
*George*

## 32 The lost year

It feels as though I've closed my eyes and an entire year has withered away - gone in a flash. A year of nothingness: empty, desperate. The war drags on and we are all so tired. Bombings are thankfully rare now, though a daytime raid not long ago took us by surprise, flattening swathes of London. Turner Street was spared, but even without the bombs, we're weary of the restrictions - starving for a proper meal, longing to buy something nice, to feel normal again.

But nothing is normal. There's this quiet - stark, lifeless - in me and on the street itself. We just get by, keep going, though to where nobody knows. It's the loneliness that gnaws at me. Nadine's a good girl, but not the company I ache for. Sheila's been down once or twice, but only for short, hurried visits. She was beside herself when I told her about Eddie, and she can tell I'm still torn apart too.

Eddie's one letter remains tucked inside an old Bible - my dirty secret hidden in the holiest of places. It sits there collecting dust, haunting me. I thought about writing back. I even put pen to paper, poured out the loss, the heartache, the distrust I'll never shake. How can I believe his words - spoken or written? I spelled it all out, not knowing if any of it made sense, until finally I threw it into the fire, back into the flames - like that night when Eddie first kissed me, thoughtless and euphoric. I look back now and wonder where my senses were.

True to his word, Eddie hasn't written again. Only a birthday card, with a single kiss, the front showing a panda bear like the one from Whipsnade. I knew it was him. I can't decide if he's holding on, waiting for me to write, or if he's forgotten me altogether. I imagine us both standing outside, staring at the same sky, hoping we might find each other again. But in truth, he's probably with Beatrice. Married, even. It's been nearly a year since he left Turner Street - plenty of time for everything to change.

Nothing really has for me. Still the same shifts at Lyons. I even put myself forward for a supervisor role, thinking it might take my mind off things. It wasn't to be. Lazy Lorraine got the job - can you believe it? Of all people. We're convinced Mrs Miller had a hand in it. Chatterbox Catherine then said Mrs Miller liked her hand *in* Lorraine a lot. I spat out my tea at that - filthy words - but you've got to laugh. We've started calling her Crude Catherine now.

Dad and Joy follow every scrap of war news, eyes fixed on the papers, ears glued to the wireless for the latest from the BBC. Sometimes they even go to the pictures together, hoping for an unlikely glimpse of Henry or George. I usually look after Mary, which I don't mind at all. She's a darling - just turned three and full of beans. She can chatter all day, though we both worry she can't picture Henry. We keep photographs everywhere, pointing him out as if she truly understands. Every few weeks Henry sends a letter addressed to her alone, so she'll have them when she's older - or, dare I say it, in case he doesn't come home. It's an awful thought, but I know what he's thinking. Things have been hard out there, even if he's not on the very front line.

Joy has been trying her best with me - inviting me for food and games. She senses my misery but mistakes it for longing for George, when it couldn't be further from the truth. I went to see her the other day, in fact. She insisted on painting my legs. Honestly, it's what girls are doing now to replace stockings, since the materials are impossible to come by. Amazing what people come up with. You've got to laugh - it tickled a bit, but she did a fine job. Not that I've much reason to show them off. Little Mary just stared at us like we'd lost our minds. That child brings such light to my life - badly needed in a year when it feels as if the sun has rarely shown its face.

And then came another ray of light: Rita and James, back from their Cornish exile. The tiny pair are not so tiny anymore. Four years is a long time - but for children, it's a lifetime.

Rita is eleven now, her face changing, shaping into that of a young woman. A slight Cornish twang clings to her voice. She's only been back a few weeks, but Violet already fears a coldness in her, a distance. Rita shuts herself away, offering little, as though she blames them for this whole dreadful business. Violet's greatest fear has always been that her children would return unrecognisable, and perhaps, in some way, that fear has been realised.

James is a different story. Nine now, though nearly twice the size I remember. He's much the same - restless, cheeky, eager. He's brought home a love of the sea and fishing, clearly well adapted to the place he called home for half his life. Despite the worry, there's relief in their return, though Violet is cautious, weighed down with guilt as the posters still command us to *keep children safe in the countryside.* For her - the obedient ARP warden, the hero of Turner Street - it must have taken real nerve to defy the order. But I sense she thought if they didn't come home now, they never would.

And so here they are. Altered, but not strangers. Changed, but not lost. It shows how tired we all are of this war. We behave as if, by living as before, it might simply fade away. Yet we remain bound by the ration book, stuck in queues, blighted by the blackout. But we want our children home now, and even Violet has turned a deaf ear to the demands of authority.

The children's return coincided with Stan's leave, and it's he, not the children, who's changed most. Stanley looks worn to the bone, eyes sunk deep like he's stared too long into the dark. Violet says the Merchant Navy has stripped him down to something harder, quieter. He tells us of endless nights on blacked-out seas, ships vanishing in fire, the cold terror of torpedoes. No trenches, no front line - just the ocean itself turned enemy, and nowhere to run. He was home, safe, for a while at least. Normality returned for Violet - but only briefly. The sea called Stan back again. It's all become a loop - arrival, departure, waiting.

For a time, with Rita and James back on Turner Street, little Mary in my care, and Nadine growing fast into a young woman, I am distracted by the business of looking after children. I do enjoy it, though it fills the empty place where my own child should be. Comforting and distracting, both at once. When I'm playing with them, I sometimes forget myself - for a moment I forget Eddie, forget the dread of George's return. Perhaps I become a child again too. Innocent, naïve.

But the fear of George never really leaves me, and it came roaring back with those letters - first Henry's, telling me of a quarrel between them. The panic that rose in me as I read his words, as if my heart might tear through the page. How foolish I was to burden Henry with the truth before he went to war. I told myself it was to prepare him for when he came home. But now, with Eddie's betrayal, I see I've left Henry carrying a weight he never asked for - and me with nothing to lean on.

I want to leave. God knows I do. But the thought of being alone, of having nowhere, no one - of choosing *nothing* - terrifies me just as much. Turner Street is all I have, even if it means living with George's shadow. And he *will* be back one day. This war will end - it must. And then what? How could I possibly go on with him? And if no baby comes, the one thing he's so desperate for, I dread what that might lead to.

So I pray. Though I don't know what for. To escape? To find courage? To give Eddie another chance? Or to hope, foolishly, that George will come back a changed man and we can begin again. But I fear

God doesn't answer prayers round here. He just sits back and lets it all be.

And then George's most recent letter arrives - careful on the surface, but seething beneath every line. He's furious that I confided in Henry. He must know. He must sense the truth in me - that if I can speak it once, I can speak it again. That boldness only leads one way: to leaving him. His words make it clear enough - I belong to him.

So while I sometimes imagine staying, making do, clinging to faint hope, Henry's revelation has set me straight. It cannot be. George will come home for revenge. And I fear him more than I ever feared a Blitz - an extraordinary thing to admit, but true.

And so, as 1944 approaches, I know it will be the year I must vanish. How or to where, I've yet to work out. But go I must.

# *1944*

# 33 Return

The year turns, and I can sense a dramatic change upon us. Victory? Loss? Who can tell. The war has dragged us all through the mud and left us gasping, and I don't think any of us can do another twelve months of the same. Something has to give. I have to escape, I have to love, I want to be free. Even Turner Street, wrecked and weary, repels me like never before. It no longer feels like home - but then I don't know where home is. A constant restlessness grips me, relentless, gnawing, like the enemy itself.

My anxious feeling about the year is not eased when I'm woken one damp January morning by tragedy.

Mrs Henderson comes over, shawl crooked across her shoulders, bun barely clinging on, her face blotched red, eyes streaming so heavily she looks caught in a storm. For a moment I think she'll collapse right in front of me, she's trembling so much.

'It's Arthur,' she chokes, clutching the doorframe like it's the only thing holding her up. 'My Arthur… he's been killed in Italy.' Her voice falters, broken by sobs, the kind that wrench out of the chest whether you want them to or not.

I can't speak. The words snag in my throat. She grips my hands hard, as if I might anchor her to the earth. 'They sent a telegram,' she whispers. 'My Arthur… gone.'

All I can do is hold her. My old schoolteacher, that formidable, headstrong woman, now crumbled and desperate - a sight I'll never forget.

Arthur Henderson. My first love, my first glimpse of what a future might be. Of course, it was never anything real, but he was part of my life growing up, and now he's been torn away. Folded into the endless roll of names that mean everything to one family and nothing to the machine that swallows them.

Turner Street has lost another son. His poor twin brother Ken is beside himself. I can only imagine - for him it's like losing another part of himself. And it strikes me as extraordinary - almost cruel - that Battersea Power Station has kept Ken safe all this time, working in a place so many once thought would be the first to fall, yet it's barely scratched. This war feels so unpredictable.

That day, Turner Street seemed to sag, as if the weight of another coffin had settled across its shoulders. Another boy gone. Another name carved into our memories. Another chair left empty at the table. I don't think these places will ever forget the loss, I don't think they'll ever feel alive as they used to.

Still, Sheila's arrival in February brings a smile to my face, lets me forget the sadness for a while - though she too is shaken by Arthur's death. She once had a soft spot for him, and for Ken as well, I think. Well, they are twins. I'm sure Bill would've approved of Arthur rather than Samuel. But it's Samuel who has won her heart – something that is truly confirmed when Sheila stretches her hand out to me, a ring catching the light - a gentle green sparkle set in a sea of silver. Beautiful, yes, but what on earth is she thinking?

'I told you I would marry Samuel, didn't I?'

'You did,' I reply, worry heavy in my voice.

'We won't do it until the war ends.'

'I think your wedding will start another war, Sheila,' I say, reluctant but honest.

'I'm telling Father later. He'll just have to accept it. I don't need his permission, Vera.' She's defiant, passionate, her optimism glowing as ever. But I know Bill's reaction will knock her straight back down to earth. Even her tireless service in the factory won't be enough to shift him - the only thing that would satisfy Bill is if Samuel miraculously changed his race.

Later that day, Sheila hammers at my door, pounding so hard Nadine leaps at the commotion. Sheila barges in, face flushed, cheekbones sharp and red with fury and exhaustion.

'Mind if I stay here tonight, Vera?' she says, determined.

Hot on her heels is Bill, his voice carrying down the street, a stark temper. For once his Home Guard helmet isn't on his head - caught off guard, you might say - though he looks more than ready for battle.

'You listen to me, Sheila Warner! You do not have - and will never have - my permission!' he bellows, stomping towards the house.

'Shut the door, Vera!'

'I can't do that!'

'Shut the bleeding door!'

So I do. I slam it with a thud right on Bill's furious face. He howls through the wood, fists battering the panel.

'Open this door, you hear me! I've had enough of this nonsense! Sheila! Vera! I know you can hear me!' His voice rattles.

'Oh, piss off!' Sheila yells back, words that shock even me. Luckily Bill doesn't quite catch them, still lost in his own anger.

'He's taken it well then?' I murmur, a sly smile escaping.

'Oh, he can't wait to walk me down the aisle,' she giggles, then turns to Nadine, who's peeking wide-eyed from the corner. 'I know you miss your family, Nadine, but honestly, they're not worth the hassle half the time.'

Eventually Bill goes quiet, worn out, though I half expect him to bang the door down. He leaves with threats instead, swearing he'll find some other way to bring Sheila to heel. He can't cope without control. He gave up on Pat, but Sheila he's determined to keep in line.

Only, I doubt it will work. Sheila seems more rebellious than ever. The factory's hardened her - sharper words, bolder tone. There's a courage in her now, an attitude even. Amazing what that place can do. She even strikes a match, lights a cigarette, and blows smoke like she hasn't a care in the world. Then she says we should go out the following afternoon – her, Samuel and me - a sort of celebration. Soho again, just like New Year's Eve back in 1940. Four years ago. When Eddie walked me home and it all began. And now look at me. How utterly demoralising.

On a chilly February afternoon, after my shift, I meet Sheila and Samuel in town - a place called *Victory* in Soho. A fitting name, or maybe just wishful. They're making the most of the Yanks being over here, serving American-style food. The place is lively, loud, full of chatter and unfamiliar accents cutting through the air. It feels like a film set.

As we're shown to our table, Samuel beams at us both, thrilled that Sheila stood her ground with Bill. To him, it's settled now - no going back.

'He isn't pleased. I've never seen him so angry,' I say, trying to bring them down to earth.

'Nothing he can do,' Samuel grins, gripping Sheila's hand. 'Nothing can stop us now.'

How I envy them - their romance, their hope, their naivety.

'D'you reckon I could get in the factory, even if I'm married?' I blurt, cutting across their glow. A waiter sets down a sandwich with far too much ceremony, and Sheila stares at me as if I've lost my mind.

'You don't want to go there. It's bloody awful.'

'I need to get off Turner Street. To get out, for good.'

'And what happens when the war ends? You going to stay stuck up in Birmingham?' she says. 'You're talking daft, Vera.'

'Then where else can I go?' I say, more desperate than I intended. Samuel shifts awkwardly, clearly baffled by my determination to escape, but he stays quiet.

'Why don't you go to Norfolk?' Sheila says. 'See if he really did wed that nice girl.'

'Now you're the one talking daft,' I snap back. 'Besides, I'm through with Eddie.'

Sheila scoffs so loud it drowns out the Americans gabbing beside us.

'Pull the other one. You've not stopped thinking about him for over a year.'

And of course, she's right. I dream of him day and night. Every time I see a fireman my heart jumps - could it be him, has he come back? Even the smell of smoke, the wail of a siren - it all drags me straight back to him. It's agony. But it's finished. Time has passed. I've got to live with the ache, move on, get out. Only how, and where, I've no idea. And Sheila, for all her scoffing, isn't much help.

'Maybe I'll go with your Pat. Where is she now?'

'On a farm, in the Land Army.'

'What, Pat?' I gasp.

'Yeah, conscripted like me. She's up in Yorkshire looking after cows. Doesn't want Father to know, doesn't want anything to do with him. She's settled quite well into country life.'

'I could do that. Instead of pouring milk, I could be the one doing the milking,' I say.

Sheila laughs, smoke curling from her lips.

'You? On a farm? Vera, you've got a screw loose.'

'You might be right,' I concede.

'Besides, things might be different when George comes back, when the war's over - really over. He's been gone more than a year. Time does wonderful things, Vera.'

Her words startle me. It's as if she hasn't heard a word I've said, as if my fear, my worry, my pain mean nothing. I start to doubt myself, to wonder if it's all in my head, if this is simply the life women like us are meant to endure. But then I see her in Samuel's arms, his tenderness, the way he looks at her with such kindness, and I can't fathom how she can dismiss me so easily.

I do love Sheila - she's a true friend - yet she often lives in her own universe, blind to what others feel. The East End once knocked her about, left scars on her spirit, dragged her to a harsh cruel reality. But now? She floats again, wrapped in her own happiness. I say nothing. My frustration must be clear as day, but Sheila wouldn't notice; she's too dazzled by Samuel, too lifted by the glow of the Victory restaurant.

Before long, we're heading home and I'm no wiser about what I ought to do. Sheila reminds me that Nadine's still with me, and I can't simply up and leave without first seeing her safe with Esther. Esther, who now writes of plans to sail to Chicago once the war ends - of leaving Turner Street entirely. If that happens, I'll be left with nothing. Me and George, without a roof. Perhaps my hand will be forced anyway.

On the journey home, Samuel is brimming with his usual optimism.

'The Germans are on the run. Look at Stalingrad! It's all falling apart. This time next year it'll be over, and me and Sheila will be husband and wife,' he says, sliding his arm around her.

'Don't count your chickens,' I mutter, trying to dim the glow.

'Don't be so negative, Vera!' Sheila snaps, her voice suddenly sharp.

'Negative? I live in the real world!' I fire back.

Sheila scoffs.

'I'm the one in the factory morning, noon, and night, keeping the war effort alive. You're still stuck in Lyons as if nothing's changed - like the war's just background noise!'

'Why are you being such a cow!' I shout.

'Me?!' Sheila squeals, offended.

'Ladies, please,' Samuel cuts in, firm but gentle. 'Stop this now. This is meant to be a celebration.'

We walk on in silence, the air between us cold and thick. Samuel stays with us still; I assume he means to spend the night, though truthfully, I'd rather he and Sheila didn't.

As we near the house, I spot two figures standing close to my front door. Their lingering silhouettes send a shiver through me. The blackout makes it impossible to see their faces, but I know at once they're not from round here. Then, glancing left, I catch sight of another man further down - standing motionless beneath a shaded lamp. His flat cap hides most of his face, but I feel his eyes on us.

The two by the door move forward. So does the one from the other end of the street. Three men, closing in. My stomach knots with dread, but Sheila and Samuel don't seem to sense it.

Within moments, they've blocked our path. My home is just yards away, yet unreachable. The third man now stands behind us. Samuel steps forward, gently unhooking Sheila's arm.

'Excuse me,' he says, calm, polite.

'What's the problem, darkie?' one of them spits - then lashes out, a vicious punch cracking against Samuel's eye. The sound echoes down the street. Sheila yelps. Another blow follows and Samuel crumples, clutching his face.

Before we can move, the man behind us barges through, knocking Sheila sideways. He joins the assault, boot swinging with cruel precision as Samuel lies on the ground, trying desperately to protect himself. The kicks come hard and fast - the thud of leather against bone, a frantic, merciless rhythm. A cruel, brutal frenzy.

'Stop! Please stop!' Sheila screams, her voice tearing through the night.

And then, out of nowhere, a figure bursts through the darkness - like a hero from a comic book. He doesn't come to join them, but to drive them back. With astonishing force, he barrels in, shoving one man aside, striking another so hard it makes me jump. The third man hesitates, then slinks off quickly. In seconds, all of them are gone, running like hunted dogs.

Samuel lies gasping on the ground. The stranger bends to lift him with steady strength, and it's then, in the dim light, that I see him.

At first just a shape, a shadow - broad - shouldered, sure-handed. Then a flash of his face under the moonlight, the unmistakable set of his jaw, the curve of his mouth, the eyes - those eyes.

My breath catches. My body jolts. It can't be.

Eddie.

But it is. Eddie. Protective, fierce, solid as ever. He eases Samuel into Sheila's arms. She weeps over her fiancé, but my gaze stays fixed elsewhere.

Eddie turns - and for the first time in what feels like a lifetime, his eyes meet mine. They hold me there, burning into me, stopping time.

He's back. Not a dream. Not a ghost. Eddie is here. A blessing, or perhaps a curse.

# **34** Faith

We get inside quickly, Eddie half-carrying Samuel as we scramble for towels and rags. Blood streams from the gash above Samuel's eye, swelling so fast it's near closed. Sheila is beside herself, shouting, sobbing, pacing like a mad thing, while Nadine hovers in the corner, pale with worry. Through it all, I keep my eyes fixed on Samuel. I daren't look at Eddie, though I can feel him watching me.

'We should take you to hospital,' I tell Samuel, pressing a cloth to his brow.

'I'm fine, really,' he groans, teeth clenched against the pain.

'You don't look fine,' Sheila says, tears streaking her cheeks.

'I'm a doctor. Trust me, I'm fine.' Samuel insists.

'Father did this,' Sheila snaps, spitting the words like venom. 'I bloody well know he did. Those blokes will be in the Guard with him, I swear by it.'

'You don't know that Sheila.' I say, trying to offer some reason.

'I bloody well do! You heard him yourself - those threats on the other side of the door. Rotten, awful bastard.' She turns to Eddie, who stands quiet in the corner. 'If you hadn't come, it would've been worse. You showed up like an angel sent from God.'

'He's no angel,' I mutter, loud enough for all to hear.

Sheila stops pacing, her voice softening.

'You two should have a chat.'

'I'm looking after Samuel,' I say quickly.

'I'm fine, Vera,' Samuel insists, holding the rag to his brow, blood seeping through. 'Honestly, I'm fine.'

Slowly, I rise. My chest pounds as I glance at Eddie. One look and I feel myself weakening. I force my legs into motion and step into the kitchen. Nadine sits at the table, concern etched in her young face.

'Give us a moment, love,' I say gently. She looks bewildered, seeing Eddie back after all this time, but nods and slips away.

I sink into the chair, too drained to stand. Eddie follows, hovering like a shadow.

'What are you doing here, Eddie?' I ask.

'To see you,' he says.

'Yeah? And what for… why now?'

He hesitates, takes a breath.

'Do you want a cup of tea?'

'I want to know why you're back here!'

'Because I'm back in London, and I couldn't not see you. I only got in this morning.'

'Back in London for what? Picking out a wedding ring?' I snap, spite cutting through before I can stop it.

'There's talk of a new threat,' he says. 'Not like the raids before. I don't know the full of it, but it's enough they're calling men back to the city. I jumped at the chance.'

'Bet Beatrice will miss you.'

His eyes flicker.

'Me and Beatrice are no longer together. Haven't been since last summer.'

'And I'm meant to believe that?'

'No… but it's the truth.'

'I don't know what's true anymore,' I tell him, my voice trembling, 'I don't know what's real. I don't know anything.'

'I understand,' Eddie says softly. 'But one thing I do know, Vera - since the day I left Turner Street, I haven't stopped thinking of you. I've…' He falters, steadying himself. 'I've cried at the longing. I've never felt emptiness like it. Not in all these months.'

'Well,' I say, bitterness rising, 'if you felt like that, you took your time about it.'

'I wrote,' he blurts. 'You got the letter, didn't you? I didn't want to be a pest. I thought you hated me. And you'd every right - '

'I don't hate you, Eddie,' I cut across him, firm, deliberate. 'I can't hate you. I love you. That's why it hurts so bloody much. Esther was right - if you love, you hurt. And it's true.' I lean forward, my voice steadying with the truth. 'I was ready to throw my whole life away for you. To be cut off from my family, shamed, ridiculed. I was ready to do all that for you. And you… you couldn't even be honest with me.'

'And I'll never stop hating myself for it,' he says. I see a tear slide down his cheek before he turns his back, unwilling to let me watch him unravel. 'Every night, every day, I think of what I could've done to put it right. And to think of you here, with him - that animal -' His voice cracks. '- I thought I might lose you.'

'Well, you did, didn't you?' I fire back, my anger shaking in my throat. 'And now I've got to stay here and suffer, knowing that when this war ends, I'm shackled to George for the rest of my days - however long that might be. Stuck on this blasted street. You were the reason I had hope, belief, faith. And you destroyed it. Talk of a blitz? That's nothing compared to the wreck you left me in. I don't know if I'm coming or going, only that I'm still here, always here, petrified to leave, scared to stay. And then you come swanning back like some knight in shining armour, only you'll vanish again when it suits. I'm not your plaything, Eddie. You got me all wrong.'

The silence after is thick, heavy. I'm half certain Sheila and Samuel can hear every word through the walls, but I don't care. Let them. My pain is no secret. Eddie hesitates, eyes shadowed, as though weighing what's left to say. Maybe my temper has convinced him it's hopeless. I almost hope it has - though I'm not sure that's what I truly want.

'I'll go, Vera,' he says at last, voice low. 'I won't trouble you again. I'm sorry. But you should know, from the bottom of my heart - I love you more than words can tell. I'll never stop loving you. I may build a life with someone else, but they'll never be you. And I'll carry that till the day I die.'

He turns to leave, and something in me breaks. I rise without thinking, words spilling out before I can stop them.

'I don't want you to go, Eddie. I want you here. I want you. I just can't bear to hurt like I have.'

He stops. Hope flickers across his face, a smile fighting through the sadness.

'I can be here,' he says. 'We can go wherever, whenever. I'll never leave you. I'll wait, I'll stand by you, no matter what names they call us. I love you, Vera. Vera *Wright. Not Hopkins.* You should never have been his. This - this is what was meant.'

'It cannot be,' I whisper.

'It's what we want. Why refuse it?' Eddie insists.

I nod as he steps closer, his chin resting lightly atop my head. His scent, warm and familiar, rises from the stubble of his neck. I sink into his shoulder, his hold steady - not tight, not claiming, but sure, protective. I tilt my face up; he lowers his to mine. Our lips hover, breath mingling, eyes locked. Then we kiss - slow, certain, aching with everything lost and found.

Time shifts. Night folds into day, clouds breaking as though my heart itself has leapt free. We go on, needful, frantic, desperate to make up for all the time stolen.

And then I notice movement at the door. Out the corner of my eye, I see Sheila standing there, a faint smile tugging at her lips.

'I see you've made up, then,' she says.

## 35 Telegram

I can't believe he's back. My everything. The man I haven't stopped thinking about, the face I feared I might one day forget - fading into memory as though none of it had ever been real. But here he is. Bold. Proud. And already, my secret feels as if it's slipping from my grasp. Sheila, Samuel, Nadine - they all know now. They welcome it, even. But too many people knowing means it cannot last. Still, after one taste of him again, I know this is the life I must choose.

Despite Eddie being back, things aren't as simple as they once were. He hasn't returned to Eve Morris's at number eighty, but is lodging with another fireman in Putney - closer to my work, though further from home. Perhaps that's for the best, away from the prying eyes of Turner Street.

Even so, I miss him. After more than a year with nothing at all, I should be grateful he's here in any form.

The moments we steal together are precious. Intimate. We talk for hours about what life might be when the war ends and I'm free of George. Eddie keeps mentioning Norfolk - how we could start afresh there, away from gossip, away from judgement, with nothing but open sky and quiet. It's easy to dream. Perhaps naïve, but dreaming is what keeps me going.

And then, as ever, life drags me back to earth with a thunderous crash.

I'm walking home from Lyons when I see him: a young chap in a neat uniform standing by my door.

'Mrs Hopkins?' he asks politely.

'Yes…'

'You have a telegram.'

He hands it over and I take it in the doorway, my heart already racing. George. It must be George. And news of George is never good.

I tear it open. My hands tremble; the small printed letters blur as I try to focus. The words are stark, merciless.

*Regret to inform you your husband, George Hopkins, service number 7925739, has been severely wounded in action.*

The line swims before me. I search for more, for comfort that isn't there.

*Injury significant. Repatriation to Britain initiated. Will be transferred to Netley Military Hospital.*

The telegram slips in my hands. I slump against the doorway, weeping - alive, yes, but terribly hurt. And that, perhaps, is worse. Because now he'll come back broken and angry, and I cannot leave him. How could I escape while my wounded husband lies in a hospital bed? I'd never be forgiven. Not by them. Not by God. Not even by myself.

I fold the telegram carefully, my fingers shaking. The words burn through the paper, through me. And there, in the stillness of my narrow hallway, I make a decision - one I am not proud of.

I will keep this to myself.

No one must know. Not yet. And so, alongside Eddie's secret letter, I hide the telegram in my bible. Now becoming a book of secrets. It must be news just for me, until I find a way forward. Because George is coming home - and I know what that means.

There's a ticking clock now.

Time is not on my side.

## 36 The lie

The sense of unease is almost unbearable, knowing George will soon be on these shores - perhaps he already is. The specifics of his condition remain unknown. I could head south to the military hospital near Southampton where he's due to be admitted, but the thought fills me with dread. I don't want to see him, what's left of him, knowing what my intentions are. I carry this exhausting guilt - already heavy from my adulterous ways, now sharpened by the fact George is hurt. I keep reminding myself who he is and how he's treated me, but I cannot ignore that he is my husband. I have a duty. Perhaps this horrific injury is God's way of making me stay. Eddie's return was a cruel temptation, a glimpse of happiness I was never entitled to.

So I keep George's status private, though I worry it may leak through Henry's letters to Joy and, with it, the family and the whole street will know. I mull over telling them - and even visiting - assuming I'll hear more when his arrival at the hospital is confirmed.

The long wait, the terrible indecision, stretches into weeks, and quickly summer arrives. Despite my panic there's a quiet hope in the air about the war, a sense that the tide might be turning, a light at the end of the tunnel. I wish I could feel it. Nobody dares say too much, in case we tempt fate, but optimism hangs on the news of a great operation between us and the Americans - they're calling it D-Day. Word spreads of success, though never without heartbreak; lives lost by the thousands. We almost expect it now, as if sorrow has become part of the air we breathe.

I soon receive a letter and, for a moment, I'm certain it will be further news of George. But it is Esther instead, writing about her American sweetheart Jacob, caught up in D-Day. She is once again left waiting in the dark. First her brother in France, now her lover. Her letter also contains a plea to coax Nadine to return with her, but Nadine is rooted here more than ever. She'll be fifteen this year and has become a young 'Nippy' in training. I nearly fell over when Mrs Miller agreed to take her on, but with so many women called up for war duties they're desperate for staff. Nadine has taken to it like a duck to water - she does the small jobs with such confidence, and her good English, along with her habit of keeping quiet, keeps her German roots safely tucked away. Most of the girls would never guess until chatterbox Catherine blurted it out.

Eddie has been quick to notice the shift in my mood, from passionate lover to a woman burdened with worry and shame. He insists we have a proper discussion, where we can plan and decide what to do next. It feels like the ideal time to tell him of George's injury, and I am torn between loyalty to a wounded - if no less violent - husband and the man I am so in love with but should never have.

So, perhaps incredibly brazen of me, on a Sunday night I stay at Eddie's while the fireman he lodges with is on an evening shift. I am confident Nadine will be fine; she knows where I am and there's a quiet, knowing trust between us. When I get to Eddie's, I tell him the news I've been holding on to for weeks. He is shocked, concerned, driven.

'We have to leave, Vera, together, you and me,' he says, the most eager I've ever heard him.

'I don't know, Eddie…'

'We have to.'

'Friday?'

'What - this Friday?' I ask, complete shock in my voice.

'Yes. We'll go to Norfolk. We can stay with my uncle in Cromer. You'll love it there, Vera - beautiful beach, fresh sea air. It'll be temporary, but it gets you away. Means we can start a life.'

'You make it sound like it's easy,' I say, panic threading my words.

'If we don't do it now, we never will.'

'Do you realise what I'm faced with, Eddie? I will be the most hated woman to walk this earth if I simply run off, with George in the state he's in.'

'Don't feel sorry for him, Vera,' Eddie says, stern, his voice rising.

'He's been to war,' I snap.

'And I've suffered it to, maybe not oversees but at war no less' he says defensively, hurt in his voice, I can sense I've touched a nerve 'All of us are suffering, but you can't forget how he treats you, how he makes you feel.'

'I'm not the only one with a troubled marriage, Eddie,' I shout back.

'Listen to yourself, Vera. Please, listen.'

'I don't know what to do, Eddie,' I plead, collapsing on the bed and turning away. 'I'm fed up with feeling like this. I want to leave - of course I do - but I don't know if I can.'

I then slowly turn back to look at him. His face is overwhelmed with disappointment, as if he's losing his grip on me, as if I'm losing my senses. Perhaps all of that is true.

We spend the night in the same bed but in different worlds, pulled apart by what may be and what might not. Nothing is clearer; it's all a mess. And I feel I've run out of strength to decide.

A couple of days later I'm sitting at Violet's; Joy has joined us too. It should be a special moment - rare, stolen time - but instead I'm thinking of the mess I'm in, and the taut words with Eddie. His insistence that we leave in a matter of days still rings in my ears: impossible to ignore, impossible to actually do. That evening with him was meant to be something, but it only left me with more to figure out, another weight added.

'Where were you on Sunday evening, Vera?' Violet suddenly asks, casually but still deliberate. My heart thumps in my chest. I try to steady myself.

'Oh, I was working late. Stock take. What stock we actually have these days.'

'Strange. Nadine says you were staying with a friend…' Violet says 'You see, I knocked by to tell you James has written his own story - *The Magical Train*, like the one you told him before they were sent away.'

Violet slips to the kitchen to fetch James's work; I try to pull myself together. She returns with a proudly written tale with delicate handwriting and small illustrations. 'I had to tell you as soon as he showed me. I think you've inspired him, Vera.'

I look through the pages - rough but full of imagination. For a moment I'm lost, until Joy brings me back.

'So, Vera, where were you then? Like Nadine said?' she asks.

I try to conjure something. Quickly.

'Er, yes... I was with a friend like she said.'

'Why say stock take then?' Violet presses, curious.

'Well, I was worried you might frown on me for leaving young Nadine alone,' I say in a rush, scrambling something together.

'She's a working woman. I was courting with Stanley at her age. Married a couple of years later,' Violet says, matter-of-fact.

'I know, I know. I'm just protective of her,' I mutter, not wanting to justify myself too much.

'Which friend then?' Violet asks, her eyes alongside Joys both on mine.

I stagger once more; fearful she suspects something untoward.

'Sheila. I went to see Sheila.'

'What! up in Birmingham?' Violet's voice rises with genuine shock and surprise.

'… yeah. I finished early and went to surprise her. She's been tucked away in those huts she's staying in - I haven't seen her properly since Samuel was beaten up on the street.'

Joy tuts and shakes her head at what happened to Samuel while I desperately try to change the subject.

'What about these new weapons then? Quite a few have fallen - it's frightening.' I ask.

'It is rather,' Joy says with Violet nodding along. My attempt at deflection works as Violet's face turns to worry.

'Unmanned rockets,' Violet says glumly. 'They just drop from the sky. There's not much we can do; we can't sound a siren, they're too quick. Honestly, I thought we were past all this.'

'Heck of a noise too,' Joy adds.

'It's not the noise, it's the silence,' I tell them, repeating what Eddie warned me. 'If it goes quiet you take cover and hope for the best.'

'Wickedness,' Joy says, and she's right. What kind of mind invents such a thing - a weapon designed for pure despair? Perhaps it's a final act, a weapon of revenge. But for all of us it feels far too familiar.

'They're calling them doodlebugs, because of the noise,' Violet says, fidgeting beside us. Her questioning of my whereabouts drifts away for now. 'I don't know if I can do it all over again. Not like last time. I don't have the strength.'

We all nod in unison.

And then Rita and James come bustling in with little Mary, digging through old toys they'd left behind before they were evacuated, now perfect for Mary. The children are so gentle with Mary, so considerate and caring.

'They'll have to go back,' Violet says quietly as the children leave the room, tears forming in her eyes.

'They were right. I never should've brought them home. I was so stupid.'

'No you weren't. There are loads of kids about round here now - most of them home. Don't talk nonsense,' I say, trying to reassure her as Joy echoes my words of reassurance.

'Nobody could have predicted these rockets would become a reality. It's like something from science fiction,' Joy says.

Violet forces herself to agree, but fear shows in her face.

'Still, I can't keep them here. It will be too dangerous. Stanley would never forgive me but I don't know if I could bear them gone again,' she whispers, wiping her tears.

'Will you stay here if these rockets continue?' I ask Joy. 'Or go back to Canterbury?'

Joy considers for a moment.

'Well where's really safe? We'll just have to take our chances, I suppose…'

'I don't feel safe here,' I add, thinking of both the rockets and George's eventual return. 'I might have to leave.'

'And where would you go?' Violet asks, her eyes sharp on mine.

'Anywhere away from here.'

'I could never imagine you not on Turner Street, Vera.' Violet says.

'Neither can I,' I confess.

A short while later there's a knock at the door. I'm curious who it might be. Violet bustles up, complaining that she's off Warden duties as I peer down the hallway, staring at the door, a mild panic settling through me - surely it can't be my George, looking for me.

Luckily it isn't. But I'm just as surprised at who it is.

Standing on the doorstep are Sheila and Samuel. My stomach drops. What on earth is she doing here?

'Is our Vera in?' Sheila calls as Violet leads them into the kitchen. 'Surprise!' Sheila shouts as she enters, euphoric, loud. Sheila holds out her small, bony hand - a ring gleams on her finger. Samuel's smile is enormous. 'We did it. I told you we would - we're married,' she says, tears of happiness at the corners of her eyes. Samuel's grin is a startling contrast to the swollen, bruised face he'd had the last time I saw him.

'You're having us on,' I say, incredulous.

'No, look. We just thought, why wait for this madness to end? War can't stop us loving each other. It's not like my old man is going to be won over,' Sheila says. I stand and hug her but am overcome with a genuine feeling of sickness. I can barely stand, my head swirls.

'Sorry we didn't invite you ladies. It was last minute. A couple of girls from the factory joined, and Pat rushed over from the farm. Nothing major,' Sheila adds, apologetic to us all, as I fight a wave of queasiness.

'We'll do a proper thing when the war's over,' Samuel says, while Violet and Joy chorus loud congratulations, fussing over the ring as if it were the happiest news in the world.

'I assume you haven't informed your father of this information?' Joy asks.

'I've come to tell me Mum but not him. Don't care about him,' Sheila says, bright and defiant.

I manage a smile, my lips pressed tight. A dull disheartenment settles over me - Sheila, my supposed best friend, has done something enormous and I've been left in the dark.

'So, when was the big day?' Joy asks.

'On Saturday,' Sheila says, eyes wide. 'The factory gave me a couple of days off. I suppose you could call this our honeymoon,' she giggles.

'That doesn't make sense. You were with Vera on Sunday and yet she's only just found out about it?' Violet says, and suddenly their faces turn toward me. The room narrows; the air feels thin. The net is closing in.

'I haven't seen Vera since that awful night Samuel got ambushed,' Sheila adds, as innocently as she can.

The whole room falls silent. They just look at me - at my face, my eyes - searching for the truth. The spotlight burns. My throat tightens.

'I'm going to be sick,' I say and stumble outside. I barely make it to the garden before I'm retching, leaning over Violet's Anderson shelter, heaving until my ribs ache. This vile, desperate mess - I've never been so ill. Shame, fear and panic tangle together; everything feels as if it's collapsing.

The ladies hover in the doorway, watching from a distance - Violet, Joy, Sheila - their faces threaded with concern and suspicion.

'She was rather unwell like this on my wedding day,' Joy says quietly, as though she's trying to put the pieces together.

Sheila stands closer to me, resting her head on my shoulder for a second. Her face holds a faint disgust at the smell of vomit. I try to lift my head but the world skews; everything blurs and tilts. My legs give way. I slip down, the ground rushing up, and then, darkness - I fall into my own private blackout.

## **37** The issue

The hours that follow are an unnerving haze - shifting shapes, blurred colours, half-familiar faces drifting in and out. I am sick, there's no doubt, confused and disoriented, petrified the entire street now knows my secret. Slowly, things begin to steady. I blink into focus and find myself back home, lying on my bed. Dr Clarke looms beside me, his large frame blocking out the light from the window. He speaks as though we've been in conversation for some time, though this is the first moment I'm aware of it.

Sheila slips in briefly and places a glass of water on the table.

'You've got your colour back' she says softly before slipping out, closing the door behind her.

Dr Clarke resumes his checks - pressing on my stomach, shining a light into my eyes. He works in silence now, methodical, his bloated face serious, a flicker of confusion shadowing his features.

'Hmm,' he mutters as I sip the water and watch him settle down on the edge of the bed. The frame creaks under his weight. He takes a long, wheezy breath, gathering himself. 'I think I know the issue, Vera… though I must admit, I'm quite curious about it.'

My heart quickens.

'What do you mean?'

He rises again, uncomfortable, his knees cracking as he pushes himself upright. His breath rattles.

'It is only my opinion,' he says carefully, 'but I believe you are pregnant, Vera.'

The words send a jolt down my spine - fear, worry, and some terrible spark of jubilation. Proof my body works. Proof, too, of my betrayal.

Dr Clarke's eyes fix on me.

'You see,' he says slowly, 'that would be quite unusual, considering George is away… supporting this war?' His stare is cold, knowing, full of judgement. 'Unless, of course, George had a moment of leave I wasn't privy to?'

I just stare back, mute. What can I possibly say? He knows. Of course, he knows. I try to hold steady, but the tremble in my lip, the tears welling in my eyes betray me, let the mask slip.

'You've got yourself in quite some bother, haven't you?' Dr Clarke says, his tone flat, unsympathetic, cold as stone. 'What will your father make of all this?'

The mention of Dad is deliberate, meant to twist the knife. His gaze doesn't waver. And so, I pluck the courage to say something back.

'You shan't utter a word to my father about this,' I manage, trying to sound calm, controlled. 'This is my burden to carry.'

'I've the utmost respect for your father, Vera. We've known each other years. This would break him. Not to mention George.'

'Well, it's not confirmed, is it? Just opinion,' I reply, defensive, scrambling.

'Your face says it all, Vera, and you know it.' His words are firm, damning. 'I suspect you've been hiding the gravest of betrayals. Now you cannot hide it.'

He gathers his things, a flush rising in his cheeks, temper beneath the surface. At the door he lingers, looking back at me with that same unyielding stare.

'I suggest you come to my surgery on Friday Vera. For now, get some rest.'

And then he's gone, taking my secret with him - fragile in his hands. I curl on the bed, arms wrapped around my stomach, trying to believe what I've just heard. Fear floods me, but underneath it, faint as a whisper, something else: hope. How can it be there? And yet it is.

Sheila slips in, sits by my side, rubbing my back.

'Are you all right, Vera?'

I bury my face in the pillow; my words are muffled through the damp fabric, but I manage to confess.

'I'm expecting…'

'Say that again, Vera?'

'I'm pregnant!' I cry, lifting my head, my voice filling the room.

Sheila stares at me, frozen, then finally nods, a flicker of a smile forming.

'Well… that explains it then.'

'What am I going to do, Sheila!?'

She hesitates, uncertain, but refuses to show it.

'You'll figure it out. Maybe… maybe this is what you needed.'

'What do you mean?' I demand, pushing her to finish.

'To find your happiness. It's what you've always wanted, Vera.'

'Not like this. You know what this means - I can't have it... I can't, I can't - '

Distress surges. I rise, pacing, the nausea never far away, though now it's worry that grips me tighter.

'Vera, calm down,' Sheila says, standing to steady me. 'You'll get through this. You've got Eddie.'

'What will people say?'

'The same sort of things they say about me and Samuel. And the more they say it, the more I realise how real our love is. Denying who we love, shutting it down for other people's comfort, it only kills us. Love's a bloody pain, it isn't easy.'

'I'll have to leave. With Eddie.'

'And I'm leaving with Samuel. Turner Street doesn't need us,' Sheila replies proudly.

I almost laugh through the tears.

'Look at us, eh? Neighbours. Rebels. Who'd have thought it?'

'Must be something in the tea at Lyons,' Sheila says with a crooked grin. She pulls me close, hugging me tight. I am overcome with odd feeling - relief, perhaps. Realisation. Maybe even joy.

Maybe this child isn't a curse at all. Maybe it's God's way of pushing me to do what I was starting to doubt.

I dash over to Eddie's lodgings too early and loiter outside, pacing like a fool - panic, excitement, worry all wrapped into one. I must look a sight. Minutes stretch until finally I see him. I rush up; he can tell something's wrong by my eagerness and the pace of my breathing.

'What's going on, Vera?' he asks, worry etched across his face.

'I'm… I'm pregnant, Eddie,' I say, trying to hold back the tears and keep my voice steady so he understands.

'…Bleeding hell.' His mouth drops open at first, then cracks into a smile that lights up his whole face. His eyes go wide, as if he's stepped into a new world. 'Oh my God, are you sure Vera?'

'The doctor thinks so. I've been feeling sick… it would make sense. What are we going to do, Eddie?'

He pulls me into his arms, holding me tight, his hands steady and warm.

'We'll do what I said,' he says.

'Which is?'

'Escape to Norfolk on Friday. I know you had your doubts, I know you were worried, but this…' he points to my belly 'this is it. God's will, I reckon. What are the chances? You can't stay now, George will know, the whole bloody world will.'

'They'll know if I run off.'

'But you'll be safe with me. Together, Vera. You know it's what we have to do.'

I nod. He's right. Of course he is.

'I'm scared Eddie, really scared'

'Nothing to be scared of, this is meant to be, I have never been so certain of something in all my life'

'Friday then…' I say, my decision made. My world changed.

We hold each other, meaningful, determined. We lose ourselves for what feels like forever. Home is wherever my Eddie is.

And so I wander back home, the sky turning grey, a coldness wrapping around me like a winter skin. I shiver despite it being mid-June. Perhaps it's the nerves and apprehension of knowing what comes next - or the sickness still clinging to me.

I step inside and immediately sense a change, a stark unnerving feeling, a brutal instinct of worry. I walk slowly through the house into the kitchen.

And there he is. Sitting in the chair, head bowed. George. Christ, it's George.

He raises his head slowly and I see a man I can barely recognise. No longer a man, but a monument to destruction. He is all angles and broken lines. His right arm is nothing but a sleeve - a sad, empty flap of fabric pinned to his chest like a flag at half-mast. The face I remembered is gone, replaced by that of a stranger. Half of it hidden behind a clean white dressing, stark and final as a tombstone. One of his eyes is entirely covered, disguised by layers of desperate bandages. His other eye remains, cold and hard, holding me in its unwavering, burning grip.

He says nothing. He doesn't need to.

I see his pain, his anguish, his horror - and his sacrifice. And in that moment the weight of my own callousness bears down.

What on earth am I meant to do next?

## **38** Hollow man

George tells me how it happened. His voice is low, halting, every word dragged up from some deep pit inside him. He says they were running convoys through the Italian Apennines, narrow mountain roads where the trucks clung to the edge of cliffs, the air thick with dust and the smell of petrol.

'We'd been shelled plenty, but this was different,' he says, his good eye fixed on nothing in particular. 'This raid was sudden. Merciless. Mortars raining down, the whole sky on fire. Before I knew it, I was blown clean out of my truck, the noise and heat tearing through me - burning, searing - and then nothing. When I came to, this was gone.' He strokes the empty sleeve pinned across his chest, rubbing the creases with his thumb. 'Just this ugly stump. And the strangest thing - it feels like it's still there. Then I realised I couldn't see properly.' He looks at me with that one remaining eye, his face half-shadowed but his pain laid bare. 'We weren't trained for heroics, Vera. Just keeping the lads fed, fuelled, moving along. But out there, we're all soldiers. They don't care who we are or what we do. We're all just targets.'

I touch his face gently, tracing the fresh scars and bandages. Tears rise in my eyes - guilt and sorrow for him. He is not the man I once feared, at least not now.

'I'm torn in half,' he says.

'We'll get through it, George. You're alive. You're home.'

'You'll still love me like this, won't you, Vera?' His voice breaks, revealing a vulnerability I've never witnessed.

'You're being daft. You're my husband.'

He suddenly grabs my hand, presses it to his lips, and kisses the back of it.

'That I am,' he says, with a grim sort of certainty. 'Your Henry is lucky, if you can call it that. They pulled us apart months ago - said our skills were better suited elsewhere.' His voice drips with sarcasm, and for a moment I fear he'll open the old wound of why they argued so bitterly. But he holds back. Instead, he tells me how his driving kept him on the road - hauling fuel, rations, and shells through the mountains, day and night. Henry, with his butcher's hands, was stationed in a field kitchen, carving and cutting, feeding men by the thousand. A safer post, George mutters, and I can't disagree, not when I look at George now.

I spend that whole evening close to him, watching. His vulnerability feels so at odds with the man I knew - like a wounded animal you can't help but pity, even if it might still bite. So I stay present, not talking too much, careful not to say the wrong thing but making it clear I'm here.

I make him dinner; he can barely eat, every chew agony. I bathe him; his wounds are brutal but will fade with time. His eye, beneath the wrappings, is less likely to mend - a dead, red swell, like raw meat left too long in the sun. Angry and wet, impossible to look at for long.

The missing arm changes everything - his shape, his posture, his presence. He speaks now and then, slowly, with the careful weight of a man who feels decades older.

During the night he is restless - tossing, groaning, trapped in dreams of where he has been, what he has seen. I'm restless too. Though he has not been cruel or violent, not loving, or tender either, which I wouldn't expect, his calm manner unsettles me. Is it the quiet before the storm, or has this destruction changed him for good? If he's now someone to tend to rather than fear, how could I possibly leave? That selfishness feels unbearable.

As much as I love Eddie, I don't think I could live with the guilt - the worst betrayal imaginable, abandoning a man already broken. I place a hand on my stomach and the reality hits me again: I can't simply change my mind and stay. Not with this life growing inside me, a life that doesn't belong to George, something everyone will know.

I am faced with an impossible choice: stay and fulfil my duty, forced to live beside the living reminder of my sin, or take the path I'd sworn to only hours ago - leave forever, never knowing if the man I once loved has finally returned, fragile and hurt, yes, but human again.

The following morning, George is pacing round the house, hunting for something. He startles when he sees Nadine, all in her Nippy uniform, herself careful and watchful of him.

'You've grown up quick,' he says as she passes, perhaps realising how long he's been away. 'You not working?' he asks, turning to me.

'I'm here to look after you.'

'I'm fine, Vera. We've got to get on. Where's the whisky?' he mutters, rifling through the cupboards.

'In the kitchen.'

'Everything's moved round - everything's changed!' he snaps, growing agitated.

At that moment, there's a knock at the door. Sharp. Purposeful. I answer, and there stands Dad.

'We need to talk,' he says at once, his voice tight with anger. Then he steps inside and stops dead when he sees George.

'George!' Dad breathes, the word almost a gasp.

George looks down at the empty sleeve and tries a smile.

'More than a blighty wound, eh Bertie?'

'Bloody hell,' Dad murmurs, pale as chalk. I slip away into the kitchen, my heart hammering. Dad's sudden, determined arrival makes me wonder if Dr Clarke has spoken to him - about the *issue.*

I pace the kitchen, straining to hear their voices through the thin wall. George retells his story, more open now than he ever was after Dunkirk. Perhaps the realisation that his war is truly over brings a strange relief to him. Dad listens mostly in silence; his few words slow and steady. Two wounded men, battered by different wars, marked by the same scars. History repeating itself in the cruellest way.

After a while, Dad comes into the kitchen. His face says it all: anger, disgust, knowledge.

'My God, that poor sod, Jesus, listen Vera..when you've got a moment, you must come to the shop,' he says tightly. 'We have to talk - urgently. In the meantime, look after George, please, Vera.'

There's pressure in his voice I've rarely heard. Then, in total contrast, he turns and calls out to George, all cheer and relief, telling him how glad he is he's home.

He shuts the door, and I'm immediately overcome with WORRY. That wretched Dr Clarke - I'm convinced he's opened his mouth.

Later on I head to the butcher's. Every step is heavy with apprehension; every second blighted with dread. When I get there, the usual queue snakes outside the shop - locals waiting for their tiny meat allowance. I walk straight to the front, tell them I'm not a customer, and slip inside.

Dad looks up, his face as stern as I've ever seen it.

'You'll be all right for a minute, won't you?' he says to Mr Sharma, who is busy weighing trotters. Mr Sharma nods as Dad gestures for me to go down into the cellar.

I follow along, the smell of meat, blood, and sawdust as strong as ever. In the basement carcasses lie unbutchered; a pig hangs from the ceiling. The cold bites. The grey walls close in.

Dad looks at me. The disappointment in his gaze will stay with me forever.

'What have you done, Vera?'

It confirms it. Tears spring to my eyes and, for the first time in many years, I am afraid of my father - petrified of what he might do.

'What have you gone and done?' he asks again, every word sharp.

'Dr Clarke had no right - ' I begin.

'He's a decent, good man,' Dad cuts across me, his voice rising so much I'm sure he might wake the dead we're surrounded by. 'How could you be so stupid? So… so cruel. My daughter, my Vera - she's a good married woman. She's no whore.'

'Dad, I need you to understand - '

'I never will, so don't try it,' he snaps. He looks down at my belly. 'And now poor George is back, wrecked by this war, and now…' He shakes his head, disgust written all over him. 'Now we've got this problem.'

'It is my problem,' I say.

'It is my family - what's left of it! How could you do this to our George? You're possessed. You need a priest as well as a doctor.'

I take a breath, try to steady myself.

'You don't know what George can be like.'

'Don't you dare put this on him,' Dad barks, closing the distance until I can feel the heat from him. 'That man's been good as gold to you.' I shake my head, hard. 'Don't you try and put him in a bad light, Vera. It won't wash with me. This is you and you alone and your adultery.'

'He hurts me, Dad. He can be relentlessly cruel.'

'Well, if this is how you behave, you deserve it.' His words cut me to the core - cold, brutal.

'Henry believes me.'

'Henry's gullible,' Dad spits. 'I know what George is and I know what he isn't. Don't try and justify your actions by blackening his name.'

'I'm not justifying,' I cry. 'I'm explaining.'

He scoffs and paces, trying to marshal his anger into control.

'You're just like your mother.'

'What do you mean?'

'A liar.'

'Mum wasn't a liar - that was Doris.'

'Your mother was unfaithful,' he shouts. Every word lands heavy and final. 'She was. I stuck by her. I loved her, for all my sins.'

I shake my head, refusing to accept it.

'I know Mum. She wasn't like that.'

'You don't know. You were a child. I knew your mother. I knew of her ways. There are sides to people we don't see. We don't know, but they're there.'

'And *that* is George!' I shout, throwing the word back at him, hoping it see sense and for a moment he goes quiet, taken aback by my brashness. For a heartbeat I think he's taking in what I'm saying, all of it coming into focus. But then his face turns, his attention moving to something else.

'Who's is it then?' he says, glaring down at me. I refuse to answer. 'I'll find out, Vera. You know I will. There's one person who doesn't need to know any of this, and that's George. Now he's back, it hasn't made it easy, but we'll figure it out.'

I look at Dad, searching his face for some mercy, some meaning, some hint of what he intends.

'I know the pain of knowing,' he says quietly. 'I wish I never did - about you, about your mother. I need to protect George, more so with the state he's in.'

'What are you saying?'

'You've made the biggest, almighty mistake and you'll carry that to the grave. But…I've spoken to Dr Clarke and we can have it arranged. The problem can go away.'

His words are unexpected - Dad drifting from rage to a resolute, nasty kind of practicality. A problem solver, to save his George.

'You mean… terminate?' I ask gently.

Dad nods.

'Dr Clarke knows someone respectable - as respectable as the matter can be. If you hold on to this, George will know; the street will know. And that can't happen. You'll go to Dr Clarke's on Friday. He'll tell you where to go. It's been *decided.*'

'But that's not *your* decision to make,' I say.

'I'm sorting this out, Vera. For you, for George, for the family.' He moves to leave, then turns back. 'And I will find out who did this…' His gaze flicks to the strung pig. 'He deserves the same fate as that, as far as I'm concerned.' His voice lowers to a threat. 'Friday it goes away. Disappears. Then you can work on being the wife that George deserves.'

He leaves me alone in the blood - slick basement: cold, broken, torn between escaping and starting again, but destroying the life within me to keep the life I have.

I walk home in a daze, two futures battling inside me like a storm. One path is paved with the cold, hard rock of duty: a life of silence, of tending to a hollow man, burying a secret so deep it might one day consume me, living in constant fear of doing wrong. The other path is a narrow, dangerous trail that promises freedom and true love, but it is lined with the thorns of judgment and the bitter taste of betrayal.

My father, in his rage and love, has offered a solution I had not even considered - one that would extinguish the hope growing within me but protect the man I am meant to love. I am a ship caught between two currents, one pulling me toward the familiar shoreline, the other toward an open sea I had never dared to cross. And the compass, the one thing meant to guide me, now points in two directions at once. It is an impossible choice.

## 39 If the threat comes

When I get home the sense of unease is back, that family instinct I can never ignore. George is slumped in an armchair. The record spins but no sound plays. A glass of whisky hangs in his only hand, just a swig left. His eye patch is off, exposing the raw, red swell, wet and piercing. He looks straight at me.

'You'll never love me,' George says, the first words as I enter. 'Look at me. LOOK AT ME!' he shouts. 'How could you love me?' His voice is bitter as bile.

I stay silent, panicked once more at saying the wrong thing - but maybe my silence itself gives me away. George lurches to his feet, unsteady, the drink clouding him.

'We can't not talk about it,' he mutters.

'About what?' I finally manage.

'About what you said to Henry.' His voice is slow, deliberate, knowing. 'About the lies you told him. He was horrible, Vera. Made some dreadful accusations.'

I insist I've no idea what he means, feigning innocence - my safest option considering Henry is not here to defend or deny.

'Don't pretend. You told him lies about me. Horrible lies. Awful gossip.' His temper sharpens, cold and familiar, so like my father's that I had just witnessed. 'You don't get it, do you, Vera…'

'Get what?'

'This is on you,' he says bitterly.

'What is?' I ask, though dread already twists inside me.

'If me and Henry hadn't had that fight, me and him would still be together. I'd be with him - not forced on the trucks day and night, not in the firing line. It was you - opening your mouth, discussing private matters, personal. You betrayed me. My trust. You… you lied.'

I shake my head.

'I never lied.'

'Yes you fucking did, you lying bitch!' he explodes.

He hurls the whisky glass with such precision and force I have a split-second to turn, but it catches me on the side of the forehead. The thud smacks my skull as the glass hits the floor and shatters. I stumble against the wall, fingers touching my head. Warmth blossoms under my palm; a small trickle of blood seeps to my temple. Before I can properly assess the damage, George is over me, his curses raining down.

'You betrayed me,' he screams. 'You're a liar, Vera - a cold, worthless liar.' He kicks at me as I curl into the corner, protecting my head that's exploding with pain. His feet are clumsy but the force still lands.

He stops, breathes, takes it all in. He must see the blood on my face, even with only one working eye.

'You never loved me, Vera. I've done everything for you and you're never grateful,' he says.

'Grateful?' I snap, fear drowning under something harder. I hold out my hand, showing the blood from my head.

‘Everything I told Henry was true - and he only knows half of it.’ I spit out the words, because if nothing else, the truth is mine to give.

George turns red. As red as the blood that lingers on my fingers. I have done it now; I deserve what comes. This is how it ends.

He slumps on top of me, pinning me down and calling me every name he can think of. The absence of his arm works against him as I claw with my bloody hands to free myself. He sits on my stomach and I feel terror for the baby inside me in ways I never imagined. For a moment I find the strength to try to lever him off, but soon he takes control, slapping me with the back of his hand and then closing it around my throat, fingers pressing until my breath tightens.

‘It only takes one hand, Vera. That’s all you need,’ he says quietly, with pride and arrogance. He squeezes until the world narrows and then - abruptly - he lets go. Air rushes back into me in a jagged gasp. My neck aches where his fingers bruised it; my head throbs like I’ve never known.

He moves to get up and his hand meets a shard of broken glass on the floor. He yelps, clutching his hand to his chest; red beads stain his palm and smear on his shirt.

‘Fuck’s sake, bloody hell,’ George mutters, his anger still burning. He looks at me like he might continue, as if even the broken glass is somehow my fault.

He s about to shout again but he is interrupted by a knock at the door.

I scuttle into the far corner of the room, out of sight, while George cracks the door open just enough to speak through, hiding his blooded head and shirt.

'Yes?' George says.

And then I hear that unmistakable voice.

'Oh… erm, sorry. I wasn't expecting you.'

Eddie. No. God, Eddie is here.

'Who were you expecting?' George asks.

'You're back, then?' Eddie replies, unease creeping into his voice.

'Do I know you?' George says, sharp and curious.

'Not really… I used to live on this street. I was hoping to speak to Vera.'

'About what?' George snaps.

'Well - ' Eddie fumbles, scrambling for an excuse. This is my moment to scream, to beg for help; he could rescue me, save the day just like he did for Samuel - but I can't speak. Noise cannot leave my mouth. I am paralysed.

Eddie tries to figure out what to say.

'Er… it's not Vera specifically. Just anyone. I'm a firefighter and I've been told to make sure folk are aware of the new threat.' He leans, trying to look past George, searching for me, but George keeps the door tight.

'Go on…' George says.

'These rockets. Menacing things. You'll hear their distinctive sound - but if they go silent, that means they're dropping.'

'Yes, we all know this,' George growls, agitated.

'Just make sure your wife is aware,' Eddie presses, his voice firm now. 'If the threat comes, she must do what she has to in order to survive.'

'Right,' George says, and slams the door without a goodbye. He looks at me 'Something about that bloke… has he been pestering?' he questions.

I shake my head quickly, but suspicion flickers in his eye as he disappears into the kitchen to wash his cut hand.

I look at the door. Eddie's words echo in my aching skull: *If the threat comes, do what you have to do to survive.* For now, though, I stay still, waiting for George to return.

When he does, his hand is bound in a bandage. To my surprise, he throws me a towel.

'Put that on your head,' he says. 'I'm sorry, Vera.'

I press the towel to my forehead and George fumbles with a cigarette, his bandaged hand clumsy, and in a collapse of reason - drained, numb - I rise to help him light it. He takes a deep drag, smoke curling, and a small, ugly smile tugs at his lips.

'I shouldn't have done that,' he says, almost casual. 'But you do get me worked up.'

'We all make mistakes,' I answer, because the sound of my own voice steadies me, and because I need him calm. Just for now.

'What will you say?' he asks, pointing the cigarette towards the gash on my head.

'The blackout,' I reply without thinking. 'Dangerous, isn't it?'

'Yeah,' he says, admiring my quickness. 'I'll get better, Vera. You'll see. Don't you worry.'

I force a smile - optimism, hope - but it's all put on. I tell him I'll make some food and I escape to the kitchen, burying myself in duty, creating a scene of normality while my head pounds. A swelling and bruise are forming at my hairline, though the bleeding has stopped. My neck is red and purple, forming a map of relentless aggression.

When I return to living room, George has fallen asleep, slumped in his chair; blood still stains his hand. He snores, a new sound from him, heavy and whole. Despite that, I carry on the act: cleaning the glass from the floor, wiping away spots of blood, doing the ordinary things. I tidy as if nothing has happened.

Once I'm sure he's asleep, I move beyond tidying and begin to pack: a few clothes, small necessities, each movement deliberate and careful. I have to go. I cannot live like this any longer - he will not get better; he will almost certainly get worse. Why live a life of daily terror when I can risk a life that is frowned upon but free?

I keep checking the clock, making sure I have time to fetch Nadine from work. I keep glancing at George; each slow exhale panics me, each slight twitch like the monster stirring. With a small bag of essentials, a cluttered handbag, and my trusted gas mask, I creep toward the door - tiptoeing, doing my best not to make a sound though the bags rattle with every step.

I look at George one last time, braced for it to be my final glimpse. He looks peaceful, despite his broken face and body; the handsome line of him remains, and it's easy to forget the cruelty underneath. Even scarred, he appears so charming.

I close the door gently. Fresh air circles me. Turner Street goes on as if nothing has happened. I stand on the doorstep with my life in bags but no longer balanced on a knife-edge. I have done it.

It is time to leave.

## 40 Selfish

Putney is frantic, the rush hour in full swing. My bags drag at my arms, but I'm determined to push through the crowds and noise to get to Lyons. When I arrive, I see Nadine through the window, her apron crisp and spotless, as though it's never known a stain. She looks impossibly grown-up, a proper young woman now, a world away from the little girl who arrived on our doorstep all those years ago. I gesture for her to come outside, and she does, confused and concerned.

'You'll be coming with me, Nadine,' I tell her firmly.

'Where? What's happened?' she asks, her eyes fixed on the cut at my forehead.

'I'll explain. Come along.'

She follows a few steps before the booming voice of Mrs Miller cuts across the street.

'Vera Hopkins! Where on earth have you been?' she calls.

'I've been sick,' I shout back.

'You don't look sick. You look like you're running away,' she barks, loud enough for all to hear. 'Come back here and explain yourself.'

'Sorry, I can't do that, Mrs Miller.'

'I beg your pardon?'

A few of the girls gather behind her now - even lazy Lorraine, taking a rare break from sitting down.

'Vera! I can take disciplinary action!'

'Shove your job!' I yell, striding away. The girls gasp in unison - another moment of madness - but God, how liberating it feels. Mrs Miller's face is a picture I will relish forever.

Nadine keeps up with me, her face twisted in confusion.

'I've packed some of your things in here,' I tell her, lifting my bag. 'You'll have to go back to Barnstaple.'

'No. No, I will not,' she snaps, determined.

'You will, Nadine. What I say goes. Home isn't safe. You'll go back to your aunt's first thing tomorrow, and I'll write or call to explain.'

She says nothing more, only outrage in her eyes and a stomp in her step - still a child, for all her grown-up looks.

We arrive at Eddie's lodgings, a small apartment block on a Putney side street with beautiful art deco features. I knock, praying he's home. Nadine waits beside me, anger in her expression. Eddie opens finally opens the door and his face lights with joy and relief. He sweeps me up at once.

'Thank God, thank you. I was so worried,' he says, holding me, cupping my face in both hands. 'I should've burst in the moment I saw he was back.'

He catches sight of the cut on my head, the bruising at my neck.

'The lunatic, the bastard,' he growls. 'I'll kill him. I knew it. I should've come in. I'm so sorry - I stood there babbling about rockets like a fool while he - ' His voice cracks with fury. 'Pathetic, I was pathetic.'

'It's fine, Eddie,' I say, trying to calm him. 'I'm here now. I'm not going back, as much as I tried to convince myself I should.'

'Why?' he asks softly.

'Because he's my husband, Eddie. He's a ruined, desperate man. It's horrendous. I feel a guilt I'll never be rid of.'

'You can't pity him, Vera. Look what he's done to you!' Eddie points to my neck, frustration trembling in his voice.

'I know. I know. But for a moment I believed things might be different - and then I was reminded of who he is.'

As we make our way inside I drop my heavy bags in the corner.

'I've done it Eddie. I'm here. But we need to get Nadine out of London before *we* can leave. I can see her off tomorrow. It'll take most of the day for her to reach her aunt, but she found her way to London - she can find her way back to Barnstaple.'

'So… Friday then, like we said?' Eddie asks, hope flickering in his voice.

'Yes. Friday it is.'

'I'll work my shift that day, then we'll leave in the evening. I've got the weekend off - they think I'm heading home to Norfolk. I'll tell them Monday I can't come back to London. It's all sorted, Vera. I've figured it out.'

His words soothe me, a rare occasion after days of chaos. For a moment, everything feels like it might actually fall into place. Nadine's mood, though, stays sour and tight - annoyance, fear, defiance all bound up together. But I'm doing this for her, whether she knows it or not.

The next morning we arrive at Waterloo Station as early as possible. London is just waking. Nadine hasn't spoken a word since we reached Eddie's. She's furious, and I can't blame her. She's finally found her footing at Lyons, carved a place for herself, and now I'm uprooting her again - sending her back to a place that holds nothing but sadness, where she was cruelly bullied at the school.

I map out her journey to Barnstaple: a complicated tangle of changes and long waits, with no certainty the trains will even run under constant threat. It's risky, but we've no choice. I tell her she can explain to Esther that George has come home injured and needs space. Esther knows his behaviour well enough; she'll understand my eagerness to send Nadine away. And with her American sweetheart still overseas, she could do with the company.

'I don't want to go, Vera,' Nadine says at last, her voice filled with frustration and sadness - the first words she's spoken properly all morning. I keep my eyes ahead, pushing towards the platform, resolute in my decision. 'This is my home,' she says again, firmer now.

'Yes. And it will be again. It's your aunt's home, and you'll return with her when she comes back. She can evict George no bother. But right now, it isn't safe - not while I'm not there.'

'I can't believe you'd run away,' she says bitterly.

'I'm not running, Nadine. I'm escaping. There's a difference,' I tell her firmly. 'You should know - you escaped Germany when you could.'

'I didn't have a choice. I was sent away to survive. You're running away for love.'

'For both,' I say quietly, hoping she might understand.

We reach the train. Steam billows across the platform, the noise and heat closing around us.

'Will I see you again?' she asks with a tremble in her words.

'Yes. I'll make sure of it,' I promise, though doubt curls in my chest.

'I don't think I'll ever see my mother and father again,' she whispers, tears cutting down her cheeks. 'I'm sad that so many people I love disappear.'

'You'll see them again, when this ends. And it will end - they reckon not long now.'

'I think they're gone,' she says softly, and I can't find the words to answer. I hug her tightly, wishing I could take the weight she carries. 'This is my home, Vera,' she says again. 'I'm old enough to choose where to live.' Her English is flawless now, clear and precise. I nod at her with a smile as the whistle blows and she steps reluctantly onto the train.

'This isn't forever. Nothing ever is.' I call out.

The train jolts, shudders, begins to move. I wave, holding my smile, but she doesn't wave back. She just stares at me - eyes heavy with accusation, as if I've failed her. Because I have. Steam swallows her, and she fades into the distance. Another goodbye.

I wander through Waterloo, relieved she's safe from George's frenzy. Tomorrow it will be me on a train - saying goodbye not to one thing, but to everything. I feel ready. And terrified.

Outside the station, I spot a familiar face: Violet, standing alone, eyes lost in thought. She's out of uniform, perhaps heading somewhere herself.

'Violet?' I call.

'Vera… what are you doing here?' she asks.

I hesitate, then realise the truth can no longer hurt me.

'I've seen Nadine off. She's gone back to stay with Esther.'

'Really?' Violet says, surprised.

'And you? What are you doing here?'

'I've just goodbye to James and Rita' she says. 'These rockets keep coming, so it's safest option, their foster family have been very understanding.' Her tone carries irritation, exhaustion, something brittle.

'You didn't tell me they were going so soon,' I say.

'You were occupied,' she says sharply.

'Occupied?' I echo, confused.

'Occupied with whatever it is you're up to, Vera.'

'I don't understand,' I say, though dread prickles in me.

'The lies about being with Sheila. Something isn't right. You haven't been yourself, not for this entire war,' she says.

'Is anybody themselves?' I ask.

'We try,' she snaps. 'Most of us do our bit.'

Her last words sting.

'What are you saying?' I ask quietly.

She turns to me, disappointment clear - the same look Nadine gave me - and then the dam bursts.

'What have you done for the war effort, Vera? Really - what have you done? Poured more tea? Taken an extra shift? That must have been so difficult,' she sneers.

'I don't know what you're talking about,' I manage, barely.

'Think about it,' she presses. 'While we've been tagging bodies in the rubble and missing our children, you've been living in a different world. You could've volunteered. You could've done something - but no, it's always been about you. You're selfish. The girl I knew from Turner Street is long gone.'

'I'm sorry the war is cruel,' I whisper. 'But it isn't my fault, Violet. There are things I've been battling -'

She freezes, her judgment sharp and unwavering.

'Well, at least your George is home, eh? Wrecked but alive - poor soul. He came looking for you yesterday, wasn't sure where you were. I couldn't tell him. You're a mystery to us all. So where were you, Vera? With Sheila again?'

Her last words cut like glass. She turns and walks away without a goodbye - only a final, contemptuous glance over her shoulder.

The clock continues to tick. I have no allies left. The street has turned. Tomorrow can't come soon enough.

## 41 Friday

The years of struggle, pain, guilt, and dreaming have led to this. Friday arrives with rain in the sky and tears in my eyes. It's hard not to feel overwhelmed - knowing what's to come, yet still facing the complete unknown.

I've had little sleep, trapped between panic and whispered discussions with Eddie, who does his best to soothe me. I tell him about Violet and her harsh words. He's quick to dismiss them, saying she's only taking her sadness and stress out on me. But there's truth in what she said - an echo I can't quite silence. She isn't wrong. I've been living in my own world, surviving both the war outside and the one at home, resisting Eddie and then surrendering to him.

For people like Violet, there's been no room for personal choices - only service and sacrifice. Her words plant a new guilt in me, another weight to carry. And another push towards the truth I've been denying, Turner Street is no longer home. It's a street I shall never see again.

As morning settles, Eddie readies himself for work.

'You'll stay here until I'm back this evening, then we'll leave?' His tone is half order, half question. 'Don't go near Turner Street, Vera. Do not go near him. You can write to your father once we're in Norfolk, to tell him you're safe.'

I nod in agreement.

'I'm going to pop to Joy's,' I add.

His brow tightens. 'Vera…'

'Just to give little Mary a cuddle,' I say quickly

'I'm not sure. It doesn't feel wise.'

'I shan't say a word. Joy's in Wandsworth, it's no bother,' I reassure him but Eddie still looks uneasy. 'Besides,' I add, 'I can use her telephone - to call Esther. To make sure Nadine got back safely.'

'See? You're not selfish,' Eddie says gently, trying to undo Violet's sting. 'You're always thinking of others.' His kindness lifts me, if only for a moment. 'Just be careful, Vera. Really careful. In a few hours we'll be gone. Our new life can begin.'

He kisses me, his hand brushing my tummy - tender, hopeful, full of promise.

'I love you, Vera.'

'I love you, Eddie.'

I make my way to Joy's, slow and steady, hoping for one last glimpse of Mary - her eyes a mirror of Henry's, her giggle a trace of his mischief. I shall miss her terribly. But knowing Henry knows the truth about George gives me comfort, a sliver of hope that the door isn't closed - that I might see them again when he comes home.

I toy with telling Joy about my escape, but what good would it do? I could telephone her once I'm in Norfolk, even hear Mary's voice. That would be something - proof that we're not entirely apart.

I knock at Joy's door. Moments pass before it opens - not briskly, but slowly, warily, which is unlike her. Through the narrow gap appears a face I barely recognise. No brightness. No optimism. Her striking red hair hangs dull and unbrushed, covering part of her face. One eye is bloodshot, ringed with grey.

It's not the look of exhaustion from motherhood. It's something darker - grief, perhaps even horror. My stomach drops. Not Henry. Please, not Henry.

'Are you all right, Joy?' I ask as she lets me in. She doesn't answer - just drifts into the kitchen and sinks into a chair. The room is a mess: dirty plates, unwashed knives, the air stale with neglect. I can hear Mary playing faintly in the other room. 'Is our Henry all right?' I press. Finally she nods, and relief surges through me. 'Then what is it? You look dreadful, I'm sorry to say it, but you do.'

'I'm tired, Vera. That's all,' she says, but the lie is written all over her face. She looks haunted.

I touch her shoulder in comfort, but she flinches, shrugging me off. I retreat, unsettled, and wander into the living room. Mary is sitting on the floor, playing quietly with a wooden train, and I ache to hold her close - to remember this small moment of calm.

But Joy's silence presses through the walls so I return to the kitchen, determined to get to the bottom of it.

'Are you unwell?' I ask again.

'Please, Vera…' she says softly - a plea, a warning, and a refusal all at once.

I busy myself, clearing plates and scraping at Mary's makeshift banana concoction - parsnip mash sweetened with sugar and banana essence. Nothing like the real thing, but Mary doesn't what the *real* thing is. Then, as I lift the bin lid, something catches my eye: a white bandage, mangled and speckled with blood. My heart lurches. I pick it up and hold it in my hands, and the smell hits me at once - acrid, familiar.

It's George's. He has been here.

I hold the bandage up to Joy.

'George's been here, hasn't he?' I say, certain. Joy looks at me and breaks down, her body heaving with shame and sorrow 'Did he hurt you, Joy? Did that rotten bastard hurt you?' I beg, crouching beside her. She takes a deep breath and closes her eyes for a moment.

'He came here looking for you,' she says, voice breaking. 'He looked so awful. I thought I was seeing a ghost. Mary screamed at the sight. He didn't like that. Not at all.'

'I'm sorry you didn't know he was home, wounded like that,' I say, trying to steady her. 'But he didn't touch you, did he?' I ask again, gasping for the truth.

Joy's words come in small, broken pieces.

'He said he loved me.'

I pause, searching for the right thing to say. What can I possibly say? I should have protected her, but I never imagined George would turn on someone else, even if his eyes had fixed on her for so long.

'I don't think George really knows what love is,' I tell her, forcing down my own pain.

'No, you don't know what he was like,' she interrupts, shouting. Then, calmer, as if my admission has given her permission, she continues in a small voice.

'He asked me to do things to ease his pain.'

'What things?' I ask, voice raw.

She looks at me as though she's ashamed to speak them aloud.

'Inappropriate things,' she whispers.

'Oh bloody hell,' I cry.

'He even begged. Of course I said no - no - but he was forceful. He said, even with one arm, he was twice the man Henry would ever be.'

I stare at her, torn and broken, trying to find something to put her back together. She glances toward the kitchen counter where a bread knife still lies, then shuts her eyes as if to block the memory.

'He said I had no choice,' she whispers. 'I kept saying no, and then he grabbed the knife and I... I really did think he might hurt me, or Mary. So I... oh my God, Vera.' Her breath stutters. 'I just had to do what he asked. God forgive me. But I would never have - I... I - ' Her whole body trembles.

'That shit, that evil lunatic,' I shout.

'He told me to promise I'd never say a word. I was certain I never would, and yet here I am. This is dreadful.'

'He doesn't deserve silence. He deserves nothing,' I tell her, urgent.

'How long has he been like this?' Joy asks.

'Too bloody long. This must end,' I say.

'What are you going to do?' she asks.

'Leave, it's finished,' I answer. 'I can seek a divorce on grounds of cruelty, and I might need you to help me, Joy. I am so sorry. I never thought he would turn on someone else. This is all my fault.'

'You're talking nonsense,' Joy sobs.

'No. It's true. If I'd been home, he wouldn't have come here. I'll never forgive myself. I can't leave you like this, with him the way he is.'

'I can go back to Canterbury, but Henry must never know,' Joy says. 'He can never think I did this willingly.'

'George doesn't deserve protecting,' I say.

'I fear for Nadine,' Joy adds.

'No, it's fine. I saw her off to Devon,' I reply, trying to steady my voice.

'That doesn't make sense,' Joy says, confused.

'Why?'

'Because George said last night that even if you weren't home, at least he had someone to cook his dinner. He said Nadine promised she would do it for him. He even mentioned what he was having.'

'No... no. I saw Nadine off first thing yesterday morning,' I stammer.

A cold dread uncoils in me. Surely Nadine hasn't gone back to the house. I fumble in my bag for my address book.

'I need to use your telephone, Joy,' I say.

She leads me to the hallway and points out the home phone on the sideboard. My hands shake as I flip to Esther's number and dial, praying George's words aren't true. After a few rings a woman answers, not Esther but the friend she has been living with.

'Cooper residence?' the woman says.

'Hello. I'm calling to check - to make sure Esther's niece, Nadine, returned to your home safely yesterday evening.'

'Er… sorry, no,' the woman replies. My stomach drops.

'She should've been with you by five o'clock, give or take an hour. Are you sure?' I press.

'No, she isn't here. Esther's working, but Nadine hasn't been back here since she ran off to the city some time ago.'

I lower the receiver slowly. Panic wells up. Nadine might be with him, alone and vulnerable.

Mary scatters into the hallway as Joy scoops her up. Holding her tightly.

'She's back there, isn't she?' Joy asks.

I nod, a nod I never wanted to give. I wonder back into the kitchen as Joy remains in the hallway, gripping Mary. My hands tremble as I slip the address book back into my bag and then my eyes falls on the bread knife on the counter - the same knife George had threatened Joy with. Without thinking, I tuck it into my bag. Just in case.

Joy joins me in the kitchen.

'What are you going to do, Vera?' she asks, voice small.

'I'll sort it out. You stay here, Joy,' I say, panic rising.

'I'm coming with you,' she insists.

'NO!' I plead 'You stay with Mary. I'll be all right - I'm used to this,' I fling the door open and step into the street my bag heavy with the unthinkable. I must get Nadine out of there - even if it means doing the one thing I swore I wouldn't do. I must go back to Turner Street.

## 42 Anywhere but here

My home stands before me - a place that no longer gives comfort or solace but fills me with dread. A place I swore I would never see again, and yet here I am. This street seems to drag me back, damned, and unrelenting, its noises still familiar: Clapham Junction ticking on, a thin fog blurring the edges, making me squint.

There's no reason for me to stay. My father doubts me, judges me, is disgusted by me. Violet watches my every move. Sheila has gone. Bill remains vile. Even Mrs Henderson - once a constant, welcoming face - has all but vanished, shut away and grief - stricken by Arthur's death. The bomb damage still lingers. Doris's house is a grave of rubble; the Butlets' home a ditch of unimaginable tragedy, now a cruel playground for the few children who have returned. We carry on, yearning for normality. But this street is not normal. This is a war street. It has expelled me. I am ready to leave. But first I must get Nadine out.

I approach the door, my belly twisting as if the secret inside me is trying to escape. My handbag concealing a stolen weapon - there for one reason. In case. In case he tries to kill me. Because this time I will not let it happen. A life with Eddie, away from here, is too promising to give up.

I open the front door. It gives a long creak, as if it wants the whole street to know I'm there. And then silence greets me. Emptiness. The house is cold, dark, lifeless. I step inside carefully, each step measured, searching for any trace of Nadine.

In the kitchen, I find her. So foolish, sitting at the small table with her head in her hands. Her hair is unkempt; she looks up at me, eyes weary and glazed, cheeks red - an echo of Joy's. She looks defeated.

I approach her carefully, my voice a whisper.

'You silly girl, Nadine. What on earth are you doing back here?'

I take her arm, trying to haul her up, to get her out of this dangerous place.

'I'm sorry,' she whispers, her English fragile. 'I… this was my home.'

'What has he done, Nadine?' My voice rises, no longer a whisper.

She looks past me. Through me. I turn, and there George stands in the doorway, still in yesterday's clothes, a new bandage across his eye, his armless sleeve hanging loose.

'I didn't hurt her, Vera, if that's what you're thinking' he says.

I look back at Nadine.

'Is that right?'

She nods - but it's a nod that tells me nothing, a nod that hides more than it reveals.

'We just had a chat,' George says, pride curling his words. 'A real nice chat. Her English is so good now - wouldn't know she was a jerry.'

Then his face shifts. Hatred, cold and bitter, flickers across it like a switch.

'So tell me, Vera, my darling wife - who is this fireman?'

I glance at Nadine. Fear is across her face . She looks at me with pure regret.

'I'm sorry,' she stammers. 'He made me say…' Every word hurts her.

'Get out, Nadine. Get out now.'

'Where?'

'Anywhere but here!' I shout, my voice hard and unfamiliar even to me.

She leaps up, brushing past George - who, thank God, lets her go. The front door slams behind her. My body trembles. He knows. Almost everything. I feel trapped - but if Nadine could escape, surely I can too.

'It was that cunt who came to the door, wasn't it?' George roars.

Without thinking, I make for the door, but George's one arm swings out, blocking my path. With a force I didn't think possible, he pushes me across the room.

'That's where you've been,' he spits, eyes blazing. 'While I'm blown to pieces, dying in a foreign ditch, you've been fucking someone else. You bitch. You whore!'

'Maybe I wouldn't have if you'd treated me better,' I shout back, my throat raw with anger, my head throbbing with the ache of it all.

'I've been nothing but good to you, Vera,' George says.

I let out a bitter scoff.

'Look at me!' I scream, pointing at the bruise on my head, the marks on my neck.

'I don't know who you are, Vera,' he announces. 'You've been lost for years - corrupted, broken. You don't work properly, up here.' He taps his temple. 'Certainly not down there. You're a faulty bitch without morals.'

'I work, George,' I snap. I falter for a second, then force the words out, petrified but determined, as if I've nothing left to lose.

'I'm pregnant.'

The look he gives me isn't rage but something colder - a dead, flat stare, as if the last piece of him has snapped away.

'You're lying,' he says, voice cracking under the weight of it, sounding for a moment like a man breaking apart. On the surface he'd win sympathy, and yet he's turned so cruel I can't grant it. I don't give him a moment to breathe.

'I'm in love with another man, and we're going to start a family. I deserve a world away from you, George.'

'You're going nowhere.' His teeth clamp together. He smells like a predator. And in that instant, I know what's coming.

He lunges. His hand clamps around my throat and drags me to the floor. I try to push him off, but his strength is monstrous. My handbag slams from my shoulder; we collide with a sickening thud to the floor. In a second he's on top of me again, his good hand aiming for my neck with the same brutal intent as before.

He pauses only to clench his fist and drive it into my nose. Pain explodes behind my eyes; blood floods my mouth. Another blow follows, crushing my eye - as if he's trying to blind me like him. His accuracy, even with one eye, is terrifying. A fist scrapes across my already - split forehead, reopening the wound. Then his hand returns to my throat, pressing harder, fingers digging into the same place as before, as if they belong there.

I can't see properly. I can't breathe. All I taste is blood. In those vanishing seconds I fumble blindly through my bag. The contents scatter across the floor; my fingers find fabric, coins - then metal. I close on the knife I stole. Gripping the handle like I'm holding on for dear life - because I am - I raise my arm and jab. Not aiming for one spot, only desperate and wild, like the aimless pokes I used to make at meat in the butcher's shop. The blade finds flesh: shoulder, neck - I don't know where. He flinches. His hand flies from my throat to his own wound. He scrabbles off me, howling in pain.

I crawl backwards, every inch a small victory. Breath comes back in ragged draughts - air, sound, the bright sting of blood and shock. I drag myself upright. George is slumped against the wall, his hand clamped to his neck, blood pouring through his fingers, soaking his filthy shirt.

'Vera...' he rasps between gasps. 'Help me... Vera...'

He tries to steady his breathing but chokes, drowning in his own blood.

I'm on my feet now, though the room spins. I stagger to the door. When I wrench it open, the fresh air hits me - freedom. I stumble out onto the street, blood pooling at the back of my throat.

A distant sound grows in my ears - a pattering rhythm, like Clapham Junction magnified - but I'm too dazed to make sense of it. I stagger forward, away from the house, when I hear my father's voice behind me.

'You're supposed to be at Dr Clarke's,' he bellows, stern and warning as ever.

I turn to him, my face streaked with blood - mine and George's. His eyes flare wide.

'What's happened?!' he cries. 'Where's George?'

The sound swells, louder now. Not the station at all but the dreaded clatter we've all learned to fear - that putt-putt, motorbike stutter in the sky. A doodlebug.

I try to look up, to find it, but pain locks my neck in place.

'Vera, speak to me' Dad shouts, grabbing my shoulders, trying to shake sense into me. 'Where's George!'

'I think I might have killed him,' I say.

Dad aims for the house, his limp slowing him down - just as the sound cuts out. That dreadful silence. The rocket must be falling.

'Get down, Dad!' I scream, racing across the other side of the road, covering my bloodied head.

Then an almighty bang shatters the earth around me. I crouch low as a flash of chaos and light blinds me - freezes me - until a deluge of rubble crashes down. Dad is hurled forward, flying like a rag through the air before being swallowed by debris and flames.

Smoke engulfs everything. Shards of glass and splinters of burning wood rain around me, pelting the ground. Flames roar like a disturbed beast.

I crawl again towards freedom - only a yard further now - dragging myself past jagged wood and scorched pavement. Through the smoke I see a figure running towards me. Nadine. She drops to her knees and wraps her arms around me, holding tight, weeping as our home burns to ruin. I watch the smoke rising and rising - a black curtain with no end.

Then, through the wreckage, Dad emerges - defiant, immortal. He staggers to his feet, dust and dirt clinging to him, a fresh cut above his eye promising a new scar to join the old. He must have been inches from death. He takes one look at me, then lifts his head to the sky and cries,

'George!'

The name echoes, ghostlike, down the broken street. He tries to push towards the burning wreckage but men who appear from nowhere, wearing helmets step into the smoke to hold Dad back. He keeps calling for George, his voice cracking - rage and grief entwined.

Sirens wail. People crowd around me, checking for injuries, but I absorb none of it. My eyes are fixed on the house that burns - and on my father, grieving, frantic, crying for George and not for me.

Another fire engine screeches to a halt. Men leap down with hoses and axes. And there in the smoke - Eddie. His eyes find mine, relief flooding his face.

With Nadine's help I stagger to my feet, limping towards him, careful over the rubble, until I fall into his arms. Flames rise around us like the night of our first kiss. He holds me. He kisses me. He doesn't let go.

I stay there for what feels like forever, safe at last. The threat is gone.

Then Dad appears, tears stinging his eyes, words catching in his throat.

'It's him, isn't it?' he says, staring at Eddie. 'You've destroyed our family, you bastard!'

He lunges towards Eddie, but another firefighter holds him back as he fights to break free. Eddie tightens his arms round me, defiant.

Violet now appears, her ARP helmet back on, her face stricken - bombs once again so close to home. Her eyes flick to me in Eddie's embrace, and I can see everything slotting into place in her mind.

'Let's go, Vera,' Eddie says quietly. 'Let's go now.'

I give him a hopeful smile and turn to Violet. 'Look after Nadine, please,' I say.

Violet doesn't answer. She only stares, her gaze heavy with judgement.

Eddie takes my hand, his grip firm. Behind us Dad shouts words of anguish into the smoky street, calling for George, calling for me.

'Vera! Vera!'

But I don't listen. I don't look back. I limp on with Eddie - who has abandoned his duty, and so have I.

I will never know if George's end was by my hand or by the hand of fate. Perhaps it was both. That unknowing will curse me forever. Yet the chance of freedom - the knowledge that George is gone - lifts me somewhere else. That man may still haunt me, but I will be guarded by the one I love.

And so we walk on, determined, resolute. Eddie glances at me; our eyes meet. He offers a smile - a promise, a way out at last.

We reach the end of Turner Street, its down end lost in smoke, its posh end battered and burnt. My home is gone. My old life is over.

But now, a new one can begin.

## NOTE TO THE READER

While *Secrets on War Street* is a work of fiction, it is rooted in the lived experiences of those who endured life on Britain's Home Front during the Second World War. The events, characters, and locations have been imagined, but every effort has been made to capture the atmosphere, hardship, and spirit of the time with historical accuracy.

The details of air raids, rationing, and daily life were informed by extensive research, including first - hand accounts, museum archives, and historical records. I have taken care to honour the truth of that period, while allowing space for the fictional lives that carry this story.

This book is, above all, a tribute to the courage, endurance, and humanity of ordinary people in extraordinary times.

## ABOUT THE AUTHOR

N. R. Downs is the pen name of Nick Withers, a storyteller and television producer from South London. After studying scriptwriting at university and working for many years in comedy and unscripted television, Nick turned his attention to fiction. Secrets on War Street marks his first full - length work of historical fiction.

He also writes children's books as N. Withers, keeping his writing worlds separate but united by the same love of character, humour, and heart. Nick lives in South London with his wife and their three children.

**If you enjoyed this book, why not subscribe to my mailing list for updates and giveaways:**
backstorybooks.beehiiv.com/

**And for more of my work check out**
***Backstorybooks.com***
**And follow Backstory Books across social media.**

Printed in Dunstable, United Kingdom

79748054R00211